YOU WISH

MARK SCOTT PIPER

BLUE ZEBRA PRESS

BLUE ZEBRA PRESS

ISBN: 978-0-578-21425-2

Library of Congress Control Number: 2018968451

PRINTED IN THE UNITED STATES OF AMERICA

Dedication

*To Amber, without whom neither this book
nor its author would be the same.*

ACKNOWLEDGMENTS

Writing a novel is always a labor of love. Sometimes it feels more like labor than love, but no matter how many years, or decades, you've spent writing, rewriting, editing, and re-editing, it's always worth it in the end.

Reaching that end, though, is not a solitary journey. I owe a huge debt of gratitude to Amber Miller for her unrelenting editorial expertise and for her refusal to accept anything less than my best. Donna Banta provided invaluable help polishing the final draft. Donna, Ruth Wildes Schuler, and Jon Shearer—faithful members of our longstanding critique group and talented writers all—have critiqued the early versions of the novel with patience, support and indispensable suggestions. Theron Yeager was an invaluable contributor when the genesis of this story existed only as a fledgling screenplay.

A special thanks to the members of The Internet Writing Workshop, especially Virginia Anderson, Winter Garrett, Don McCandless, Brent Salish, and Bob White, who stayed the course through the several months of weekly submissions. Every writer needs a benevolent editor, and I was lucky enough to have several.

My children—Robyn, Michelle, Colin, and Courtney—supported me through the long process. I have loved each of them every minute of their lives.

CHAPTER 1

An icy tingle slithered down Jake Parker's spine.

He checked the dilapidated scoreboard behind right field: the Santa Necia High freshmen were down three runs with two innings to go. And Coach Michaels made sure everyone got into the game. If Jake had been good enough for varsity or JV, he wouldn't be sitting here. Thing was, even in this pile of rejects Jake was near the bottom. Pretty much where he fit in the social order at school. And in life. A freakin' nobody.

A quick glance told him his mom, Jill, had made the game. He gave her a subtle wave. Jake knew taking time off work to come to his ball games sometimes meant trouble for her with her boss, but she'd never missed a game—not even back in T-ball. His brother, Kevin, was sitting in the rickety stands next to Kev's two buddies, Max and Brian, both bent over their cell phones thumbing out texts, probably to each other. It would take some kind of miracle for his dad to show up—he never did—but Jake checked anyway. Now that his mom and dad were separated, he didn't know why he even hoped for his dad's support. He just did.

A couple of his bench-mates were checking out the freshman

girls sitting on the well-worn risers behind home plate. Jake recognized the girls, but he doubted they had a clue he existed. Lester Woo nudged Jake and tilted his head down the bench toward another scrub who looked like he'd fallen asleep. Lester was Jake's best friend and the only other guy on the team as short as he was—both were stuck at five foot three. And in a few months, Jake would be fifteen. It sucked to be a late bloomer.

Santa Necia's right fielder raced after a fly ball. It took some impressive acrobatics to avoid tripping over the chuckholes in the outfield, and Jake would likely be the one dodging those hazards next inning. The right fielder ran down the ball just before it rolled through one of the holes in the outfield fence, which leaned inward in several places. With so many boards missing, the faded green fence looked like a gap-toothed monster about to devour the outfield. The broken-down sign atop the scoreboard in right read "Sa ta Nec Littl eague," as if it had the hiccups. The freshman team had to play on this piece-a-shit field because the varsity and JV teams got the good one. Jake figured it all would seem freakin' hilarious to someone who didn't have to play here.

Jake was fast and a pretty good fielder, but he couldn't hit for crap. He'd always loved baseball, and he'd figured it could be his best shot at success. Guess not. He didn't expect stardom, but he'd settle for not looking like a total dweeb at the plate. He really needed somebody to work with him on the finer points of hitting, but he wasn't getting any help at all. Michaels was okay as a biology teacher, but he didn't know dick about coaching baseball. And his dad? Well, he wasn't that kind of father, even before he walked out on them. Jake squeezed his eyes shut and eased a pent up breath between clenched teeth.

When he opened them, Lester was staring back at him, biting

his lip. Jake recognized that look. Les wanted to help get him out of his funk.

"Dude, I was thinkin'," Lester said. "What if you could like change yourself into anything you want? To, you know, maybe become a six-foot-tall chick magnet or somethin'?"

Jake stifled a smile. "It's lame to want stuff that'll never happen."

"Yeah, I know," Lester said. "But it'd be so cool if you had like a magic wand or somethin' and you could just—"

"Jesus, what are you? Ten years old?"

"I'm just sayin'…"

When Jake noticed Coach Michaels glancing down the bench, he pulled his green baseball cap down tight in an attempt to look like a real ballplayer; it also helped keep his unruly mass of brown shoulder-length hair in check. He turned to Lester and affected his best sports announcer voice: "Well, sports fans, it looks like Michaels is about to make a move. The Terriers are down three, and they're runnin' outta innings."

Lester adjusted his glasses, assumed a game face.

The first scheduled batter this inning, Petey Barnum, donned a batting helmet and began his elaborate, well-rehearsed warm-up routine. Jake rolled his eyes. By consensus, Barnum was the team's best player and biggest asshole.

Petey's father, Big Pete, clutched the wire screen in front of the risers. "All right, slugger, show this pathetic bunch of clowns how it's done."

"Jake! Grab a bat," Michaels said. "You're hitting for Petey."

Jake donned a batting helmet. Showtime.

"You gotta be kidding, Michaels!" Big Pete bellowed. "What the hell are you thinking?"

"Can it, Pete. You know everybody gets to play on this team.

Petey's had more at-bats than anyone this season."

Petey gave Jake a shoulder on the way past. Jake regained his balance, but didn't bother to react. He was used to guys like Barnum.

Petey flung his batting helmet against the dugout wall. "This totally blows! Parker hasn't hit a ball out of the goddamn infield all season!"

"Pick up that helmet, Petey," Michaels said. "And watch your language."

Petey smirked at Jake. "Hey, Parker, if you're lucky he'll walk you. It's the only freakin' chance you got, you pathetic dweeb."

Jake and Michaels ignored Big Pete's belly laugh.

"Don't listen to them, Jake," Michaels said. "Just go up there and…and do the best you can, okay?" He pointed to Lester. "Lester, you're up after Jake. Bat for Kyle."

Grabbing a bat with a flourish, Jake marched to the plate. He wiggled his bat and glared out toward the mound, to try to strike fear in the heart of the pitcher. The asshole just laughed.

Jake swung as hard as he could at the first pitch and missed. Yes, he knew the batter's mantra, "just meet the ball," but he couldn't hold back. What he really wanted to do was break the freakin' ball in half. He missed badly again, and the pitcher smirked, as if Jake were no more than an irritating bug. Jake wanted to wipe the smug look off his ugly face. A line drive to the forehead would do it. Jake managed to make contact with the next pitch, sending a one-hop grounder right back to the pitcher. At least he got the location right. Jake raced down the line. He didn't have to look to know the pitcher was mocking him when the dickweed fired the ball to first just in time to get Jake by a step.

He strode past Lester on his way back to the bench and tilted his head toward the mound. "Dude, this guy's got *nothin'*."

"Yeah, I can see that."

When Jake passed the bleachers, Big Pete sneered. "Way to go, *loser.*"

Jake grabbed his helmet by the bill and waved it to the spectators as if he'd just single-handedly led his team to a World Series crown.

"You shoulda stuck to dissecting frogs, Michaels." Big Pete plopped down hard on the weathered riser. As if it, too, had had enough of Barnum, the split plank gave way, sending him to the ground with a thud.

Jake chuckled when his mom stood up and started a round of slow clapping.

CHAPTER 2

By the time Jake and Lester caught up with Kevin and his buddies at the edge of the ball field parking lot, the spewing of minivans and SUVs out of the lot was reduced to a trickle.

The boys watched Angie Woo glide toward them. Angie was just finishing her junior year, as were Kevin, Brian, and Max. To them, Angie moved in slow motion; her long, silky black hair swayed sensuously, and her dark eyes glowed somehow. She had all the right curves in all the right places and a megawatt smile that could turn a guy to mush. She'd be in their dreams again tonight.

When Angie drew near, the boys' conversation stopped. Kevin and his buddies demonstrated the full extent of their social skills by studying the fascinating patterns they were making in the dirt with their sneakers, while weighing the advantage of jamming their hands into their jeans pockets against casually scratching something.

"Hey, guys," she said.

The older boys mumbled incoherent grunts, likely meant to convey what Jake said, which was, "Hey, Angie."

"C'mon, Les. We gotta bounce, Mom's getting anxious." Angie swung around and started back across the lot.

"See ya, Jake." Lester trotted after his sister.

As soon as Angie was out of earshot, Brian and Max offered an enthusiastic "Woohoo!" and exchanged fist bumps. Jake witnessed the same ritual at Santa Necia High when guys spotted Angie Woo a safe distance away. On the other hand, he'd noticed that when the girls did the "woohoo!" thing, they meant it ironically. Jake wasn't surprised; girls saw things differently.

Kevin, oblivious to his friends' antics, wiped the loose strands of dark brown hair from his forehead, never taking his eyes off of Angie. Max and Brian shook their heads in unison, confident they understood the pitfalls facing their smitten companion. The casual observer wouldn't have associated such insight with either Max or Brian.

What Max lacked in brains he made up in enthusiasm. Lanky and thin, with spiky red hair that seemed to be fighting to escape from under the baseball cap that he always wore well off center. A constellation of freckles failed to hide the fact that his battle with acne wasn't going well.

Brian never hesitated to point out that, while shorter than Max, he was still a half-inch taller than Kevin. Brian claimed to be growing a mustache, though he'd simply never shaved. Since he was blond, his mustache appeared to be little more than a rumor, and an ongoing dispute between Brian and his bathroom mirror.

The boys headed down a familiar trail into the undeveloped forest next to the ballpark. Long ago, local Miwok Indians named it *Hojamu Hale*, but these days everyone just called it "the Wood." It was a lot easier to pronounce. Almost two miles across at the widest point, the Wood featured a small pond near the middle, and a few overgrown hiking and biking trails that crisscrossed the terrain in no apparent pattern. In a more affluent community, it long ago would have been turned into a golf course country club. But few people here even noticed the Wood anymore.

Cutting through the trees saved the boys more than a half hour on the walk home, more important now as the sun sank behind the hills surrounding Santa Necia.

The four of them followed a winding trail that led to the west edge of the Wood, where the foliage seemed to simply run out of enthusiasm by the time it reached the rutted, dirt alley directly behind the Old Addison Place.

The boys stared at the crumbling Victorian and its once-impressive landscaping that had given way to waist-length overgrowth. Yellow caution tape surrounded the building, which seemed to be leaning over, an old man reaching for his cane. The veranda tilted dangerously outward, and all the windows they could see were boarded up. The shadows masked the faded colors that once made this place a thing of wonder.

"I've always thought this ol' place was kinda cool," Jake said. "Bet it was awesome back in the day."

"Yeah, well, pretty soon it's gonna be history," Max said. "My dad told me the town's gonna like sell it to some developer or somethin' for a shitload a cash."

Brian snorted. "Wrong, lizard breath. It doesn't even belong to the town. It was Old Lady Addison's, so it goes to her family. Obviously."

Max raised himself up to reinforce his height advantage. "Not if there isn't no family, dipstick."

"Max is right." Jake nodded toward the dilapidated building. "Our mom's the real estate agent who's gonna be handling the sale of the property."

"I thought she worked at that used clothes place," Brian said.

"Clarke's is a discount clothing store, you tool," Kevin said. "Besides, Mom's gonna quit that job once she gets her real estate career going."

"I don't see how you could get much for this old place," Jake said. "*Look* at it."

"I'm guessin' somebody just wants the land," Kevin said.

Brian smirked. "Seriously? This broke-down ol' yard looks like a freakin' bombsite."

"Yeah, well, like I told you, this whole place is gonna be gone." Max waved his arm in a wide arc to include the Wood.

"No way!" Jake groaned. "Not the Wood!"

"That's just a rumor." Kevin punched Max in the shoulder. "Jesus, Max, you'll believe anything!"

"Oh yeah? Well, my uncle says it's no rumor. He told my dad he heard it from a guy he works with."

"Come on, they can't destroy the Wood." Jake pulled off his cap and ran his fingers through his hair. "Can they?"

"Probably," Kevin said. "But why would somebody wanna do that?"

Nobody had an answer.

"Jesus, I gotta get goin' pretty soon," Max said. "Remember, Kev, you're gonna take my shift at Stan's tonight."

"I already told you I'd cover for you."

"Me and my brother are gonna pick up my wicked cool new ride," Max said. "It might need a little work, y'know, but it's like totally awesome."

"Yeah, we know," Kevin said. "You told us about it like a *hundred* times." He and Brian both had their driver's licenses, but they knew neither of them had a chance in hell of getting a car any time soon.

Brian took a shot at changing the subject. "Man, the Old Addison Place is pretty cool inside. At least it was the last time we busted in."

"Yeah, remember how creepy it is in there, with all the furniture and shit gone?" Kevin asked.

Max scoffed. "I also seem to remember Brian about pissed his pants."

"Yeah? Who tore off like a spastic duck when that window slammed shut?"

"Oh right, dog log, like you weren't—"

"Wanna go in one more time before they tear the whole thing down?" Kevin nodded toward the building.

"I dunno. What about the crime scene tape?" Brian asked.

Max grinned. "You scared?"

"I just don't want to end up in jail, jagoff."

"Dude, it's *caution* tape. This isn't a freakin' crime scene." Kevin started toward the house.

Max nodded to Jake. "What about the dwarf?"

Kevin stopped. "Max is right, Jake. It might be kinda, you know, dangerous."

"We wouldn't want you to get scared out of your tiny, impressionable mind," Brian said.

"Yeah, right." Jake chuckled. "I doubt I'd pee myself, though."

"Very funny, dickweed."

Brian and Max ducked under the tape.

"Maybe it *would* be better if you stayed here, Jake," Kevin said. "We won't be gone long." He hurried through the overgrown weeds to catch up with the others. The late afternoon shadows swallowed up the boys as they disappeared around the side of the house.

—∿∿∿—

Jake glanced down the alley, then back at the Old Addison Place. A broad grin crossed his face. He stuffed his baseball cap into his backpack, yanked out a worn red watch cap, and pulled it down over his unruly mop—effectively transforming himself into his alter ego, Captain Hawke, a heroic adventurer who sailed the oceans of the world and survived the frozen north in search of excitement and riches. Jake was a big fan of Jack London.

He slunk toward the gloomy structure. "It takes more than danger to keep the Hawke from his share of the treasure!"

Jake tore around the side of the house and located the window where the others had pried off the boards. He peered into the darkness, let out a pent-up breath, and climbed over the sill. When he paused to let his eyes adjust to the darkness, he heard a scraping sound coming from deeper inside.

As soon as he could see well enough in the dim light, he pressed his back against the wall and slid down the hallway toward the rear of the house. He came to a halt at the doorway to a huge kitchen. A perfect place to hide and pounce.

This late in the day very little light came through the kitchen window, but he made his way slowly toward what looked like some kind of pantry. He slipped inside and heard a thump on the far side of the kitchen. He peered out into the room as cabinet doors banged shut.

"Aaaaahhhhhh! Help me! It's got meeeeee!" shrieked a high-pitched voice that could only be Max overacting.

Even so, it startled Jake enough that he jumped back and slammed hard against the shelves. The wall emitted a painful screech and swung open, and Jake fell backward into blackness.

Kevin knew his claim to have dropped his Swiss Army knife inside was lame, but at least Max and Brian had pretended to buy it. He sprinted back to the open window and climbed inside. "Jake!" he shouted into the darkness.

No answer.

Kevin bit his lip and hurried down the hall into the kitchen. Jake was nowhere in sight. Kevin yelled again, "Hey, bro! Not funny. Where the hell are you?"

Jake leapt out from behind the pantry shelves.

Kevin shrieked.

"Damn, Kev, you all right?" Jake grinned. "You screamed just like a girl there."

"Shut up and quit screwin' around. Let's blow this place before it collapses on us."

"Wait a sec, Kev." Jake tilted his head toward the wall behind him. "You gotta check this out."

Jake pushed on the shelves, which creaked open enough to reveal a small room. "It's like full of old stuff. I think it was some kinda secret hiding place."

Except for some odd shapes and dark shadows, Kevin couldn't see much. He stepped back. "Yeah, well, it's probably just the old lady's worthless junk."

"Hey, maybe she's got some real old magazines and valuable old-time baseball cards. That stuff'd be worth a shitload of money now."

Kevin rolled his eyes.

Jake shrugged. "Well, she *could've* saved stuff like that."

Kevin marched down the hall. "Move it, Jake. We gotta be home when Mom calls to check on us."

Jake pulled the shelves back into place and took off after his brother.

CHAPTER 3

Charley Krock relaxed in the passenger seat, while his boss, Councilman James Wahdle, docked his silver Cadillac Escalade across from 17 Mozart Street, the Old Addison Place.

Wahdle unlatched the seat belt, freeing his substantial girth, and wheezed with relief. He leaned back and stuck his elbow out the open window. He reached into the Donut Delight bag resting on the console, eased out a chocolate cream donut, and half-heartedly tipped the bag toward his assistant.

Krock waved away the offer and stared out the window. He'd seen his boss stuff donuts into his face too often. Not a pretty sight.

Oblivious to the glob of cream slithering down his chins, Wahdle closed his eyes, lost in a state of greasy chocolate ecstasy.

Both gazed at the Old Addison Place, once an architectural showplace, now a victim of vandals and time. It barely held together—windows broken, gaping holes decimating the roof, and chunks of the siding and trim barely hanging on. The once-magnificent grounds surrounding the building had long ago given way to weeds and neglect.

Wahdle wiped his chin with a forefinger, and pulled a cruller out of the bag. "How could a dump like this cause me so much grief?"

"Not any more," Krock said. "With that crazy ol' bag Charlotte Addison dead and buried, there's nobody to stand between you and a boat load of cash." He knew better than anyone that the substantial, untraceable payoff Wahdle stood to gain from this latest venture would make every other crooked deal his boss had brokered look like chump change.

"We should have just burned her damn will." Wahdle finished off the cruller.

"Relax. The fact she left everything to this 'Ben' character won't be a factor much longer, sir. We've done the required search, and if he hasn't shown up by now, he sure as hell isn't going to."

"Probably some senile fantasy of hers anyway." Wahdle chortled. "Hell, all pathetic old broads spend their time dreaming about romantic heroes." Swallowing a grin, he shifted the donut bag to his lap and studied the remaining selections. He pulled out a maple bar.

"So, don't worry. The last of the contracts were signed this morning," Krock said. "Bulldozers are ready to roll. By the time anyone figures out what's going on, this'll all be gone." He swept his arm to indicate the neighborhood, the Old Addison Place, and the wooded area behind it.

"That's what I want to hear, Charley. Who the hell's gonna complain about losing a bunch of useless trees and ramshackle houses?" Wahdle licked chocolate from his lips. "Gonna be the biggest damn shopping-slash-business complex in this part of the state. It'll put Santa Necia on the map." Wahdle pulled a powdered jelly donut from the bag. "Write that down, Charley. I oughta use that line when I make the announcement."

Krock slipped a small, leather-bound notebook from his inside jacket pocket, flipped it open, and scribbled. "Point is, you're sitting pretty. The will's in probate, and its two-year statute-of-limitations is up in a week. Soon as the Town Council officially claims the place, it'll all be yours."

Wahdle blew donut shrapnel onto the steering wheel. "Can it, Charley! I'm a damn *silent* partner in this!" His eyes darted back and forth out the open car window, as if he expected a *60 Minutes* crew to leap from the bushes, cameras rolling.

Krock winced. "Sorry, I meant *Forest Glen Development* is poised to grab this property as soon as it's legally up for sale. Trust me, everything's going according to plan."

"It sure as hell better be." Wahdle added a growl for emphasis, an effort that would have been more effective if he hadn't had a mouthful of jelly donut. He checked again to make sure no one was lurking within earshot. "Montoya's people are getting edgy. They've already moved a small fortune from you-don't-want-to-know-where into Forest friggin' Glen. They're gonna be very unhappy if we don't get this…this *laundromat* up and running when we promised."

"Good one, sir." Krock smiled with practiced sincerity.

Wahdle laughed at his own cleverness. He plunged his hand into the bag and came up empty, except for powdered-sugar-covered fingers. He licked them clean. "What time ya got, Charley?"

"Four twenty-one."

"Close enough to five. Let's grab some dinner. We'll expense it."

CHAPTER 4

Saturday morning, Jill Parker drove past the ornate wooden Walt Staley Realty sign into the parking lot. Ever since she'd passed the Real Estate exam a few months ago, Jill had been working part time for Staley. Not much of a clientele yet, but if the real estate market continued to grow as predicted, she'd soon be making some real money. She couldn't wait to quit her assistant manager's job at Clarke's. For now, though, the paycheck she brought home from selling discount clothing was the only thing that put discount food on the table for her and the boys.

Jill could feel her luck changing, though. She had the listing for the Old Addison Place, and when the town seized the property in a couple of weeks, she'd be taking it into escrow. Even though the old woman's will left everything to someone she called "my dear friend, Ben," no Ben had shown up. No doubt Forest Glen Development intended to tear down the house as soon as the sale closed. It didn't matter to her what they did with the property. The buyer had made a very generous cash offer, and her commission on this sale alone would net her more than triple her salary at Clarke's.

When Jill checked the voice messages on her cell phone, she discovered she'd missed one from yesterday afternoon—a request from the high school guidance counselor that Jake's parents come in for a conference on Monday. Crap, she normally kept on top of messages. She'd just been so damned distracted lately. But if she expected to stay on top of two jobs, two boys, and a deadbeat ex-husband, she needed to focus.

What could be important enough to call a conference now? There were only a few weeks left in the school year. Jake was a good kid. A little impetuous sometimes, and he tended to day-dream. So what if he'd been a bit moody since he started high school? Jill chalked it up to normal teenage growing pains. As far as she knew, he'd never caused any trouble at school. His report cards weren't spectacular, but he managed passing grades.

Whatever the problem was, this conference meant she'd have to call Steve—they were supposed to be co-parenting. A joke. It also meant taking more time off from Clarke's. That wouldn't sit well with her manager; he'd probably dock her pay.

"Everything all right, Jill?" The deep male voice startled her.

She looked up to see Walt Staley leaning against the door-frame of her office. "Oh sure, Walt, just a school thing for Jake is all."

He strode over to her desk and stood a little too close to her. "So, have we got all our docs in a row?" Staley never got tired of his pet catchphrase, although he was the only one in the office who still chuckled at the pun.

"Uh huh, I have them all right here." Jill pulled a bulging folder out of her briefcase.

"Nice job on the Addison property, Jill. I'm impressed." Walt put his hand on her shoulder and squeezed. "Looks as if you've got everything under control."

She wanted to pull away; instead she sighed. "God, I hope so. We're ready to begin escrow the minute the statute of limitations runs out."

Walt leaned down close and offered his best seductive grin. "Tell you what, when the deal's done, how about I take you out to dinner to celebrate."

She looked away, hoping he hadn't noticed her flinch. "Oh, I don't know, Walt. I mean, um…that wouldn't—"

"Jesus, Jill, I'm not asking you out on a *date,* for Christ's sake. It's strictly business all the way."

"Of course. I know, Walt. I didn't mean to imply you meant anything."

He winked. "Bet it's been way too long since you've had some adult company."

"Almost two years." She wished she hadn't responded so quickly.

"Good, it's a date then."

Jill blanched.

Walt pointed his finger at her like a pistol. "Gotcha!" He chuckled his way into his office.

So far she'd been able to pretend his advances were simply innocent flirting. He hadn't yet crossed the line with her, but he'd sure as hell bumped up against it a few times. She hoped he wouldn't push further. Not with so much riding on her commission on the Addison sale. She closed her eyes and massaged the bridge of her nose.

If she overreacted to Walt's innuendoes, she could blame it on the fact Steve left her and the boys for some cheap slut from *his* office—blowing up their marriage of almost eighteen years. The bastard. Still, co-parenting meant letting him know about the school conference, even though he'd probably beg off.

Jill slumped back in her chair. Steeling herself, she picked up her phone. Somehow, talking to Steve always reduced her to a whining shrew. But, damn it, if Jake had gotten into some kind of trouble at school, *both* his parents should be there. She dialed Steve's cell, managing to keep her fingers from trembling.

"Helloooooh?" A female voice breathed into the receiver.

Had to be Steve's girlfriend. Jill swallowed a breath. "Let me talk to Steve, please."

"Honey, wake up. It's for you. I think it's your *ex*-wife."

Why couldn't the little tramp dial down the fact she was in bed with him? Still, Jill was determined to not let it upset her. She didn't care about Steve anymore. She really didn't.

"Hi, Jill, what's up?" Steve asked.

She could hear him yawn.

His girlfriend moaned in the background. "Um, looks like *you* are, lover."

Steve gasped.

Jill rolled her eyes. "Jake's guidance counselor wants us to come in for a conference."

"What's the problem? I thought school was over."

"No, Steve. It's not. I'd think you'd keep a little better track of the boys' activities. Like bothering to show up at some of Jake's ball games. He always looks for you, you know."

He sucked in three rapid breaths. "Gimme a break, Jill. I've been busy. Gotta make a living, don't I?"

"Which reminds me, when do you intend to start paying at least *some* child support?"

"*Stop* that, baby." He did his best to muffle the sound with a hand over the mouthpiece. "I'm tryin' to...oooh, god!"

Jill squeezed the phone so tightly she was surprised it didn't snap in two. "Look, I can tell you're *busy*, Steve. I'll let your sons know that their father just doesn't have time for them, because he's too busy trying to keep his nympho slut happy."

"She's not a…" His voice deep and raspy. "I'll try to…um, make it to the meeting thing."

"Sure you will, Steve. As long as you're pretending to care, the meeting is Monday at noon."

"Umm what?" He moaned. "I'll try…ooooh-my-god. I… um—"

"Damn it, Steve. This is *important*."

"What? Uh-uh-uh-uh—"

"Forget it, Steve. You know what? I don't even *want* you there." She punched OFF on her phone. Hard. She prided herself for not slamming the phone into her purse. Instead, she buried her face in her hands. At least she didn't break into tears this time.

CHAPTER 5

Jake swung his legs over the edge of a crude but sturdy platform nearly twenty feet up an ancient oak. In his mind he sat on the deck of *The Snark*, named after the boat built by Jack London himself.

Back when Jake and Lester were kids, they'd discovered this place near an overgrown hiking trail well into the Wood. They'd quickly claimed it as their secret pirate ship, *The Black Ghost*. They'd outgrown the pirate thing, hence the name-change to *The Snark*. Still, it would be embarrassing if any of their classmates discovered that Jake and Lester still sometimes played out sea-faring fantasies here—as Captain Hawke and First Mate Slade. Kinda lame, but really *The Snark* was just a cool place to hang out.

Jake surveyed his domain. A trapdoor in the floor served as the entrance. A rickety ladder nailed to the trunk was the only choice to reach *The Snark*. The ends of two thick ropes loosely wrapped around the makeshift railing were secured high up in the branches of a couple of taller trees several feet away. Tied to one of the ropes was a small red flag, to the other, a blue one.

Jake pulled his red watch cap down tight and flipped up the collar of his well-worn leather jacket. He'd discovered the jacket a couple of months ago at Goodwill, and it looked a lot like the one worn by London in the famous photograph of him sitting at a ship's wheel. Maybe the cap and jacket didn't transform Jake into a real seafarer, but they sure made him feel ready for action.

Jack London wasn't Jake's *idol* or anything. Not really. But ever since he'd read *The Call of the Wild* in seventh grade, Jake was hooked. He'd read every story of London's he could get his hands on. No other writer let him experience adventures in the balmy South Seas or the frigid Yukon like Jack London. No chance Jake would ever sail the world, drive a team of huskies, pan for gold, or ride the freights the way London had. He knew that. Sometimes, though, London-inspired fantasies helped him escape the boring reality of his life, if only for a while. It was a chance to be somebody special.

He eased back, hands behind his head.

Captain Hawke is exhausted from this rigorous trek through the godforsaken jungle—but he cannot let his men see him struggle. He is their leader, and they have come to expect more from him than from a mere mortal. It has been thirteen days since they set out from The Snark to seek the secret cavern that hides the famous Tongan Treasure, reputed to hold more riches than any ship's hold can carry. But they are close now. Hawke can feel it.

He calls for a halt to give his men a chance for a much needed break. But Hawke will not rest. He climbs to the top of an enormous banyan tree and scans the landscape with his telescope. In the midst of the overgrown jungle he spies what he's been looking for. A dark hole, a cave, several feet up on the side of a cliff and less than a day's march away. He feels a rush of excitement, as he checks his map. Yes! This is the place they've been seeking.

Hawke slides down to the ground and dashes back to his loyal crew. As he has come to expect, each man looks up at him with respect and awe, but Hawke senses something new. Excitement tempered with fear—

———

The ringing of his cell phone brought Jake back to the moment. A text from Lester: 1st mate slade rprt 4 duty. permission 2 cm abrd sir.

Jake grinned and texted back: permission grantd, mr slade.

Lester leapt into the clearing below *The Snark*. He raced up the ladder, shoved open the trapdoor, and hopped onto the platform.

"Prepare to go ashore, Mr. Slade."

"But I just got here."

Jake shot Lester a pretty good menacing glare, instantly reestablishing the ship's pecking order.

"Aye, Cap'n." Lester saluted. "Preparing to go ashore. Um, so you wanna play video games at my place? Or we could—"

"Belay that, Mr. Slade," Jake growled. "There's real adventure afoot."

"No shit? What?"

"You'll be seein' soon enough, Mr. Slade." Jake grabbed the red-flagged rope, ready to swing down to the ground. He turned to Lester. "Beware the blue flag, mate."

Jake swung with practiced ease to the ground and flipped the rope in an arc up to the deck of *The Snark*. Lester grabbed the rope and secured it to the railing before he pulled up the trapdoor and scrambled down the ladder to his bike hidden in the brush.

Just as Lester was about to pull ahead in their impromptu bike race, Jake cut down an alley and came to a skidding halt at the edge of the caution tape surrounding the Old Addison Place. Lester followed Jake's lead, ducking under the tape and stashing his bike out of sight in the shadows next to the building.

Lester glanced around. "I don't think we're supposed to be messing around here."

Jake grinned. "What's the matter, Mr. Slade? Afraid?"

"No. Not really, it's just that, you know." Lester gestured toward the caution tape.

"Dude, that doesn't mean shit. Me and Kevin and his backup band were in here yesterday on the way home from the game."

"Really?"

"Yep. So step lively, Mr. Slade. Exotic riches await." Jake raced to the familiar open window, tossed his backpack inside, and lifted himself over the windowsill.

"Come on, Les. I promise it's totally cool inside."

Lester handed Jake his pack and hoisted himself up to the windowsill.

Jake grabbed Lester's arm and helped him inside. "C'mon, dude. You gotta see what I discovered. You're not gonna freakin' *believe* it."

With Lester following close behind, they made their way down the hall and into the kitchen. The late morning sunlight filtered through cracks in the boarded-up windows, revealing a large empty room. Dust motes danced in the shafts of light. A thick layer of dust and grime covered every surface. Doors were missing from half the cabinets, and there were no appliances in sight. Even the sink had been taken. Empty beer cans and cigarette butts were strewn among the discarded syringes and fast-food containers on the cracked and broken linoleum floor.

"Seriously? *This* is what you're so freakin' excited about?" Lester scrunched up his face at the musty smell.

"Nope." Jake stepped toward the pantry. "Les, you gotta see this."

"Jake, this whole place is way too creepy. Everybody says old lady Addison was some kinda witch, or devil worshipper, or somethin'."

"The Hawke's in command here. No witches or goblins'll be willin' to show their faces around me."

"You're just weird." Lester shook his head.

"Weird...but *feared*!" Jake charged into the pantry.

Lester took a deep breath and followed.

"Check *this* out, dude." Jake leaned back against the shelves.

Lester gasped as the wall of shelves began to move, exposing the small dark room behind it. Shards of sunlight seeped in just enough to reveal unrecognizable shapes.

"Whoa! What is this place, Jake? I mean, are you sure we—?"

"Booty from exotic ports o' call, Mr. Slade."

Lester chuckled.

"Dude, what's so funny?"

"I'd love to get me some real booty."

Jake smirked. "Stop dreamin', Les. Our luck's not *that* good." He marched into the secret room.

Lester followed, determined to ignore any demons that might be lurking nearby.

Jake pulled a flashlight from his pack and shined it around the room. Some large wooden crates were stacked next to a couple of old steamer trunks. A tattered sheet covered something that might have been a desk or a bureau.

Lester grabbed Jake's arm and pointed to a dark corner, wide-eyed. Against the wall stood the body of a headless woman. She wasn't moving. Yet.

Jake turned the light on the apparition.

"Chill, Les. It's just one of those things that women used back in the day for like makin' dresses. My grandma had one like this in her attic, I think." Jake sauntered over and held out the skirt of an old-fashioned, tattered gown on the dressmaker's dummy. "Dude, this looks like it's at least a hundred years old."

"Wonder why she saved that grungy old dress, anyway."

"I bet it wasn't in this bad a shape when old lady Addison stashed it here. Might a been a pretty cool dress back then."

Lester maneuvered around the small space, taking it in bit by bit, careful to avoid physical contact with anything. Jake looked inside one of the crates, pulled out an ancient dinner plate and a chipped teacup, and set them aside. Lester rummaged around in one of the large trunks. Nothing but old clothes.

Against the far wall, Jake spied a table, partially draped with some kind of fringed, shawl-looking thing that had probably once been very colorful. "All *right*."

In the center of the table, a young man in a Navy uniform smiled at them from a faded photograph. Arranged around its tarnished gilt frame were various medals, a set of dog tags, a decaying American flag folded in a triangle, and a few other relics of a sailor who never returned home from a war.

Lester and Jake stared at the display, as if this called for a moment of silence for the plight of a fellow seafarer.

Then something toward the back of the table caught Jake's eye. "Ha! I told ya there'd be treasure here, Mr. Slade." He picked up three coins and handed them to Lester.

Lester studied them, shaking his head. "These sure aren't American. The letters are all snaky-lookin'."

"They're obviously from a far-off port o' call." Jake gently pulled aside a faded cloth, unveiling a small, old-time ship's lantern. "Ah ha!" He held it up.

"What's that thing?"

Jake studied it. "It's some kinda old-school ship's lantern." He held it out for Lester to get a better look. "See? It has the word 'Port' engraved on it."

"Port means left, doesn't it?"

"Yep. They woulda had lanterns like this on sailing ships like a hundred years ago." Jake rubbed the dust off the red glass window. "This is somethin' right outta *The Sea Wolf.*" He handed the lantern to Lester.

Lester hefted it in one hand. "Wow, I thought it'd be a lot heavier."

"Me too, but it's gotta be an antique. A little grungy, but it might be like brass or somethin'. Bet she shines up pretty good."

Lester's eyes lit up. "Dude, seriously, you could clean it up and score mega-bucks on eBay." He handed the lantern back.

"Yeah, it's gotta be pretty valuable. If it wasn't, why would old lady Addison keep it hidden away in a secret room?"

"Maybe 'cause she was a few Bradys short of a bunch?"

"Chill, dude. You worry too much." Jake used his sleeve to wipe away as much of the heavy dust layer as he could and headed toward the open wall.

"Jake, um, you sure we should be takin' this stuff?"

"Code of the seas, Mr. Slade. Whoever finds the treasure, claims it." Jake flicked off the flashlight, stuffed the lantern into his backpack, and strutted out.

Lester tossed the coins into his own pack and ran after Jake.

Pedaling like mad, the boys raced down the alley. They swerved to avoid a beat-up green pickup jouncing along the rutted surface of the alley towing an ancient Airstream trailer.

—⁓⁓⁓—

The pickup pulled off to the side directly behind the Old Addison Place. The elderly driver dragged himself out and stretched his large frame, as if his entire body were cramped and sore. He shook his head back and forth, trying to get rid of the cobwebs. Keeping his eyes on the boys, he removed an old Brooklyn Dodgers baseball cap and ran his fingers through his thin white hair.

CHAPTER 6

Jake and Lester raced their bikes through Babylon Park, where they both lived. It was one of Santa Necia's less affluent areas, although in all honesty, there weren't many affluent sections of Santa Necia. Babylon Park was usually referred to as B-Park, which may have had more to do with its second-rate status than a shortening of the name.

That didn't mean the residents of the neighborhood didn't take pains to maintain their homes. Some did. It would be easy to miss these efforts, though, unless a driver slowed down and looked. Since most cars used B-Park as a shortcut to somewhere more important, most people noticed only rows of run-down one- and two-story wooden structures, with small lawns clutching broken sidewalks. Several houses, including the Parkers', sported driveways and detached garages.

The Parker house may not have been the nicest on the street, but it wasn't the worst. The original sky-blue paint had faded toward chalky gray, but it showed no signs of peeling or chipping. The small, newly mowed lawn managed to hold its own in the ongoing border dispute between the grass and the horde of dandelions and other interlopers. Jill had recently planted red, orange, and yellow zinnias along the walkway. That helped.

The boys came to a stop in the alley behind the Parker house. They heard a basketball bounce off the rickety rim over the garage. Kevin. They leaned their bikes against the side of the garage, and Jake signaled Lester to follow him toward the driveway.

"Ready, Mr. Slade?" Jake whispered.

"Aye, Cap'n."

They peeked around the edge of the garage to watch Kevin, in red gym shorts and a sweat-drenched LA Clippers T-shirt, provide running commentary as he dribbled the basketball and eyed the hoop. "Four seconds left on the clock, Marv. It's now or never for the Clips, and everyone in the Staples Center knows who the ball's going to."

Kevin bounced the ball off the garage door, scooped it up, and faced an invisible opponent. "Parker fakes left, then right. He shoots!" The ball hit the rim, bounced against the backboard, and fell through the net. "He SCOOOOOORES! The Clippers win! The crowd goes wild! Haaaaaaaah, haaaaah!" Kevin emulated the roar of the crowd as he thrust both arms into the air, acknowledging the adulation of the fans. He strutted under the basket pantomiming high-fives, low-fives, and chest bumps with imaginary teammates. With perfect timing, Jake leapt from the shadows and jumped up to complete a high-five with his brother.

Kevin was startled, embarrassed—and pissed. "Where'd *you* come from, dweeb?"

Jake hopped out of reach. "We were attracted by the roar of the crowd."

"Yeah? Well, next time you just might end up with a basketball enema, you little…" Kevin spotted Lester. "Hey, Les."

"Hey, Kevin."

"So, Les, um, how's your…um, how's—?"

"Angie's doing okay."

"The Hawke strikes again!" Jake took off for the house.

Kevin didn't notice. "Um, so…are she and Robert Cahill like still a thing? I heard they might—"

"Naw. He turned into a total cokehead. The bastard started gettin' rough with her too. So she dumped his ass."

Kevin beamed.

"She was too good for that dickweed, anyway," Lester shot back as he took off after Jake.

Jake and Lester stormed the cluttered kitchen and tossed their backpacks on the table.

The boys rummaged through the refrigerator, discovered nothing more appealing than a couple of slices of suspect cheese, and moved on to the cupboard. Jake pulled out a box of Honey Nut Cheerios, claimed a fistful, and offered the box to Lester.

Lester plunged his hand in. "Jeez, you guys always used to have great munchies."

"Yeah, I know."

Jake was well aware money was tight. Especially since his dad didn't help with expenses anymore. Then again, they'd never had much even before his dad left. But Jake knew the trouble between his parents went beyond money issues. His dad having a girlfriend upset his mom a lot. Even though she tried to hide it, he sometimes heard her crying in her room. He wanted to go in and try to make things better for her; he just didn't know how. He didn't think a hug would be enough.

Jake rummaged around under the kitchen sink among the collection of mysterious cleaning supplies. "Ah-*hah*!" He emerged with a plastic bottle of Uncle Glitz's Liquid Metal Polish. "This stuff might work for cleanin' up that old-school ship's lantern."

"What *is* that crap?" Lester asked.

"I think maybe it's somethin' my dad polished his car with."

"The old Chevy? That thing is wacked."

"Yeah, well, I'm not sayin' he used this stuff *recently*."

The boys bounded up the stairs to Jake's room. Jake plopped down on the bed, and Lester planted himself on the chair of a beat-up desk where an outdated laptop rested. A small television sat on a chest of drawers against the wall across from the bed. A few clothes were hung haphazardly in the closet, and an equal number of T-shirts, socks, and underwear were strewn on the floor under the room's only window. The uneven patches on the tan walls were evidence Jake had painted the room himself some years ago. He didn't even notice the flaws anymore.

Lester booted up Jake's old computer. "I'm gonna find out what the hell this thing is."

Jake peered over Lester's shoulder. "Good idea, dude. Look for pictures of antique ships' lanterns or somethin'."

Lester googled it. "Man, there's way too many kinds of ships' lanterns here to be able to find…wait! Here it is."

Jake leaned closer. "Click on it. See what it says."

Lester skimmed the text. "It says you had to have one of these or they wouldn't let you into Hong Kong Harbor back in the day."

"And see," Jake pointed to the screen, "it burned oil…so it has to be pretty freakin' old!"

Lester read on. "These lanterns were generally small, usually about nine inches high, five inches wide, often weighing no more than a pound or two." He seized a wooden ruler from the desk drawer and held it up to the lantern in Jake's hand. "Yep, this is it all right."

Grinning, Jake lifted the lantern triumphantly. "So this sucker is totally an antique." He checked the T-shirts on the floor, picked one he didn't mind ruining, and plopped down on the bed. Squeezing a little of the metal polish onto the T-shirt, he worked at removing the oxidation from the metal surface of the lantern. The red glass would have to wait until later. He stopped polishing and stared at the top of the lantern. "Hey, check this out!"

"What?" Lester slid over to the bed.

"There's some kind of writing on this thing!"

Taking the lantern from Jake, Lester examined the brass top. "Naw, it's just more of those squiggly symbols like on the coins we found. But, dude, that lantern's startin' to look *tight*. You're gonna get a shitload a cash for this thing."

"No, wait." Jake grabbed it back. "Here, look down at it from the top, like this." He tilted the lantern toward Lester.

Lester read. "Oh brave lib…liberator of this sacred beacon." He glanced up at Jake, wide-eyed, then read on. "Three wishes only to thee be granted."

Jake tilted the lantern back and finished. "Woe be unto him who would reveal his wish. For it will soon be re…recanted."

"What's 'recanted' mean?"

"Hell if know." Jake set the lantern down on the bed and hopped to his desk. He pulled up dictionary.com.

Lester peered over his shoulder while Jake found the word and scanned the definition.

"Withdraw, um, revoke…cancel."

The boys spun around and stared at the lantern. They were much too old to believe in magic crap. But no one was watching. Their concerted effort to maintain an air of thoughtful skepticism lasted about ten seconds.

"All riiiiight!" they both yelled at once, exchanging a vigorous high-five.

"So this thing supposedly gives you three wishes, just like in all the stories, right?" Jake looked to Lester for confirmation.

"Yeah, that's gotta be what it means. But the brave liberator can't tell anybody what he wishes for."

"What's a liberator again?"

"I'm pretty sure that means the one who found the lantern... the guy who gets to make the wishes. *You!*"

Jake shrugged. "I knew that."

"So let's try it out. Maybe there'll be like a genie or somethin'."

"Right." Jake chuckled. The only genie he could think of was the crazy-weird guy in the Aladdin cartoon with Robin Williams' voice. Jake would have preferred something more...real. And less blue.

"Come on, we *gotta* see if it works. Try makin' a wish."

"Okay, but...um, like what?"

"How about a Corvette? No, no, a turbo Porsche! Red!"

"A real one?"

"Duh. Of course a real one."

"Dude, that would be so *cool.* But I gotta wait more'n a year before I can get my license."

"It'll be freakin' awesome anyway, Jake! Once the word gets out that you got a sweet ride like that, you'll be a total chick magnet."

Both boys took a moment to absorb the implications of such a status.

Jake sucked in a quick breath. "Okay, here goes." He reached over, picked up the lantern from the bed, and looked it over, unsure exactly how to go about it. Holding the lantern in both hands, he leaned down next it. "Hey, ol' lantern," he murmured. "How about a tur—"

"Wait!"

Jake looked up. "What's the matter?"

"It's gonna recount."

"Re*cant*, you mean."

"Whatever. Anyway, you can't tell anybody what your wish is."

"Oh yeah, I forgot." Jake squeezed his eyes shut, scrunched up his face, and made his silent wish. He looked up expectantly.

Lester glanced around the room, then back at his friend. "I don't see anything."

"Of course not, dude. It'd be in the driveway…probably." Jake took off for his mother's room and the window that overlooked the driveway. Lester was hot on his heels.

Nothing in the driveway. Not even Kevin.

"Damn." Lester shook his head. "Guess it doesn't work."

"Let me try again." Jake repeated the ritual, this time more deliberately. He scanned the driveway. "Crap. The thing is bogus."

The boys shuffled back to Jake's room in silence.

Jake slumped onto the bed.

Lester plopped down in the desk chair again. "Maybe you have to do it like under a full moon or somethin'."

Jake rolled his eyes. "Get real, dude, that's only for werewolves."

"Oh, right."

Jake turned the lantern in his hands, examining it.

"Hey, tip it up like that again."

"Like this?" Jake flipped the lantern, exposing the bottom to the light.

"Seriously, dude, it's just a joke."

"What do you mean?"

Lester took the lantern and tipped it so that it caught the light just right. Etched on the bottom was some kind of symbol that looked suspiciously like a smiley face.

"Crap. But who cares if it's not really magic anyway? It's still damn impressive swag." Jake went back to polishing the surface, determined not to reveal the depth of his disappointment.

"I guess so." Lester slipped over to the computer and called up YouTube music videos. A fuzzy image came into focus, revealing a high-energy music performance by The Skidd Markz. He shook his head. "Their act is so wacked."

"Yeah, Mom doesn't even like *Kevin* to watch these guys. But they're like his favorite band."

Kevin strode into the room, grinning, and sauntered over to Jake on the bed. "Jesus, you dorks, did you forget I can hear everything you're sayin' from my room? And, spoiler alert, I'm totally over the freakin' Skidd Markz." Kevin grabbed the lantern and looked it over.

Jake's shoulders drooped. "Looks like the stuff on there about three wishes is just a bunch of bullshit."

Lester shook his head. "Yeah, it's like a practical joke or somethin'."

"Well, *duh*." Kevin rolled his eyes. "We're not livin' in a freakin' cartoon here."

"Come on, bro, we totally knew it wasn't really magic or anything."

"Yeah." Lester folded his arms across his chest. "And I was only kiddin' about the genie."

Jake snatched back the lantern. "I'm keepin' it anyway 'cause it's wicked cool."

The Skidd Markz finished their video with a flourish. Jake absently began polishing the lantern again, as a commercial for Pluto's Pizzeria began.

"God! There's more commercials on the Internet than on TV these days," Lester said.

"Who cares? This one is seriously makin' me hungry," Jake said.

The image of a Pluto's Super Colossal pizza filled the screen.

Kevin licked his lips. "That would taste so freakin' *great* right now."

Lester's eyes widened. "Man, it's so real it's like you can even smell it."

Jake glanced over at the Pluto's Super Colossal pizza box nestled on top of his bedspread. He turned back the lantern, wide-eyed, then lifted the box lid to reveal a steaming hot pizza. "Sweeeet! It freakin' *does* work!"

Lester and Kevin slid over and gawked at the pizza.

"What the *hell?*" Kevin reached over and poked the pizza.

"What did you do different?" Lester asked.

"Um, well, I was polishing it, and I guess I…" Jake looked at the stained T-shirt in his hand. "Maybe you gotta be rubbing it when you make a wish."

"Oh yeah, now I remember," Lester said. "That's how they usually do it in the fairy…um, in the old legends." He glanced around the room and puffed out a sigh.

Jake noticed. "What's the matter, Les?"

"No genie." Lester shrugged. "But I totally knew that part was a bunch of crap."

Jake laughed. "This is real life, dude."

"Well, this pizza sure as hell is real." Kevin grabbed one of the huge slices and began to devour it.

Jake and Lester followed suit. After a few bites, Jake looked around for something to wipe his hands on. "Guess I shoulda wished for some napkins too."

"And a pitcher of Coke," Kevin said.

Lester nodded. "And some of those awesome bread sticks."

"Yeah, with that special sauce to dip 'em in," Kevin added.

Jake studied the lantern next to him, but the elation drained from his face. "That was *stupid*."

Kevin smirked. "You kidding? Those bread sticks are epic!"

"Pluto's Super Colossal is the best pizza in town." Lester took a huge bite.

Jake sighed. "No, I mean…now I only have two wishes left."

The front door closed downstairs with a bang. The boys looked at each other in a panic.

"Jacob Daniel Parker, are you up there?"

"Yeah, Mom, we're in my room." Jake jammed the lantern, soiled T-shirt, and polish into his backpack.

"Uh-oh, she sounds pissed." Lester swallowed the last of his slice of pizza and wiped his mouth with his sleeve.

Kevin slammed the pizza box shut and slipped it under the bed.

All three boys spun around to face Jill as she walked in.

"Would you guys excuse us please? Jake and I need to have a little talk."

"Sure." Lester nodded. "Time to get goin' anyway. See ya, Jake."

"Um, I should get back to my homework." Kevin escaped to his room.

"What's that smell?" Jill scrunched up her nose and marched over to the window, absently picking up discarded clothing and dropping them into the clothes hamper next to it. "Jake, how many times have I told you that you have to air out your room once in a while?" She opened the window as far as it would go.

"Sorry, Mom."

She twisted around to face him. "Jake, what am I going to do with you? As if I didn't have *enough* trouble!"

"Jeez, Mom, what did *I* do?"

"Why can't you at least make an *effort* to live up to your potential, Jake?" She closed her eyes and massaged her forehead. "You're clever. You're smart. But you just don't apply yourself in school."

"I don't know what you're talkin' about, Mom. I'm gettin' mostly Cs and Bs, I think."

"So maybe you can explain why I got a phone call from the high school guidance counselor."

"I don't have a clue." He flipped his hands out to the side. The look on his mom's face told him she wasn't buying it. "I didn't do anything. Honest!"

"Really? Mr. What's-his-name didn't offer any details, but I have a feeling you have a pretty good idea already, young man."

"No...honest, Mom, I promise, nobody said anything to *me* about any problems."

The look of utter confusion on her son's face caused Jill's exasperation to melt away. She really needed to keep her perspective; *Jake* wasn't really the source of her anger. Jill strolled over to the bed and plopped down next to him.

She put her arm around Jake and pulled him close. "I didn't mean to snap at you. It's just...I have a lot on my mind these days. And your father is obviously more concerned with that tramp... than with his family."

"Honest, Mom, I don't know what's going on. I mean, school's almost over anyway."

"Well, I guess we'll find out." Jill kissed Jake on the cheek and stood. "You know? I'm just too worn out to cook tonight. Let's all go out for dinner. I kind of feel like pizza. How about you?"

"Um…sure, Mom. That'd be great."

CHAPTER 7

Jake and Lester agreed to keep the whole three-wishes thing quiet. Who'd believe them anyway? They spent most of the night texting back and forth options for the other two wishes. The list grew like crazy, and Jake's adrenaline rush didn't wear off until after two.

As soon as Jill left for the real estate office Sunday morning, Kevin and Jake gathered around Jake's computer. Online, they examined everything from ridiculously expensive cars to the coolest new games for PlayStation and Xbox.

Kevin plopped down on Jake's bed. "This is fun, but no way you can wish for this much stuff. You'd need like a thousand wishes."

Jake leaned back in the chair, hands behind his head. "Remember when you were a little kid, and you went to see the fake Santa at the mall?"

"I guess so, what's that got to—"

"You're sitting on his lap, right? And he asks you what you want for Christmas. So you tell him, I want this and this and this and this and that. You know, give him your whole Christmas list.

Maybe I could do something like that."

"You mean if you wished for a lot of different stuff, but put it all in one sentence?"

"Uh huh."

They pondered the idea in silence.

Jake scrunched up his face. "Probably doesn't work that way."

"Yeah, everybody knows you can't wish for more wishes, I doubt you can get away with sneaking a whole bunch of 'em into one long wish."

"Besides, in the old fairy tales it's always just one thing per wish."

Kevin shrugged. "You know, bro, maybe you oughta just wish for like a shitload of money...for everyone in the family."

"Yeah. I was kinda thinkin' that too. It'd sure as hell be a hun-dred-and-eighty-degree shift from the way we're living now."

Kevin rolled his eyes. "Got that right."

"Anyway, me and Lester are goin' over to the Crowne Pointe Mall...just to kinda check out some possibilities."

Kevin hopped to his feet. "Cool, but talk to me before you make any wishes. I'll make sure we don't end up with any more accidental pizzas."

"Gimme a break, Kev. I didn't know the freakin' lantern really worked."

"Course not. Who'd ever figure this three-wishes crap actually existed?"

"Yeah, but wasting a wish was totally stupid."

Kevin laid a hand on his brother's shoulder. "It'll be all right, Jake. We'll figure it out." He glanced at his watch. "Listen, bro, I gotta haul ass to the Superette, or I'm gonna be in trouble."

"I just gotta think this thing through," Jake said. "It's way more complicated than I thought."

"Well, whatever you finally decide to wish for, life as we know it is about to change big time." Kevin beamed.

"Yeah, I guess so." Jake tried to return the smile, but he couldn't quite pull it off. His stomach did a flip-flop. It was a little scary that his brother was a lot surer about how things were going to turn out than he was.

Jake followed Kevin downstairs to the kitchen.

"Don't worry, Jake, I'll help you. We're in this together, bro. Just try and forget about it for a while."

Jake watched Kevin sprint out to his bike in the garage and race down the street. It occurred to him maybe Kev wouldn't have to be one of the few seniors next year who still rode a bike everywhere. Maybe he'd be able to get him a car. A nice one.

Jake picked up the cereal bowls from breakfast and rinsed them in the sink. Mom hated it when the cereal dried up and stuck to the bowl. He glanced at the broken dishwasher. Well, at least they might not have to put up with that piece of shit much longer.

The West Valley Mall in Crowne Pointe—the only large shopping center in the area—was a half-hour bus ride from Santa Necia. Local teens generally preferred to hang out at Bonzo's Burgers next to Stan's Superette, where Kevin worked. But today the upscale mall seemed to be awash with teen girls.

Lester poked Jake in the arm. "Check it out, dude." He nodded toward a clutch of four high school girls they knew, but only by name. All modeled variations of the same outfit—skin-tight designer jeans, solid-color layered knit tops, and top-of-the-line Nikes in fluorescent colors. Each of the four had a pink iPhone sticking out of her right back pocket.

"iButts," Jake whispered.

They exchanged fist bumps. "Dude, I'm gonna use that one. That's *sick*."

As Jake and Lester passed, Carrie Cartwright, the hottest of the four, rolled her eyes. Jake heard her say, "Seriously? A couple of total retardvarks." All four pulled out their phones, thumbs a-blur, as they launched into a Twitter frenzy. Probably to keep their loyal followers updated on the hottest new slang for "loser." It would be all over school by Monday.

"Freakin' stuck-up bitches," Lester murmured as soon as they were far enough away from the girls.

Jake glanced back as the four shared the texts on their iPhone screens. "But I gotta say Cartwright's got some choice boobage on her."

"The rest of her is tight too." Lester blew out a sigh. "She may be a bitch, but you gotta admit she's a totally *hot* bitch."

"Seriously. The stuff dreams are made of."

At Power Mania, they pretended to race each other on the matching Jet Skis in the floor display, imitating the roar of racing engines, much to the chagrin of the forty-something salesman, who was already annoyed at being forced to wear form-fitting cycling regalia on the job. It wasn't easy to talk normally while continually sucking in his gut and keeping an eye out for an opportunity to adjust his package.

Later, Lester strutted around Good Sports, modeling a way overpriced LA Kings jacket. Jake flopped through the shoe department in a pair of two-hundred-dollar Hondo Henry signature basketball shoes, which featured an elaborate fastening system so high-tech it came with printed instructions.

Finally the salesman had seen enough. "Okay, you've had your fun. Time for you guys to get on someone else's nerves."

The boys moved on to the mall-satellite agency of Workowski Real Estate. The prominently displayed slogan—"With *Workowski*, you're closer than you think to *your house key*"—solicited groans from potential clients whenever they noticed the painful rhyme.

Since Jake and Lester were the only people in the office at the time, the agent on duty allowed herself to be greatly amused by the boys' interest in million-dollar-plus homes. "I assume this is for some kind of school project."

Lester shook his head. "No, we're just kinda doing some research…for our parents."

"Yeah, we might be movin' soon. We're totally gonna be gettin' out of Babylon Park."

The agent raised an eyebrow. "Well, boys, I'm sure your parents would be more interested in something a bit more…*practical*, one of our more economical properties."

Lester scrunched up his face. "What do you mean by that?"

The agent rolled her eyes. These boys were cute, but *really*.

"So how would it work if we like paid cash for one of these places," Jake asked, waving his hand toward the photos of the highest-priced listings.

The agent chuckled. "Don't be silly, sweetie. *Very* few people do that."

Jake narrowed his eyes. "Oh, so you're sayin' you couldn't handle a cash sale?"

Lester scoffed. "I think we should be talkin' to somebody else. Obviously this agency is too small-time."

Both boys whirled around and marched out of the office, managing to stifle their laughter until they were out of sight.

"What a total bee-atch," Lester said.

"Yeah, but *man*, some of those houses were stupid cool."

"Totally. One of them even had *two* pools."

"And tennis courts."

"Anyway, your mom could probably find you a house like that. I mean she works for that real estate company and all."

"Maybe, but I don't think Walt Staley Realty handles mega-houses like those."

They strolled along without a word, both imagining what it would be like to live in a house bigger than their whole school.

Lester peeked at Jake, who was staring ahead, a frown on his face. He patted Jake on the shoulder. "Hey, you okay, dude?"

"What? Oh, yeah, I'm good. I was just thinkin' that maybe I shouldn't be concentrating so much on buyin' expensive shit. You know?"

"Yeah, there's like a ton of less pricey things you could get that we probably haven't even thought of yet."

"No, Les, I mean maybe I shouldn't wish for *things* at all? It feels weird to be only thinkin' about myself. Maybe I should consider, you know, other people too."

"Like your family…or your *friends*?" Lester broke into a big cockeyed grin.

Jake looked at the ground. "I could use my wishes for important stuff. I could totally do something that really matters."

"Like wishin' your mom and dad back together?"

"I dunno." Jake bit his lower lip. "I'm not sure they really want to be married to each other anymore. Besides there are… maybe even bigger things I could do with my wishes."

"Like wishin' for a cure for cancer or somethin'?"

"Maybe…I dunno *what* exactly." Jake sighed. "It's just that there's tons of stuff to think about if I'm gonna make the right wishes. In all the old fairy tales, they totally screw up and make wishes without thinking about it."

"Right. And they usually end up with nothin'."

"Yeah, and I already wasted one wish. I don't want to waste the others."

"But aren't you supposed to wish for stuff you really want… like for yourself?"

"But first I gotta figure out what I freakin' want."

"Why don't you just wish for like a hundred gazillion dollars and then do somethin' like you're talkin' about?"

Jake chuckled. "Yeah, maybe. But what if it turns us all into a bunch of mega-rich jerks, who only care about themselves and buying more expensive stuff than the other guy. I hate those kinda people. Mostly, though, I just don't wanna waste my wishes on stupid stuff that's just gonna wear out. You know, like some dumbass little kid would!"

"Dude, so would most *adults*," Lester said. "Anyway, there's no hurry to make the wishes. It's just kinda fun to think about gettin' cool stuff, you know?"

"Yeah." Jake reached back and patted his pack, reassuring himself that the lantern was still inside. "It's just that…I got a lot to think about. Maybe I should talk to my mom about it."

"Bad idea, dude. She's never gonna believe that the wishes are *real*. You'd have to use up your second wish just to prove it."

"Yeah, I know. Old people never believe in magic. Jesus, Les, until yesterday, neither did I."

CHAPTER 8

Jake dashed along Handel Street on his bike and zipped over to Strauss. Mondays were a pain, especially if he got busted for being tardy, and even worse today because his mom had that stupid meeting. He had to make up for lost time, and cutting down the pothole-filled alley next to the Wood could shave at least six minutes. Whatever trouble he already faced at school, showing up late wasn't going to help.

He slowed as he approached the beat-up green pickup and a small Airstream trailer now parked behind the Old Addison Place. The trailer's metal surface featured several dents and scratches. Jake could tell someone lived in it by the crooked stovepipe sticking out of the roof and the faded canvas awning shading the wooden steps at the door.

"Well, well. If it isn't that wise-ass Parker," boomed a voice behind him.

Jake looked back to see Buster Flatt flanked by his two thug buddies at the end of the alley, their bikes lined up like Indians on a mesa in an old Western. Buster was an oversized asshole who'd been regularly tormenting him since middle school. A freshman like Jake, Buster was almost two years older and twice his size. Buster often bragged at school that he owned a tricked-out Camaro. But since the bastard still rode his bike to school, Jake called bullshit.

Everyone called Buster's sidekicks "Tweedledumb" and "Tweedledumber." But never to their faces. Tweedledumb sneered. "I wonder what surprises the little prick has in his backpack for us today."

All three took off toward Jake.

He wasn't sure he'd be able to outrun them, but no way he was handing over the lantern to these buttheads. He glanced back; they were gaining on him. When he heard the bullies come to a skidding, tumbling halt, Jake swung around to see what happened.

An old man in faded overalls, plaid shirt, and a well-used blue baseball cap stood directly in the path of Buster and the Tweedles, his arms folded across his chest. He might have been old, but he was big, and it didn't look like he intended to move out of the way.

Jake slowed to a stop and watched Buster pick up his bike, flip it around, and climb back on. The Tweedles followed suit. When they were a safe distance from the old man, Buster yelled over his shoulder, "This ain't over, Parker."

All three raced back out of the alley, and Jake walked his bike back toward the old man. "Thanks, mister. Those guys would have had me for sure."

"You best be gettin' your behind in gear, young fella, before those hooligans make it around t' the other end of the alley."

"Shit!" Jake blushed. "Oh, um, sorry, mister. I—"

The old guy tilted his head down the alley.

"Thanks again, mister," Jake hollered as he sped off.

The old man kept tabs on the kid until he sped around the corner. Then he allowed himself a hint of a smile.

CHAPTER 9

Jake squirmed on the world's most uncomfortable wooden bench outside the school office. His mom had just arrived for the conference, but he had too much on his mind to concentrate on what might be going on in the room on the other side of the wall. If he wished for his dad to be back into the family, wouldn't he have to erase his mom's memory so she wouldn't be so pissed at him for leaving? But would it be right to force people together when they didn't want to be? And if he did that, how many wishes would it take?

The wall clock in the hall seemed to click backward, in that maddening way of all school clocks. Jake sighed and shifted his butt on the bench. Again. Finally he pulled his World History book out of his backpack. Might as well finish up the reading he should have already done. He stared at the montage of images on the cover: Egyptian pyramids, Roman ruins, a guillotine, soldiers on horseback, and some old-school sailing ships. Could be the Spanish Armada. Or maybe Sir Francis Drake or some other high-seas adventurer.

Screw it. No way he could concentrate on a mind-numbing

history text. Jake dropped the book in his lap. He leaned back against the wall, his hands behind his head, and let his mind wander.

———❧———

Captain Hawke stands at the bow of a longboat, while four of his most reliable crewmembers row toward the secluded inlet of a small island in the South Seas. The schooner, anchored a hundred yards off shore in the dense fog, is invisible from the shoreline. Their mission is fraught with danger, for, according to Tama—Captain Hawke's trusted Maori deck hand—this is the island of the notorious Warrior Women of the Solomons. There is no time to waste; sunrise will come soon. The mission is personal for Captain Hawke, for he has learned the Warrior Women are holding his own father captive. As Tama understands the legend, once the male slaves have served their purpose—to aid in producing female offspring—they are killed and eaten. Hawke vowed to save his father from this gruesome fate.

Careful not to make a sound, Hawke leads his crew through the jungle growth until they reach the edge of the village. The largest hut in the center of the clearing is most likely that of the Warrior Queen. Two heavily tattooed, nearly naked women, each with a large spear at her side, guard a smaller hut near the edge of the jungle. That, Hawke guesses, is the location of the doomed captives.

At his signal, two of his crewmen attack the guards from behind, cutting their throats with a swift flash of their blades. Inside, Hawke finds six men huddled in the corner of the hut. Most look barely alive. His men cut the slaves' bindings, and Hawke motions for the captives to follow him into the dense jungle and to freedom.

But not all heed his gesture. One of the slaves holds back, refusing to follow. It is Hawke's father. Hawke rushes back and grabs his father's frail, bruised arm and pulls him toward the door.

"There's no time to waste, Father. We've come to set you free. Soon you will be reunited with our family. Your horrible ordeal is over!"

His father offers a sheepish grin. "Actually, it's not really so bad, son. I mean there's a downside for sure…eventually, but the s—"

"We've no time for such babble." Hawke nods to the burly crewman at his side, who renders his father unconscious with the butt of a revolver. Two of Hawke's men carry the limp body through the opening and into the jungle. The ragged prisoners follow as quickly as their legs will allow.

The school secretary directed Jill toward a room to her left, where a lanky, forty-something man stepped out and offered Jill a practiced smile. Wire-rimmed glasses, brown suit, pale yellow dress shirt, thin purple tie. In fact everything about him was thin, including his mustache and slicked-back brown hair.

"Mrs. Parker, I'm Dr. Willis Everend, Vice Principal, but really I'm a jack of all trades around here." He chuckled and held out a hand.

She shook it but ignored his attempt at cliché humor.

Everend ushered her into his office and gestured to Ellen Jacobs, seated in front of his desk. "You've met Ms. Jacobs, Jake's homeroom and English teacher."

Jill nodded to Ms. Jacobs. She knew her from their parent-teacher conference back in November.

Everend dropped into his desk chair. "I don't want you to think we're ganging up on you here, Mrs. Parker." Hearty laugh. "I'm only sitting in on your conference with Ms. Jacobs as a kind of facilitator. I'm just here to answer any questions that might come up, otherwise..." He pantomimed zipping his lip and motioned her to an empty chair next to Ms. Jacobs.

Jill turned to her. "Is Jake in some kind of trouble?"

Ms. Jacobs smiled. "No, no. Not trouble exactly."

"No need to be alarmed, Mrs. Parker." Everend steepled his hands at his chin. "We do not hold back students in high school. Experts agree that it isn't a viable approach at this stage in an adolescent's social development."

"I didn't realize that was even a *possibility*." Jill kneaded the back of her neck. "Jake is a good kid, he's smart—"

"Of course he is," Ms. Jacobs said. "In fact, Jake has been one of my most engaging students. He has a lot of potential."

"So, what is the issue?"

"It's the daydreaming, Mrs. Parker," Ms. Jacobs said. "It's as if he were lost in some other place when I need him to be concentrating on class activities. It's been happening more often lately. Other teachers have mentioned it, too."

Jill stiffened. "Well, I *have* noticed he's a little more distant lately. And Jake has always had a very active imagination."

Everend leaned forward. "Ah, just as I suspected."

Both women spun around to face him.

"The literature clearly supports it. An overactive imagination can lead to...other problems."

Jill fixed on the coffee stain on Everend's tie. "What sort of problems?"

He stood, strode around to the front of his desk, and plunked down on the edge. "To put it plainly, kids today are inclined to experiment with drugs." Everend adjusted his glasses. "And, sadly, Mrs. Parker, children with active imaginations are among the most susceptible to the lure of marijuana, cocaine, opioids and other dangerous, mind- altering drugs."

Jill stared at him, mouth agape. He had to be kidding.

Everend went on. "Like you, most parents are completely un-aware of the epidemic. But let me assure you, I have confiscated a rather large stockpile of drugs and paraphernalia here at Santa Necia High." Everend smirked. "In fact, I've gained *quite* a repu-tation among my colleagues for busting drug abusers."

Jill narrowed her eyes at him. "Are you saying you've found drugs on my son?"

"Well…um, no. Not on Jake specifically. I was speaking in general terms."

Jill closed her eyes and massaged her forehead. "Let me make sure I have this straight. You're telling me because Jake is inclined to daydream, you think he's getting *high*?"

"I certainly haven't seen any signs of that in *my* class, Mrs. Parker," Ms. Jacobs said. "I'm more worried about Jake falling behind in his class work."

Everend slipped back around his desk and dropped into his chair.

Jill focused back on Ms. Jacobs. "*Has* he fallen behind? I've told him how important it is to keep up with his homework. I've tried to keep on top of it."

"Homework isn't the problem. I'm concerned that he's devel-oping a bad habit of tuning out the class and drifting off. More and more lately, I've had to call him back to reality. I hate having to do that. Other kids tease him about it."

Jill cringed. "As I said, Jake's always had a big imagination. He's still a little obsessed with seafaring adventures and man against the wilderness. Jack London kind of stuff."

"Yes, Jake already knew *The Call of the Wild* well when I listed it as suggested reading." Ms. Jacobs smiled. "So I steered him to a collection of London's other stories. He devoured them."

"He's enthusiastic about that heroic adventure stuff all right, but I assumed it was just a phase he'd be outgrowing."

"Boys this age often fantasize about performing heroic deeds," Ms. Jacobs said. "After all, identifying with a conquering hero is really what the most popular superhero movies and video games are about." She glanced at Everend. "And I'm sure Dr. Everend would concur, Jack London-type adventure fantasies are certainly a lot healthier than the violent, misogynistic rap lyrics so many kids are fascinated with these days."

Everend pressed his palms together. "Agreed, but let's not lose sight of the problem here. If Jake doesn't become more attentive in class, he's going to fall behind. And if he falls behind now, he may never catch up."

Jill took in a breath and let it out slowly. "I...I'll talk to him."

"Freshman year can be a really tough time for kids," Ms. Jacobs said.

Everend stroked his chin. "Is there anything going on at home that might be causing Jake to lose focus at school?"

"Well, his father and I separated a year and a half ago." Jill fidgeted in her chair. "He promised he'd be here today, but, as usual...um, I'm not sure Jake has really accepted it yet, but the truth is, there's no chance of a reconciliation." She blushed in spite of herself.

Ms. Jacobs reached over and touched Jill's hand. "It must be especially difficult for you."

"We're still adjusting, but we'll get through it."

Everend removed his glasses and rubbed the bridge of his nose. "Studies show some children are inclined to turn to fantasy—and often illegal drugs—to avoid a personal reality they consider un-acceptable or unpleasant."

Jill squeezed her eyes shut and took in a breath. "Thank you for your concern. I'm sure Jake will be much better once we…*he* gets through this rough period."

"I sincerely hope so." Everend rose, and both women stood. "We appreciate your coming in, Mrs. Parker."

Jill shook hands with both.

Ms. Jacobs smiled. "Please understand, Mrs. Parker. In my opinion, Jake's one of the good ones. I'm just afraid we may be losing him."

Jill nodded and hurried out. The pain in the back of her throat made any reply impossible.

Jake hopped off the bench. "Am I in trouble, Mom?"

She sighed. "No, but they're worried you're not performing up to your abilities…and that you might not be able to keep up after this year."

"Jeez, Mom, I'm not stupid!" He glanced down the hallway to see if anyone might overhear.

She followed his gaze. "Walk with me to the car."

When they'd cleared the double doors leading to visitor parking, Jill put her arm around Jake and gave him a quick squeeze. "No one thinks you're stupid, honey. You just have to quit daydreaming so much in class…stay more focused."

Jake groaned. "They're feeding you a load of crap, Mom. Besides, most classes are totally lame and boring. We don't even have that much homework. Anyway, we only got a couple of weeks left."

"Classes are going to be more difficult after this year, Jake. You're going to have to really pay attention in class."

"I *know*, Mom."

"You can do it, Jake, I know you can." She hugged him then stood back and held him at arm's length.

Jake looked her in the eye. "What?"

"Mr. Everend thought you might be doing drugs."

"That's so wacked, Mom. Seriously, everyone knows Everend is a total dickhead."

Jill frowned.

"Sorry, Mom, but he is so *annoying*. He thinks we're all a bunch of potheads and meth addicts."

"I told him you've never used drugs."

"I *haven't*. I know some kids who do grass and coke and other stuff at parties. But you don't have to worry about me. I'm never invited to the stupid parties anyway." Jake studied his shoe tops.

"Honey, I believe you." She checked her watch. "I have to scoot back to work. Too bad your father couldn't tear himself away from that...that *woman* so he could join us."

"Jeez, what did *Dad* do?"

"Everything! Nothing!" Jill reined herself in, took a breath. "Never mind, Jake. It's not anything you need to worry about." She leaned over and kissed the top of his head.

———∞∞∞———

The end-of-lunch bell rang, and the halls swarmed with a rising cacophony of yelling voices and clanging locker doors. Jake flipped his backpack onto his shoulder and headed for history class.

Lester ambled over. "So what did they wanna talk to your mom about?"

"Just some bogus shit about not payin' attention in class."

"Jesus, dude, how does that make you any different from the

rest of us?" Lester punched Jake in the shoulder.

"Totally. Especially when Grimsby drones on about random boring shit that happened like six lifetimes ago."

They bumped fists.

"Everend told her I might be doing drugs," Jake said.

"No shit? What did you tell your mom?"

"Denied it. I wasn't about to let her know we tried it a few times."

"Could happen again, I suppose." Lester offered a passable innocent expression.

Jake laughed. "Probably. What the hell? It's not even illegal any more."

As they headed into the swirling mass of students, they passed a clutch of juniors.

Bobby Grossman, a hulking, muscle-bound star linebacker during the football season, but mostly just a dick the rest of the year, called out to them: "Oh my god. Call Santa. Looks like a couple of his elves have escaped."

The entire group howled with laughter. Clearly they supported each other in their collective assholery.

Jake and Lester didn't give any indication they even heard the dig at them for being among the smallest guys in school. Besides, even though the comment hurt some, it was kinda funny.

Jake didn't flinch when Buster Flatt and Tweedledumb deliberately rammed shoulders into him as they passed.

"Y' oughta watch where you're goin' Parker," Buster said.

Tweedledumb chuckled. "Guess he musta been daydreamin' again."

For a brief moment, getting even rose to the top of the list of options for the second wish.

CHAPTER 10

The old man slumped down on one knee to attach a current-year sticker to his battered black California license plate. He glanced up at a Santa Necia Police cruiser pulling up a few feet away and returned to his task.

The older of two policemen strode to the truck. "Afternoon, sir."

A younger officer followed, his hand poised near his weapon in case the situation turned ugly.

The old man offered no response beyond pulling himself upright with a grunt and brushing dirt off the knees of his overalls. He stood over six feet tall and carried a good thirty more pounds than he needed. At one time he might have been an imposing figure, but now his back bent and his shoulders sloped as if he had spent too much time cramped in a small space.

"You're parking on private property." The younger officer gestured to the trailer and pickup. "You're gonna have to haul this outta here."

The old man's eyes shifted from one policeman to the other. He made no comment.

"I'm gonna need to see your driver's license and registration," the younger cop said.

"I ain't committed no crime."

"We'll see about that old man." The younger officer took a step toward him.

The older officer slid between them, facing his colleague. "Dial it down a notch, Otto." He pivoted back to the old man, and tapped his badge. "I'm Sergeant Patt, Santa Necia Police." He gestured toward his partner. "This is Officer Norbert. And you are?"

"I'm mostly called Ben."

Norbert wrote down the name on his pad.

Patt offered a friendly smile. "Ben, good, and what is your last name, sir?"

"Akiak."

Norbert poised his pen over the pad. "How's that spelled?"

"Same's it sounds."

"Benjamin Ackyack. Got it."

Patt nodded toward the cruiser, and Norbert sauntered over to it, mumbling, "Sure doesn't sound like an American name."

"You'll have to forgive my partner's...um, enthusiasm. He's still pretty green. Doesn't yet realize he's not a big city cop. Needs to understand we're not so strictly by-the-book around here."

Ben glanced over at Norbert talking on the car radio.

Patt eyed Ben's dusky, weathered face. "If you don't mind my asking, you don't look like you're from around here."

Ben shrugged. "That a question?"

"I mean I haven't seen you before, and, well, you look like you might have a little *foreign* blood in you."

"Reckon that depends on what a guy considers foreign."

"Good point." Patt gave the old Airstream the once-over. "So how long are you planning to visit Santa Necia, Mr. Ackyack?"

"Few days. Might be a little longer. Ain't in no rush t' move on."

"Well, sir, as Officer Norbert pointed out, this is private property. I'm afraid you can't legally camp here."

"I got permission. Charlotte told me I's welcome any time."

"Charlotte?"

"Charlotte Addison." Ben tilted his head toward the dilapidated building. "This still her place, ain't it?"

"Hold on a minute. You *knew* old lady Add…Mrs. Addison?"

"Charlotte and I were friends, you might say." Ben started toward the trailer door.

Norbert strode up to Patt. "No outstanding warrants."

Patt dismissed him with a wave. "So when was it you were here before, Mr. Ackyack? It must have been some time ago."

"Awhile back."

"Yeah, well, nobody cares about the past," Norbert said. "The point is, you're gonna have to be movin' this heap outta here, old-timer, or you're gonna end up in—"

Patt brushed Norbert aside without looking at him. "Tell you what, Mr. Ackyack. We're gonna need to check on something here. Let's say you can stay 'til some things are straightened out."

Norbert narrowed his eyes at Patt. "What's to straighten out? He's breaking the *law*."

"Relax, Otto. This might turn out to be more complicated than we thought."

Ben yanked on the door to the Airstream until it swung free. He glanced back at Patt. "We done?"

"Well, yeah. I suppose we—"

Ben banged the metal door shut behind him.

Patt clicked his tongue. "Councilman Wahdle isn't going to like this one bit."

CHAPTER 11

Jake tried to concentrate on Mr. Carlyle illustrating algebra equations on the whiteboard in the front of the room. But paying attention wasn't easy. A whole lot of questions jostled around in Jake's head; none had anything to do with algebra. What if he used one of his wishes to turn himself into a chick magnet for real? Or used one to make his family richer than a Saudi sheik? Or to transform himself into a famous writer, like Jack London? Or to really do something important like end world hunger, or stop prejudice, or cure cancer or…or something he hadn't even thought of yet?

His cell phone vibrated. They were supposed to turn them off completely in class, but nobody did. Jake pulled his phone from his back pocket and stashed it in his lap under his desk. He checked to make sure Carlyle still faced the board. A text from Lester featured a meme of a couple of handsome studs in tuxes sipping glasses of some unpronounceable liquor aboard an elegant yacht. Several gorgeous models in low-cut evening gowns gathered around the two men. Lester had added the caption "Captain Hawke and Mr. Slade." The text read: "How about this for a wish!!!???"

———⟨✀⟩———

As Jake pedaled home from school that day, he kept an eye out for Buster and the Tweedles. Although he still had to endure their well-established litany of hallway taunts and harassment, they hadn't ambushed him outside of school again. Jake knew they were just waiting for a safe opportunity. He could take the beating if he had to, but if Buster went after the lantern, Jake feared he'd have no choice but to waste a wish to save it. No way he'd let that happen.

He started down the alley at the edge of the Wood and noticed the old man scouring his Airstream with soapy water and a brush. Jake judged the alley safe enough, with the old guy already outside, so he jostled along the rutted surface toward him.

The old man acknowledged Jake's arrival with a nod and continued wiping off some obscene, if badly misspelled, graffiti.

Jake pulled up and shook his head in disgust. "I'm pretty sure I know who did this."

"Yep, I'm guessin' your *friends* paid me a visit while I's away."

"They're totally a bunch of ass...*creeps*. Can I give you a hand?"

"Up t' you." The old man gestured to his pickup. "I think there's another brush in the back."

Jake jogged over and grabbed a well-worn brush from the truck bed.

They scrubbed away side by side for a few minutes, until Jake broke the silence. "My name's Jake. Jake Parker."

The old man didn't look over. "People usually call me Ben."

As they continued to work, Jake stole fleeting glances at Ben. The old guy didn't say much, and he acted as if he didn't care if Jake was there or not. But Jake suspected Ben's grumpiness might be just an act.

"What're you starin' at?" The corners of Ben's mouth twitched with the barest hint of a smile.

Jake noticed that when Ben did that almost-a-smile thing, the old guy's eyes got sort of sparkly. Jake produced an actual smile. "I'm not staring at anything."

"I got a spider on my cap or somethin'?" Ben pulled off his cap and slapped it against his overalls.

Jake nodded at the cap. "So, um, what's the B stand for?"

"Brooklyn. The Brooklyn Dodgers." He wiped the sweat off his brow with his sleeve, and flipped his cap back on. "Great team."

Jake scrunched up a crooked grin. *Brooklyn?* The Dodgers are in Los Angeles."

Ben tilted his head to the side as if about to respond. Instead he dipped his brush in the bucket of soapy water and attacked the word "Fagut" scrawled across a window.

"So, um, did you play for them or somethin' back in the day? Those Brooklyn Dodgers?"

"Nope, just sorta picked up this cap along the way you might say. Been with me awhile. Kinda like an old friend."

"Cool." Jake had an idea there was more to the story but didn't push it.

They continued in silence, now removing the black and red letters from the back of the trailer. Jake paused only long enough to remove his sweatshirt and wipe the sweat from his forehead with it. He glanced at Ben. "So where are you from anyway?"

"Well, I been all over the dern place, I guess. I's told my great-granddad came from a little speck of a place way up north, up past the Yukon."

"The Yukon? Wow. Jack London wrote lots of stories about that place."

Ben nodded.

"London's my favorite writer." Jake studied Ben's face. "So then were your people like…Eskimos or somethin'?"

"More 'somethin' than Eskimo."

Jake swallowed a chuckle. He wasn't sure the old guy was making a joke.

"I see you're a ballplayer." Without looking at Jake, he added, "You must be a catcher."

"A catcher?"

"You're wearin' your cap backwards…like a catcher."

Jake pulled off his Santa Necia baseball cap and examined it. "Oh, naw, we just wear 'em like this sometimes. It's a stylin' thing."

"*Is* it?"

Jake switched his cap around. "Actually, I usually play outfield. I mean…when I get into the game. I suck at hitting."

"Oh?" Ben glanced over. "Hand me the bottle by your foot there. Bucket's runnin' outta soap."

Jake passed the bottle over to Ben, who squirted a green stream into the bucket and sloshed it around with his brush.

Jake didn't know why, but he was comfortable around this old guy. As if they'd been friends for a long time. But that was totally wacked. He'd been warned by his mom and his teachers many times to avoid adults he didn't know. Plus, he had to admit this Ben qualified as weird. But something about him made Jake feel safe—and not just because the old guy stood up to Buster and the Tweedles.

Ben stretched up toward the roof. "Probably all you need to improve your battin' skills is a little coachin'."

"You offering?"

"I might could teach you a couple things. Course the best idea is for a fella to see for hisself how the pros do it. Just pay real close attention ever time he goes to a ball game."

"I've never been to a Giants' game."

"Giants?" Ben scratched his stubbly jaw. "New York's a pretty long way to be goin' to see a ball game, young fella. As I recollect, though, there are some mighty good minor league teams out here in California."

"What do you mean, 'New York'? The Giants have been in San Francisco since like forever."

"They have?" Ben shook his head. "Guess I been away too long."

"So where were you?"

Ben didn't respond right away. He stared at the place he'd been rubbing, but didn't move the brush. "I just been out a touch for a while. Maybe I oughta go see these *San Francisco* Giants sometime. Guess I got me some catchin' up to do."

"It would be awesome to go to a game."

Ben focused on the task in front of him. "Might need someone to show me how to get there, though."

"Yeah, that'd probably be a good idea." Jake stifled a grin.

Ben held the brush in the air and stared at the last bit of graffiti. "What in tarnation does 'dick wod prevort' even mean? If it's some guy's name, I ain't never heard a him."

Jake moaned out a laugh. "Mostly it means those jerks are complete idiots." He reached up and helped Ben get rid of the letters. When they finished, they tossed their brushes into the pail.

With the graffiti gone, along with a lot of the road film and dirt, the Airstream looked a whole lot better. Not *good* exactly, just not as bad.

Ben let out a painful groan as he bent down to pick up the pail.

Jake reached over and grabbed it. "You know, you could get this trailer to really shine if you used some metal polish on it."

"Be a big waste of polish, y' ask me. Besides, all this tarnish kinda gives the old girl some character." Ben ran his hand along the side of the trailer. "Sometimes things that ain't all shiny and new are the most valuable."

"Guess so." The lantern sure looked a lot better after he'd shined it up, though. He figured Ben's trailer might be okay as it was—if you didn't mind living in a beat up ol' toaster.

"I got other stuff t' do, son." Ben took the pail from Jake. "So time for you to scram."

"Okay." Jake stuffed his sweatshirt into his pack and righted his bike. "See ya." He hopped on his bike and began to pedal away.

"Thanks for the help," Ben shouted after him.

Jake glanced back and waved.

CHAPTER 12

Jill squinted into the morning sun as she strolled into Walt Staley Realty. She had to be at Clarke's Clothing Options in an hour, but she often stopped by the real estate office first. It was a way to reinforce the hope that real estate would soon be her only career.

She dropped into her desk chair and powered up her computer. Even though working two jobs wore her out, she hadn't slept much recently. She felt so alone, especially at night. She knew she should be used to it by now; Steve left a year and a half ago. Sure, she had the boys, and they provided some comfort—a lot really, but trying to forge a new life still took its toll. The boys couldn't be expected to understand.

She thought Kevin was adjusting to the separation all right, but it was harder on Jake. She vowed to do something to help him through this. Trouble was, she didn't even know how *she* would get through it.

As hard as she tried, she just couldn't picture her future, except for the certainty that it wouldn't include Steve. For all Jill cared, Barbie or Bambi or whatever the slut's name was could have him.

She brought up the Multiple Listings Service website to catch up on what was happening in the local real estate scene, but the MLS couldn't hold her attention.

Sure, she would love to have someone around, an adult she could talk to. Really talk to. But the thought of trying to build a relationship with someone new was terrifying and exhausting. As tired as her hectic life made her now, how would she ever muster enough energy to try dating again? She knew even at thirty-eight, she could still turn heads. Just not as many as she used to.

"You look like you could use this."

Jill looked up into the concerned face of Sarah McRae, the office receptionist, who held two cups of coffee. She offered one to Jill.

"Thanks." Jill cradled the cup in both hands. "Is it that obvious?"

"I'm here, if you feel like talking. We're kindred spirits after all."

Sarah, too, had recently gone through a messy breakup. Jill had to admit the war stories they exchanged did help a little.

"Thanks. Some days are tougher than others. Maybe this will turn out to be one of the good ones." Jill scrolled through email on the computer.

Sarah grinned. "Well, just remember, what's good for the goose—"

"Damn it!" Jill slumped back in her chair.

"What's the matter?"

"Just got an email from Walt telling me someone's moved onto the Addison property."

"Hey, maybe it's the mystery man...um, Buck? Bob?"

"Ben...Ben Ackyack, apparently. Great. I really don't need this. Not when the Addison property sale is so close I can taste it." Jill closed her eyes and slowly massaged her forehead to stave off a full-on headache.

—◦◦◦—

Councilman Wahdle paced back and forth in front of his desk as if trying to catch up with his massive gut. Charley Krock, in a chair nearby, punched the keys of his laptop.

"You better be checking this son of a bitch out, Charley."

"I've got people on it right now."

"Any chance this is a coincidence? I mean that his name is Ben something, and he just happened to park his friggin' trailer there?"

"Come on, sir, what do you think the odds are?"

Wahdle suspended his pacing and wiped a handkerchief across his brow.

"I suppose the old codger could be an imposter," Krock said. "I mean it's not as if the terms of the will were a secret."

Wahdle's eyes lit up. "Yeah, follow that angle. Force the bastard to *prove* he's got a legitimate claim."

"But even if he *is* the right Ben. Everybody has a price."

"I don't give a damn what we have to do to fix this. We can *not* delay this project any longer."

"Quit worrying, sir. We've already hired the contractors. Bulldozers are scheduled to be on-site in less than two weeks."

Wahdle stuffed the handkerchief back into his pocket and sidled closer to Krock. "But Montoya's people are not going to be happy about this. I promised we'd have the whole friggin' thing up and thriving by early next year."

Krock tipped his head toward the office door.

Wahdle followed Krock's gesture. "You're right, Charley, let's continue this conversation somewhere more private."

As soon as Krock was settled in the passenger seat of Wahdle's Escalade, he snapped his fingers. "Hey, what about that clean-up ordinance you jammed through the council awhile back? You remember. The one we claimed was to appease the old lady's neighbors."

Wahdle hefted himself into the driver's seat with a grunt and closed the driver's side door. "What about it? The old crone died before we got a chance to serve her with it."

"Right. But I seriously doubt this Ben will comply." Krock grinned. "I hear he's not much for respecting authority."

"So we toss him in jail? Jesus, Charley, even if we pull that off, we still don't end up with rights to the property!"

"We do if he never files a claim. He probably doesn't even know he has to. And the statute of limitations is up in a matter of days."

"Right, put him on ice, and the property gets taken over by the town, just like we planned it." Wahdle smirked

"We can keep him locked up until it's too late for him to interfere with the project."

"By the time we send him packing, the whole project will be a done deal." Wahdle slammed his hand down on the steering wheel. "The town will be swimming in money. And Montoya and his people will be off my ass."

"You'll be a hero, sir. A very *rich* hero."

"You know, Charley, this could turn out okay after all. What do ya say we hit Moby's for happy hour. Love those free tacos and wings."

Inside Bonzo's Burgers, Jake and Lester slid into a booth, dumped fries onto their trays, and unwrapped their cheeseburgers. Bonzo's was the gathering spot of choice for Santa Necia High students. Even the more sophisticated teens who preferred Starbucks next door took their exotic caffeine concoctions out to the parking lot to hang with friends near Bonzo's. Today, though, only a few cliques hung around outside.

Lester began squirting ketchup packets onto the tray. "Dude, these burgers are epic."

"What?" Jake glanced down at the burger in his hand. "Oh, yeah, the Double Beefy Bonzo rocks."

"Damn, wouldn't it be great if we…I mean, if *you* wished for like all the Beefy Bonzos you ever wanted whenever you wanted 'em?"

Jake rolled his eyes. "How's that not even more stupid than the freakin' pizza?"

"Jesus, dude, the hell's the matter with you? I was totally kidding."

"Sorry, Les. It's just…how'm I ever gonna decide what to wish for?"

"Jake, according to the legends you're supposed to pick the three things you want the most and just, you know, wish for 'em."

"Two things."

"Right, the *two* things you want most." Lester dipped a fry into the pool of ketchup and popped it into his mouth.

Jake stared off into the parking lot.

As a disheveled forty-something mother tried her best to herd her brood of six children toward the booth next to them, Jake spotted Ben heading for his truck with a bag of groceries. Jake vaulted from the booth.

"Hey, what's up, dude?" Lester asked.

"I'll be right back." Jake weaved his way through the swarming mass of chattering youngsters like a halfback breaking through the line of scrimmage.

Lester held up Jake's barely touched burger. "So you gonna finish this?" he shouted.

"It's all yours, dude," Jake yelled on his way out the door.

Jake slowed when he reached the truck and affected a casual air. "Hi, Ben. Um, so…how ya doin'?"

Ben set the groceries on the front seat without responding.

Jake looked away. "So, ah, I see the Giants are in town this weekend."

"Are they?" Ben shut the passenger-side door and stepped around the truck.

Jake's response caught in his throat. Did Ben forget their earlier conversation about going to a game? He'd heard old people sometimes had memory issues, but he felt like a complete idiot, anyway. "Okay, well…so I guess I'll see you around." He did a one-eighty and shuffled off toward Bonzo's.

Ben called after him, "You feel like goin', you could show up at the trailer on Saturday."

Jake whirled around, his grin almost too big for his face.

"But you better get permission from your folks first."

"Oh yeah. Course." But Jake realized it wasn't going to be easy. He felt confident Ben wasn't a perv or anything, but his mom didn't know the guy, and mothers always assumed the worst.

"Somethin' the matter, son? Don't worry 'bout money. My treat."

"You sure? I hear it's *really* expensive. I can pay a little of it. I have some—"

"Money ain't a problem. See ya Saturday mornin' at the trailer?"

"Yeah, see ya." Jake ambled back toward Bonzo's. He thought he heard the old man chuckle to himself as he climbed into his truck.

———⟨⟩———

When Jill trudged through the door after work that evening, both boys sensed her mood and gave her plenty of space. She made them a nice dinner—baked chicken, instant mashed potatoes, and those frozen green beans with the little sliced almonds that Jake liked—but the boys could tell her thoughts were elsewhere. The dinner conversation consisted of asking each other to pass things.

"Um...so, is something the matter, Mom?" Jake finally asked, ignoring Kevin's admonishing glare.

"What?" Jill blinked. "No. Well, yes, a problem *has* come up, but it's nothing you have to worry about."

"Is it something Dad did?" Jake asked.

She flipped her hand as if swatting a fly. "Hardly. Your father doesn't *do* anything. At least nothing appropriate to discuss at the dinner table. But this isn't about him. It's just a complication with the sale of the Old Addison Place. A possible beneficiary to the old lady's will suddenly showed up out of the blue."

Kevin tried to put a positive spin on it. "Well, maybe they'll want to sell anyway."

Jill nodded. "Yes, that's what I'm counting on. I plan to pay this mysterious Ben character a visit tomorrow."

Jake perked up. "Ben?"

"Yes, Charlotte Addison left everything to someone named 'Ben.' The old man who just showed up could be the guy. Anyway, he's parked his trailer in the alley behind the Addison property."

Jake eyes widened. "Wow, what a coincidence. See, I was hoping you'd let me go to a Giants game on Saturday with—"

"We all thought this Ben was just a figment of Charlotte Addison's imagination." Jill grimaced. "But here he is, big as life."

"So *can* I?" Jake asked.

She squinted at him. "Can you what, honey?"

"Can I have permission to go to the game with—?"

"Tell you what, Jake." Jill rubbed her eyes. "Why don't you just ask your father? It's about time he participated in this family like he promised. Don't you think?"

"I guess so." Jake looked away and jabbed a bean with his fork.

CHAPTER 13

Jake stepped outside the school building for some privacy. He glanced at his cell: 10:00 a.m. He'd stalled long enough. But now it occurred to him it might not be a good idea to interrupt his dad at work. Problem, though. At night his dad would be at his girlfriend's place, and Jake might have to talk to her—that would just feel too weird.

All he knew about the girlfriend was she worked for the same company. Jake didn't even know her name.

But with the Giants game two days away, he'd already put it off as long as he could. If he called his dad's office, he might be able to just leave a voicemail. He took a deep breath, wiped his sweaty palms on his jeans, and punched in the office number.

"Herringbone Accounting and Tax Services," a perky female voice announced.

"Um, may I speak to Steve Parker, please?"

"Mr. Parker is unavailable at the moment. Perhaps you'd like to leave a message."

"Okay, can you please connect me to his voicemail."

"I'm afraid our voicemail system is shut down for maintenance.

But I will personally relay your message to Mr. Parker."

"Could you just tell him Jake needs to ask him somethin'?"

"Jake? Oh my god! She'd magically transformed from no-nonsense businesswoman to bubbly cheerleader. "You're Steve's little boy?"

"I'm almost fifteen."

"Oh, I'm sorry, sweetie. In the picture on your dad's desk, you look much younger."

"I do?"

"Must be a really old photo. I'm Cyndi, sweetie."

Wait. Was he supposed to know who she was?

"You know, *Cyndi*. Your dad's girlfriend?"

Something sharp did a somersault in his gut. This was the last person he wanted to talk to. He'd only seen her once, from a distance, but close enough to register long dark hair and some killer boobage. Now what? His mom called her a bimbo, and he had no idea how to talk to one of those. But he had to say *something*. "Hi."

"So tell me, sweetie." Her voice got husky. "Is there a problem at *home*?"

"No I, um…I just need to ask my dad if it's okay if I go to a Giants game on Saturday…with my friend Ben."

Cyndi lowered her voice as if they were sharing a secret. "So, your *mother* won't let you, huh?"

"No, I mean, um, she just said to ask my dad is all."

"Tell you what, Jake, I'm sure Steve will give you permission. He loves you, and he wants you to be happy. How 'bout we do this. If Steve needs to talk to you about it, I'll have him call you. If you don't hear from him, then you'll know he's cool with it."

"That'll work."

"Y'know? We should have you boys over for dinner sometime,"

Cyndi said. "Maybe we could go out to a real nice restaurant or something."

"Sure, okay." Except for the first few weekends after their dad split, he and Kevin had spent zero time with him.

"Oops, 'nother call. Gotta go." Cyndi clicked off.

Jake slipped his phone into his back pocket. If his dad ever did call back, Jake would tell him all about Ben. And if he didn't? Well, technically, he already had permission to go to the game.

Jill looked over the beat-up Airstream as she stood at the door. After three knocks she'd gotten no response. She'd all but given up when the trailer door creaked outward, and an old man—in a faded blue baseball cap, overalls, and a threadbare Pendleton shirt—looked down at her from the top step.

"Mr. Ackyack? Mr. Benjamin Ackyack? I'm Jill Parker, Walt Staley Realty. Sorry to bother you, but may I take a few minutes of your time?" She offered her business card, which Ben made no effort to take.

"You ain't botherin' nobody. Not yet, anyway." He twisted around and lumbered back inside.

Jill followed him.

Like the outside of the little trailer, everything inside—except for yesterday's edition of the *San Francisco Chronicle*—seemed to have been suspended in time a half century ago. Ancient *Life*, *Look*, and *Saturday Evening Post* magazines lay among the discarded clothing and empty food plates on the threadbare brown and orange sofa. An antique radio leaned precariously on top of a stack of neatly folded paper bags in a corner. Off to the side of the front door sat a small refrigerator, held closed with a wire coat hanger through the handle, a crusty hot plate nestled among the debris on top.

Ben cleared a space in the clutter on the sofa and waved his arm toward it. Jill sat down, half expecting an aged mouse to limp out from under the dusty piles of nostalgia. Ben grabbed an old wooden chair and straddled it facing the couch.

It was like being in a tiny, dusty museum. Jill released a pent up breath she hadn't realized she was holding. She nodded toward the pile of magazines. "I see you're something of a collector."

"Naw, I just ain't inclined t' throw stuff out right away."

"Right. So, um…Ackyack? That's an unusual name."

"Not back where my folks originally came from it ain't."

"Oh, so you're not from California?"

"Nope."

She waited, but he didn't elaborate. "Let me get right to the point, sir. The town of Santa Necia is poised to lay claim to this property in order to put it up for sale."

"What property's that? Doubt you mean my Airstream. B'sides I ain't about to sell this old girl."

Jill chuckled. "No, sir. I'm referring to Mrs. Addison's estate." She made a sweeping gesture with her arm. "Her deed includes the house and grounds and the large wooded area behind it as well."

"Mighty big piece a property."

She nodded. "Yes it is. The thing is, when Mrs. Addison passed away, she left a will bequeathing everything to a person identified only as 'my dear friend, Ben.'"

His face remained blank.

Time to be direct. "There is some speculation that *you* may be the 'dear friend' to whom she was referring. Is that true?"

"Might be. Lots a Bens in this world, though."

"Of course. Well, since no other Ben has yet stepped forward to claim the inheritance, the town plans to assume control of the property in order to put it up for sale."

He squinted through the small dingy window toward the crumbling mansion. "Don't see nothin' here that'd make a town or anybody else want t' buy the place."

"Actually, Mr. Ackyack, a prospective buyer is prepared to pay quite handsomely for it."

"This person got a name?"

"It's not an individual, sir. The buyer is a development corporation. And they don't wish to disclose their identity at this point."

Ben shook his head. "So, yer sayin' you got yourself a *town* that wants to grab up this ramshackle ol' place and then sell it to some big *company*. But there ain't no actual *people* in the deal. I got that right?"

"Yes, sir, that's essentially how it would work. But if it turns out that you do have a legitimate ownership claim to the property, the city would be forced to withdraw from the proposed transaction. You, then, would be in a position to sell it. It's very likely that the buyer would still be interested in going forward with the purchase."

Ben offered a half-hearted shrug.

Jill couldn't tell if his expression signaled disinterest, boredom, or dementia. "Mr. Ackyack, I'm not a lawyer. I can't advise you on what to do, but I *can* tell you it would be in everyone's best interest for you to inquire whether or not you have a legal claim to the property."

"I ain't interested in any a that legal mumbo jumbo."

"Filing a claim is pretty simple, really. All you have to do is fill out a few forms and provide some identification."

"Ain't none a that gonna matter anyway."

Jill stiffened. "Why not?"

He dismissed her question with a wave. "Just ain't is all."

What's wrong with this old codger? Claiming the property should be a no-brainer. The guy lives like a derelict, but money doesn't seem to mean anything to him. Is he certifiably nuts? Well, I've planted the seed. That's all I can legally do. Once he's had a chance to mull it over, I hope to god he'll come to his senses. I wish he'd just...but wishes get you nowhere.

"That it?" Ben asked, rising to his feet with a groan.

"Tell you what." She hopped up. "You sleep on it. I'm currently the agent for the town of Santa Necia with regard to the Addison property. If you decide to file a claim, and if you desire to take advantage of the opportunity to sell, I hope you'll consider me when you're ready to select a real estate agent. You can trust me to keep your best interests at heart."

To her surprise, when she offered him her business card this time, he took it and glanced at it. Jill felt a flutter in her belly. This could be a very good sign.

"Parker, huh? You related t' Jake Parker?"

Jill gasped. "Why, yes, he's my son." She narrowed her eyes at him. "You *know* Jake?"

"Met him."

"Where?"

"He passed by." Ben gestured toward the alley.

"*Did* he?" Jill glanced out the filthy window. What in the world could ever interest Jake about this place or this old curmudgeon? Probably he was just taking a short cut. Jake knew very well it was dangerous to talk to strangers, especially when they were as unstable as this old geezer.

She noticed Ben waiting, still expressionless. "So...what do you say we talk again in a couple of days." When she swung toward the door, she knocked a *Look* magazine onto the floor. "Sorry." She picked it up and set it carefully on the stack. "When you've had time to think it over, I'm sure things will be a little cleaner...*clearer!*"

"Like I said, Mrs. Parker, it ain't gonna matter."

She stopped in her tracks. "Why would you say that?"

Ben shrugged.

"Well, sir, I can assure you it matters a great deal to some of us." Jill started to offer her hand to shake, but decided it would be a waste of time. "Very nice to have met you, Mr. Ackyack." She tried to open the door, but she couldn't budge it.

A dusty chuckle escaped Ben. "You gotta push on 'er pretty good sometimes."

Jill gave the old metal door a couple of serious shoves without success before it finally gave way. Her first thought was how difficult it would be for someone smaller, *like Jake*, to open that door. She dropped that thought. Better to keep focused on the job at hand. The metal door banged shut before she'd taken three steps.

Driving off in her eight-year-old Ford Fiesta with the broken radio, Jill tried to clear her head of the real estate world and dumb things down for her dead-end job at Clarke's Clothing Options. The only job that actually paid her anything. A hot fist pummeled her stomach. Just when things were beginning to go her way, somebody pulled the rug out from under her. Her hope of a real estate career was imploding around her. Her soon-to-be ex-husband didn't give a damn about her or the kids. Jake was having trouble at school, and now he was somehow connected to an old man who was probably crazy—if not worse. What was she thinking? She was from humble stock—not the kind to make millions flipping properties.

When they met at Humboldt State, Steve was brash, good-looking, and fun—and the first person in her life to tell her he loved her. He dazzled her with his plans for the wonderful treasure trove that life held in store for him and, she assumed, for her.

After the boys came along, their marriage died little by little. It wasn't long before Steve blamed her for his disappointing life. He never seemed to understand why she could no longer pretend interest in sex with a man who clearly had lost interest in love. God damn you Steve Parker!

On good days she was able to smooth out the rough spots for the sake of the boys. On bad days, she felt like Wile E. Coyote in a Road Runner cartoon.

CHAPTER 14

James Wahdle unstuffed himself from his Escalade, keeping an eye on a white limo idling in the corner of the deserted parking lot. He hiked up his gut and strode toward the limo with a swagger meant to emulate a hungry lion, but he had too much body mass; it was more reminiscent of a drunken walrus. As he approached the two large Hispanics in expensive dark suits, one of them pulled the limo door open.

Wahdle glanced around the lot, then leaned inside. "This is not a good idea."

"*I* decide what's a good idea." Carlos Montoya pointed to the seat across from him. It wasn't a request.

Wahdle swallowed a response and climbed inside.

"You told me everything was taken care of," Montoya said, as soon as the door closed. His voice revealed a trace of an accent but no emotion whatsoever.

"It is." Wahdle tried to sound flip in spite of the beads of sweat forming on his upper lip. "Everything is in place. The contracts are signed. We're ready to roll. There's nothing for you to be concerned about." He attempted a confident chuckle, but it sounded more like a wheeze.

"*Oh?*" Montoya narrowed his eyes. "My people tell me you've hit a snag." He tilted his head to the side. "But *you*, you're saying there's nothing to worry about. Are you telling me that no beneficiary to the old lady's will has shown up, then? Because if what you're saying is true, I'm going to have to eliminate a couple of my most reliable informants."

"Eliminate? Um, you mean—"

"Let's just say that people who lie to me have a way of disappearing." Montoya's expression remained blank.

"Well, yeah. There *is* someone who showed up who may possibly be this Ben mentioned in her will." Wahdle squirmed; the inside of the limo seemed to have reached a hundred degrees. "But it's just, you know, a temporary setback."

"My people say the guy isn't so anxious to sell."

"Doesn't matter." Wahdle managed a half-laugh. "He hasn't claimed the property, and I have a plan to make sure he doesn't."

"I have to tell you, this is sounding more and more like a problem. A big problem."

"No, Mr. Montoya." Wahdle wiped his damp forehead with his sleeve. "It's just a little speed bump. It's not a *problem*. Not really. I'm handling it."

"I am not a big fan of problems."

"Don't you worry, sir."

"You keep saying that. But *I'm* not the one who should be worried, Councilman."

Wahdle swallowed hard.

"I have no desire to explain another delay to my people," Montoya said. "They are not nearly as patient as I am."

Montoya's smirk sent an ice-cold trickle down Wahdle's spine.

"You owe us, Councilman. And we *always* collect our debts."

Montoya was no longer smiling.

"I know. And I really appreciate the financial support you've given me."

"Good. Then you understand it's time for you to *earn* that support and prove your appreciation. If you cannot provide the means for us to clean up a sizable, ongoing influx of cash, we'll have to find someone who can."

"You won't have to do—"

"And that would mean a *substantial* immediate payback from you."

"Well, yes, working with you on this has allowed me some financial gain so far. But—"

Montoya held up his hand. "I don't want you to misunderstand me, Councilman. When I say payback, I'm not just talking about the money. It would be a shame if anything were to happen to your lovely wife…or your sweet young daughter, who's so vulnerable way off on the other side of the country at Wellesley."

"Um, yes…it would be." His throat was full of dust.

"Good. I think it's always best if all concerned parties understand the consequences fully."

"I'm taking care of this, Mr. Montoya. It'll all be over in a few days at the most. You—"

"There will be no extensions."

Before Wahdle could respond, Montoya made an almost imperceptible nod toward the door, and it immediately swung open. This conversation was over.

When the cool night air slapped Wahdle across the face, he realized just how profusely he'd been sweating.

CHAPTER 15

Perched atop *The Snark*, Jake and Lester could make out six men in the distance. One unrolled what looked like a large map, which he spread out on the hood of a pickup. He pointed to something on the paper, while one of the others made sweeping gestures toward the Wood.

"Damn. Looks like they really are gonna tear up the Wood," Lester said.

Jake slumped down on the plank floor and pulled the lantern from his pack.

Lester flopped down next to him. "Wanna talk about it?"

"Why is makin' the other two wishes so freakin' *hard*?"

"Dude, maybe you're just thinking too much."

"It'd be so much easier if there were like rules or limits." Jake absently brushed dust from the lantern's red glass window.

"Maybe a guy's just gotta go with his feelings," Lester said. "And then just, you know, make the freakin' wishes."

"But what if I screw it up?" Jake bit his lower lip.

Lester put a hand on Jake's shoulder. "They're *your* wishes, Jake. You can't screw it up."

"Bet I could find a way, Les."

Lester stood up, yanked his watch cap from his pack with a flourish, and jammed it on his head. "Whaddaya say we slip over and see what the hell those guys are up to?"

"Can't today. I gotta do somethin'."

"You do?"

"I'm goin' to the Giants game."

"Shut *up*!" Lester's eyes widened. "Your *dad* takin' you?"

"No, um, I'm going with a...a friend."

Lester focused on stuffing the cap back into his pack. "Dude, I thought *I* was your best friend."

"Course you are. I'm going with Ben, the old man I told you about the other day at Bonzo's. Remember? The guy who saved my butt from Buster and the Tweedles?"

Lester looked away. "It'd be so freakin' awesome to go to a Giants game."

"I'd ask him if you could come too, but ballgames are mega expensive. Besides, he's sorta, I don't know, a little odd, I guess."

"Odd?" Lester raised his eyebrows.

"Not scary odd, he just kinda acts grumpy sometimes."

"So, um, you have to get goin' pretty soon, then?"

"Yeah. I'm meeting him at his place. He lives in a trailer over by the old Addison place."

Lester rubbed the back of his neck. "Seriously, Jake, you sure this guy is okay?"

"Yeah, I think he's just lonely."

"I dunno, Jake. He sounds sorta creepy to me. And lonely guys are more likely to go after kids, right?"

"Naw, honest, he's cool. Christ, you think I'd even be considering going with him if I thought he might be some kinda perv? Besides, the ballpark is about the most public place you can be."

"Yeah. But promise you'll be…extra careful, okay?"

Jake gave Lester a playful punch on the shoulder. "Jesus, dude. What are you? My mother?"

Lester nodded to Jake's backpack. "You know you can't take the lantern into the ballpark, right? I hear they confiscate stuff like that."

"Shit. You're right. I'll have to find somewhere super safe to hide it."

"I could keep it for you while you're at the game."

Jake bit his lip. "What if somethin' happened to it?"

"Jesus, Jake, no one but you, me, and Kevin even know about it. Besides, nobody can do the wishes but you anyway, remember? Trust me, dude, I'll protect it with my life."

Jake grinned. "Nobody else I'd trust with it, Les." He handed over his backpack.

Lester stood up and looped Jake's pack over one shoulder, his over the other.

Jake checked his watch. "Shit, I gotta bounce."

Lester grabbed the red-flagged rope and swung to the ground. With a sharp downward motion, he sent the rope in an arc into Jake's hands on the platform. Jake tied the rope to the railing as Lester began their parting ritual. "Beware…"

"The blue flag, mate."

Officer Patt followed Norbert, who strode chest-first up to the Airstream and knocked on the metal door. When he got no response, he banged on the door harder with the heel of his hand.

Still no answer.

"Police! Open up!" Norbert shouted, pounding on the door

again with as much authority as he could muster.

Patt sighed. "Jesus, Otto, get a grip. This isn't police business. You're here in your capacity as a process server."

The door creaked open, and Ben stared down at the officers. "This a social call?"

"No, sir. I'm here on official business. For the Santa Necia Town Council." Norbert thrust some papers at Ben, who made no move to take them. "Benjamin Ackyack, since you may be about to take ownership of this property, I am charged with informing you of your potential noncompliance with Santa Necia Town Ordinance three-oh-dash-seven-one-seven-five."

Ben regarded Norbert with all the enthusiasm of a man facing a grinning horde of Jehovah's Witnesses.

Norbert read from the document. "It is required that all properties be maintained at a level that reflects local community standards." He glanced up at Ben. "Now, it's your responsibility to comply with this ordinance, sir."

"Ah! So what you're sayin' is, it's against the law t' be differ'nt."

Norbert rolled his eyes. "It's my duty to inform you, sir, that failure to comply with the aforementioned ordinance may result in a fine, jail sentence, or both."

"Okay, you informed me." Ben snatched the papers and shut the door in Norbert's face.

Fresh from her morning shower, Cyndi wrapped a fluffy towel around her and ambled into her bedroom. The sun leaking through the pink gossamer curtains caused the yellow roses on the pale green wallpaper to appear as if they had just burst into bloom. In the sunlight her image seemed to glow in the giant mirror above the robin's-egg-blue dresser. Even without makeup, she was still striking for a woman on the wrong side of twenty-five. She unwrapped the towel and broke into a sly smile. Yes, she had a body men dreamed about, and she still had a few years before that would no longer be true.

She rewrapped herself, plopped down on the edge of the bed, and nudged Steve, who continued to snore blissfully. Cyndi gazed down at him. Steve wasn't like all the others; he truly loved her. Treated her almost like a princess. She knew Steve understood her…appreciated her, for the person she was *inside*. He said so. Well, maybe not in so many words, but a girl can tell.

His special insight into her soul notwithstanding, Steve was still a guy. And Cyndi had learned by fourteen how to get what she wanted from men. Since her divorce six years ago, she'd reveled in the attentions of more men than she could count. But, then, she'd never been very good at math.

She prodded him again. When that didn't work, she bent closer and tickled him under the chin.

Steve opened one eye. "It *is* Saturday, right?"

"Yep, but that doesn't mean you gotta stay in bed all day, lazy bones." She reached under the covers to tickle his ribs.

"Okay, okay. Enough with the damn tickling. I'm not a kid, you know."

She gasped. "Oh, Jeez, I forgot to tell you, baby."

"Tell me what?"

"Your son, Jake. He called yesterday."

Steve rose up on an elbow. "Is something wrong?"

"No, no. Nothing's wrong, baby." She played her fingers along his arm. "He just called to ask permission to go to a ball game."

"He called *me* for permission?"

Cyndi smirked. "Yeah, I got a real strong impression that your *ex* was being a total bitch about it."

"So do I have to get back to him about this?"

"Nope. I took care of it. I even asked who he was going with, 'cause I thought you'd want to know."

"So, who is it?"

"One of his little friends' parents, I think."

"Which one? Lester?"

"No, that's not it." She ran her fingers through her still damp hair. "No, it was Ben. That's it, yeah, Ben."

"Must be someone new."

"Well, I told him you would give him permission 'cause you love him and want him to have a good time."

"Oh, okay. Sure. Of course I do." Steve thought for a moment. "I guess I probably need to call Jill."

"No!" Cyndi grimaced. "Um, I mean I told Jake you'd get back to him if you had any questions. Otherwise you were cool with him going."

"Sounds like you took care of it then."

CHAPTER 16

Jake squirmed in the passenger seat as Ben eased the ancient truck down the highway.

"Somethin' the matter, son?"

"What? No, I mean not really. It's just that this is the first time I've ridden in a car without a seat belt."

"Didn't make 'em back when I got this old girl."

"You could get a ticket for not havin' 'em, y'know."

"Ain't gonna matter much if I do."

"Why not?"

"It just ain't."

Jake got the message. This subject was off limits.

Cars sped past them as the old truck puttered along. A yellow Mustang full of rowdy teenagers tailgated them, the driver pounding the horn as he pulled alongside. A couple of guys leaned out the windows.

"Get out and walk, old-timer! Be a hell of a lot quicker!"

"Move that piece a shit outta the way, old man!"

Jake recognized most of them from school. But he doubted they had any freakin' idea who he was. For a second, Jake yearned be part of that "cool" posse, but now he scrunched down in the seat, embarrassed and ashamed. He *wasn't* like those idiots. They acted like a bunch of assholes. They *were* a bunch of assholes. The Mustang swerved around the old pickup, slicing in front so close Ben had to slam on the brakes. Then they took off at top speed, tires squealing.

Ben shook his head. "Them youngsters are headin' fer trouble."

"Yeah, you're probably right." Jake broke into a grin. "Course, they might be just trying to get to the game before it's over."

Ben raised an eyebrow. "You sayin' I'm drivin' too slow?"

"Well, I'd say you're about the carefullest driver I ever saw."

"Smart talk from a fella who ain't even wearin' a seat belt."

Jake didn't know why it was so easy to kid around with Ben, since the old guy worked so hard at being grouchy. But Jake felt comfortable with him, more than with any other adult these days—even his mom, given the way she'd been so pissed about everything lately. Didn't matter that he knew barely anything about Ben. Jake trusted him. There was something mysterious about him, though. Like the way he answered questions as if he was being asked to give up a body part.

Ben took a peek at his quiet companion. "What're you thinkin' on so hard, son?"

"I was just wondering…are you a relative of old lady…*Mrs.* Addison's or somethin'?"

"Nope."

"But my mom said you were the only one named in her will."

Ben sighed. "Guess Charlotte was all alone at the end."

"But how come she picked you? I mean—"

Ben kept his eyes focused on the road. "I was her friend once…long time ago."

The old man seemed lost in his memories, so Jake kept quiet

when they drove through the Golden Gate Bridge toll plaza. The FasTrak screen blinked a warning. He didn't mention the fact that the toll would show up on Ben's credit card. If he even had one.

When they stopped at a red light on the Embarcadero, Ben glanced at Jake. "So, these guys any good?"

"The Giants? Yeah, pretty good. Not that long ago they won three World Series in five years."

"Impressive. So who's your favorite ballplayer?"

"Guess I don't really have one."

"You mean you don't have any heroes, like Bob Feller or Ted Williams?"

"Who?"

"Just some pretty dern good players...from the old days."

"Oh. Well, to me, pro athletes aren't really, you know, *heroes*. They're just a bunch of millionaires who are really good at playin' ball. A hero's somebody who's not afraid to take chances...who maybe even puts his life on the line. You know? He takes on the elements or whatever no matter what might happen—even if he's scared."

Ben remained silent, eyes on the road.

Jake could feel his cheeks redden. "C'mon, *you* know what I mean."

"I reckon I do. And I guess you're right about ballplayers. They ain't actual heroes when you think on it. A real hero don't hafta make a lotta noise...don't even need a audience." Ben pulled into a crowded parking garage.

Jake squinted. "Wait. How can a guy be a hero if no one sees him do heroic stuff?"

"Son, all being heroic means is doing somethin' good, or maybe even somethin' great, 'specially if nobody else knows it. The guy hisself would know. Ain't that enough?"

"Yeah, that's kinda what I meant. Heroes just do whatever has to be done just 'cause it's the right thing to do."

Ben pointed a finger at Jake and winked. "You got it."

———❧———

They headed for a ticket booth. "Let's get us a couple a seats out in the bleachers. Good to feel the sun on your face when you're takin' in a game."

"Okay with me." Jake beamed. "I'm just stoked to be at a game." Besides, seats in the left field bleachers were probably a lot cheaper than the ones closer to home plate.

Once inside, Ben scanned the stadium. "This here's a beautiful ballpark."

"Yeah, it's a lot cooler than on TV. And way bigger."

The Giants and the Rockies changed leads several times. And as the game progressed, Ben pointed out strategies behind the action on the field. Things like: how the right-handed batter shifted his feet so he could hit the ball to right field with a runner on first; when a pitcher was likely to throw an off-speed pitch; and how the shortstop had a good idea where the ball was going to be hit even before the batter swung.

On the other hand, Jake had to explain to Ben why the batters wore plastic helmets, why most of the players let their pantlegs droop down around their shoes, and, finally, what the heck Lou Seal, the Giants' big, goofy-looking mascot, had to do with baseball.

Jake shrugged. "I guess he's supposed to pump up the crowd or somethin'."

Ben shook his head. "Don't recall ballpark crowds needin' no boost to get excited during a ballgame. Not no real fans anyway."

They had hotdogs, sodas, and peanuts and generally just enjoyed sitting in the sun on a beautiful day. They cheered when the Giants did something worth yelling about and rose up in excitement when there was a well-hit ball or a close play. Jake couldn't remember when he'd had this much fun, even with Lester.

With two runners on in the eighth inning, the Rockies batter lofted a long fly ball toward the bleachers, and everyone in the first several rows jumped up in anticipation. The ball sailed right to Jake, and he reached up to make the catch. At the last second, a big drunk guy stepped in front of him and snagged the ball. Ben and Jake kept an eye on the jerk in his gaudy orange Giants jersey, strutting up and down the aisle holding his trophy aloft and exchanging high-fives with everyone he could reach.

"Hey, that asshole stole my ball!"

"He's had too dern many beers, and he's all bluster. Truth is, Jake, you're goin' to run into guys like him just about ever'where."

Jake hissed through his teeth, squeezed his hand into a tight fist.

Ben took hold of Jake's shoulder and looked him in the eye. "It's just a baseball, son. Ain't near important enough to fret over."

With the Rockies ahead by three and only an inning and a half to go, a lot of people in the bleachers headed for the exits. Jake and Ben stayed until the last out.

Jostling along with the crowd after the game, Jake eyed Ben with a new sense of respect.

"Man, you sure know a lot about baseball. You must have played it a lot back in the day."

"When I was a young buck like you, I played wherever I could find me a game. Had some power, but I couldn't run too good. Haven't had a chance to play much since then though. Been too busy being a grown-up. But even with all them changes we seen out there today, I reckon it's still pretty much the same game."

As they reached Ben's truck, the old man noticed the faraway expression on Jake's face. "Somethin' stuck in your craw, son?"

"Did you really mean it when you said you could, you know, help me be a better hitter?" Jake asked, heart pounding.

"I might could give you a few pointers."

"That'd be so cool...I need all the help I can get." Jake managed a self-conscious laugh.

"We'll see." And there was that almost-a-smile again.

CHAPTER 17

Charley Krock slumped into the leather desk chair in his Santa Necia Town Hall office. Sport coat hung over the back of the chair, imported silk tie loosened, shirt unbuttoned at the collar. It wasn't easy, but everything was in place to take down the old codger. Time to let his boss know he'd saved his fat ass once again.

Krock pulled a burner cell from his shirt pocket and punched the speed dial key for Wahdle's. "It's all set. You can relax. Montoya won't be hassling you after tomorrow."

Krock endured another of his boss's rants, getting in a word whenever he could find an opening. "Yes. Yes I did. I got local news coverage…yes, and TV. Quit worrying. There'll be plenty of irate citizens there too, sir…let's just say I called in a few favors."

Krock stared out the window, only half listening as Wahdle tumbled into another tirade.

When his boss paused for a breath, Krock jumped in with, "Trust me, sir. By the time the old derelict is back in commission, it'll be too late for him to cause us any trouble." Krock slid out a drawer, pulled out a bottle of Glenfiddich and a tumbler. "Like I said, sir, your backers will see that you've taken care of the problem. You kidding? They won't be able to miss it." He poured three fat fingers of scotch. "Yes, sir. Of course, I'll stay on top of this until it's over." He clicked off the phone, raised the tumbler to his lips, and took a swallow.

"Good night, fat ass," Krock said to the blank phone screen and slipped it back into his pocket. He drained the rest of the tumbler of scotch and set it on the desktop, questioning once again why he took so much grief from Wahdle. *He* did all the friggin' work, and that blowhard blubber-butt took all the credit. Then again, Wahdle was the one who had to answer to Montoya. Krock grinned as he splashed more scotch into the glass.

A gangly cameraman and a scraggly-bearded video tech sipped reheated coffee from paper cups in the lounge of Channel Six, KRUT—"The Voice of the Valley." Sundays were notoriously slow news days; this one teetered on the edge of mind-numbing boredom.

Bethany DuVey stomped into the room and made her way to the coffeepot, where she filled her personal KRUT mug. An attractive brunette, in an aging-sorority-girl kind of way, Bethany's splotchy, pale skin and haphazard ponytail made it clear she hadn't done her hair and makeup.

The cameraman offered a half smile. "You look *mah*-velous, Doris. What *have* you done with your hair?"

"Can it, Mike." On location awhile back, after a few drinks, Bethany had mentioned her younger days as an ugly duckling growing up in Stockton. She'd revealed her real name in a moment of weakness she vowed never to repeat.

Bethany spiked her coffee with heaping spoonfuls of sugar

and a couple of capsules of non-dairy creamer.

"So, what have we got?" Mike asked.

"Nothing worth a damn. Some old fart refuses to mow his lawn or something and the neighbors are all bent out of shape over it."

"Wow! I live for these moments."

He and the tech stared at Bethany in mock-serious silence, anticipating her familiar rant.

"How am I ever going to get anywhere in this business if they won't let me tackle the big stories?"

Mike snorted. "Come on, Doris—"

Bethany froze him with a glare.

"I mean, *Bethany*. Get real. When's the last time there was a big story in Santa Necia? Besides, it's Sunday, for Christ's sake, and..." Mike could tell Bethany had tuned him out.

She took out her hand-mirror, checked her image, and rolled her eyes. "Damn, some major work to be done."

She caught her full reflection in the window. "Oh god. This navy blue is not working. Maybe something brighter...emerald green? Yeah, emerald's a great color on me."

——✺——

Sun broke through the clouds and flooded the Santa Necia Little League field in brightness. Jake stood in the batter's box, and Ben pitched to him from a few feet in front of the mound. Any of Ben's old, scuffed-up baseballs Jake had managed to make contact with had dribbled out between home and first base. More huddled in bunches behind the plate. Jake wiped the dust and sweat from his face with the back of his hand.

Ben pitched the remaining baseball, and Jake popped it up a

few feet in front of the plate. He threw the bat down and reached up to catch the baseball glove Ben tossed to him. Thank god nobody but Ben could see him looking like a total spaz. Face it. He'd never be worth a damn as a hitter.

Jake retrieved the balls among the debris near the backstop, collected them in the pocket of the glove, and glanced toward the parking lot. If his mom found him here alone with Ben, she'd probably never let him see the old man again. Jake hadn't exactly gotten permission to be here. His mom left early for some important meeting at the real estate office. She didn't give him the details, but he could tell she was crazy nervous about it, and Jake didn't want to make things worse. So instead, he left a message on his dad's cell. Since he hadn't yet gotten a call back from him this time either, Jake figured he was in the clear, same as when he and Ben went to the ball game. But he couldn't help looking over his shoulder like a criminal on the lam.

Jake plodded out to the mound, handed Ben the glove-full of baseballs, and let out a pent-up breath. "I'm *never* gonna be any good. You're wasting your time with me."

Ben lifted his cap and dragged his palm across his sweaty scalp. "You a quitter, son? 'Cause you don't strike me as a guy who gives up so easy."

Jake pulled the bill of his cap down. "Maybe you're wrong about me."

"Don't think so. I'm usually a pretty good judge a character." He wiped his wet hand across the bib of his overalls.

"Well, whether I'm a quitter or not, I still can't hit for sh... crap."

"Don't be so hard on yourself, Jake. Things worth doin' take a whole lotta plain ol' work."

"Yeah, I know." Jake spied three crows perched like vultures on the sagging left field fence. Smart-ass birds were mocking him. Might be some kind of a sign that all this work was pretty freakin' useless

"I'm gonna show you a little trick. Make a kinda box with your arms and your body when you grip the bat straight up in front of you." Ben demonstrated the stance. "Now let's see you do it."

Jake retrieved the bat, held it upright in front of him, and pushed his elbows out.

"Good, that's it. Now keep your arms steady and twist your hips back. No, no, don't pull your arms back; they'll move all by theirself when you swivel your hips."

Jake tried it again.

"That's it. Feel the difference?"

"Yeah, it's kinda like winding a spring."

"That's pretty much what you're doin'. You were only usin' your arms before; now you're usin' your legs. That's where all the power comes from."

Jake repeated the process a couple more times.

"You got it, Jake. Now all you gotta do is twist your hips forward real quick-like and throw the barrel of the bat at the ball."

Jake swung at an imaginary pitch.

"Don't shove the bat, fling it at the ball."

Jake tried it again.

"There, that's it. Let's try it out."

Ben returned to his position in front of the mound and tossed an easy pitch. Jake swung hard and hit a dribbler that died on the way to second base.

Ben threw again, and Jake swung hard, sending a two-hopper back to Ben, who reached down and snatched the ball.

"You don't have to try to break the dern ball, son. All you

gotta do is make contact."

Ben hurled the ball a little harder. Jake swung again, and this time he heard the reassuring "ping" of metal on cowhide. The ball shot on a line out to left field and rolled nearly all the way to the broken-down fence, sending the crows off into the sky, complaining the whole way.

"That's it, Jake. See how easy it is when ya stay focused?"

"Yeah. It really works."

More hard ones sailed toward the plate, and Jake lined most of them past the infield. On the next pitch, Jake sent a hard line drive straight at Ben, who flipped the glove up and deflected it. The ball glanced off, barely missing his face.

Jake tossed the bat aside and sprinted to Ben. "Oh god! I'm so sorry!"

"Now *that's* more like it. I think you might jess be gettin' it." The old man flexed his hand and gritted his teeth.

"You okay?"

"Never felt better." Ben took a long pull from an old glass milk bottle he'd filled with water.

He offered Jake a drink. Jake took a couple of swallows and mopped his face with his T-shirt. "Um, maybe that's enough for today."

"You're prob'ly right."

Jake trotted around the field retrieving stray baseballs and dropping them into the crinkled brown paper sack Ben stored them in.

Jake felt stronger, bigger somehow, ready to take on the world. Sure, smashing the ball was part of it, but there was more to it. He just wasn't sure what. Maybe it was just confidence. Whatever it was, it made him feel pretty damn good.

Jake handed the sack back to Ben. "Nice equipment bag."

"Yeah, well, it's what's inside that counts."

Jake nodded; he got the point.

When they reached the truck, Jake set his backpack on the seat and climbed in next to it. He didn't even notice the musty smell of the truck cab anymore.

As they were about to pull away from the lot, Ben glanced at Jake, who stared straight ahead, clutching his backpack to his chest. Ben turned off the engine. "Wanna talk about it?"

"What?"

"What's botherin' you."

"Nothing. I…" Jake really needed to talk to someone besides Lester and Kevin about figuring out the freakin' wishes. He needed to discuss it with an adult. But not his mom; she'd just shake her head and figure it was just another example of his so-called daydreaming problem. Or worse, that he'd made the whole thing up to get attention or some stupid thing. And how could he approach his dad with any kind of problem? His dad was *part* of the damn problem; he had plenty of time for his girlfriend, but none for him and Kevin. No way Jake would waste his second wish to prove its magic to either of his parents.

Ben, though, might be the one adult he could talk to about the wishes. Jake sensed that, even if Ben didn't believe any of it, the old guy wouldn't judge him. He'd understand. Without a word Jake slid the old ship's lantern from his pack and handed it to Ben.

"Ah, she's a real beauty." Ben rotated the lantern in his hands, handling it as if it were precious.

Jake pointed to the top of the lantern. "Read what it says."

Squinting, Ben read the inscription. "Well, I gotta tell ya, she sure appears t' be some kinda wishin' lantern." He handed it back.

"It's real all right. Too real. I accidentally used up the first wish on a stupid pizza. So now I only got two wishes left." Jake collapsed against the seatback. "I don't know what to do."

Ben took a deep breath and stared out the window. Finally he said, "Looks t' me like you can wish for pretty much anythin' you want."

"But that's the problem. I don't *know* what I want."

"Well then, just take yer time, son. He glanced at Jake squirming in the seat. "Ain't necessary to rush somethin' like this. After all, they's your wishes."

Jake was flailing in familiar waters. Like he had ever since he realized his wishes could change the whole world. *What if I used one of my last two wishes to end world hunger or discover a cure for all diseases? Sure, the world would be better off, but my family would still be just barely scraping by. I could save the last wish to make us all super rich. But how would we explain our sudden wealth? People would wonder for sure. We might even get investigated by the FBI or something.*

"Most people'd love to be in your shoes, son."

Jake came back to the moment. "Yeah, well, most people don't have to come up with the right wishes." He slipped the lantern into his backpack.

"Well, if I's you, son, I'd try t' just go with my feelin's. The best thing to do in a spot like this is not think on it too much. All I'm sayin' is just do what feels right."

Jake rubbed the bridge of his nose, thinking: *Great advice, but it's not as freakin' easy as he thinks. How am I supposed to know which choice feels the most right? The more I think about it, the tougher it is to know how I really feel. I gotta make a wish soon, before choosing becomes totally impossible.*

CHAPTER 18

The Santa Necia police cruiser idled at the curb on Mozart Street across from the Old Addison Place. A taco truck parked next to it, about half a block from the Channel Six News van. Several people gathered on the broken sidewalk, a few carrying handmade signs:

"Clean Up or Shove Off!"

"Keep the Riffraff Out!"

"No More Eyesores in Santa Necia!"

To most people in the milling crowd, this was a social event. Several were already lined up for tacos. Hardly anyone paid attention to the dilapidated mansion.

—∾∾∾—

Charley Krock surveyed the scene. Not a bad turnout on such short notice. His telephone blitz had worked better than he'd expected. He peered farther down the block where Wahdle sat in his silver Escalade, as if his boss hoped to lose himself in the background. Fat chance.

Jill fidgeted near the back of the growing crowd. This morning Walt Staley chided her for suggesting Ben file a claim on the property, warned her there'd be hell to pay if she continued to encourage the old man. She understood the value of taking this Ben character out of the picture before he could file—especially since he showed no interest in selling even if he did. Forcing the old man out might be expedient, but it wasn't ethical. Jill eyed Councilman Wahdle's Cadillac. She had an idea he was behind this scam. She'd never be able to prove it, but it wasn't hard to guess Wahdle was involved in Forest Glen Development. That meant he had a hell of a lot to lose if the sale of the place didn't go through as planned. Wahdle had a reputation for squashing people who got in his way. And Ben Ackyack was definitely in his way.

Besides, the old curmudgeon had been rude to her, and the fact he had some kind of connection with Jake made her cringe. How would Ackyack have persuaded Jake to even talk to him? And how many times had the old man approached Jake? She'd vowed to confront Jake about that, but she'd been so busy lately working both jobs and trying to save her commission on the sale she just hadn't had a chance. Tonight. Yeah, tonight she'd sit down and talk to Jake. Her family *needed* that commission, and getting Ben Ackyack out of their lives would be, well, a nice fringe benefit.

Ben's ancient green pickup rattled past the end of Mozart Street on the way back from the ball field.

"Hey, what's going on?" Jake nodded toward the crowd in

front of the old mansion.

"Trumped-up trouble, I s'pose. Just some local politickin' about some kinda neighborhood beauty law. Best you hustle yer butt outta here, though." He pulled the truck over.

Jake pointed to the black-and-white cruiser. "But what's up with the *police*?"

"I'll handle it, son. You better get movin' on home or your momma'll be gettin' worried."

Jake grabbed his backpack and slid out the door. "You sure I can't help?"

"Ain't nothin' that concerns you."

Jake barely swung the door shut before Ben took off down the alley.

CHAPTER 19

Bethany DuVey faced the camera with a practiced expression of concern.

"This is Bethany DuVey, Channel Six On-The-Scene, reporting *live*. We're here in the once-proud Roundhill section of Santa Necia, where we're witnessing a neighborhood dispute that's become anything but neighborly." She thrust her hand toward the Old Addison Place. "Behind me is what's left of the palatial home of the late Charlotte Addison. Once a showplace of Victorian style and charm, today it's no more than an unsightly blotch on the area." She grimaced and drew her finger across her throat.

"Is it 'blotch' or 'blot'?" she asked Mike, who rested his camera on his shoulder.

"Beats me." He pivoted toward the crowd. "Let me grab some b-roll."

—◌◌◌—

Jake rushed through the crowd to Lester's side. "What the hell's goin' on, Les?"

"I hear your new friend is in some kinda big-ass trouble. I

think they're gonna arrest him or somethin'."

"*Arrest* him. Why?"

"Dunno, dude." Lester shrugged. "I think it has somethin' to do with this ol' piece-a-crap house."

Jake gasped when two policemen escorted Ben around to the front.

⎯⎯◦◦◦⎯⎯

Mike aimed the camera at Bethany. "Goin' live."

The video tech held up three fingers, two, paused a beat, then pointed at Bethany.

She whirled toward the three men. "Approaching us now are Santa Necia Police Chief Leon MacDuff, Officer Otto Norbert, and the man, known as Ben Ackyack, who may be in line to inherit this sadly neglected estate." When they stopped a few feet in front of the spectators, she glided closer. "Chief MacDuff, could you tell our viewers exactly what's at issue here?"

MacDuff beamed for the camera. "Well, Bethany, it seems—"

"This some kinda circus?" Ben grumbled.

MacDuff swung around to Ben. "No sir. This is a very serious matter." He returned to DuVey and the camera. "Mr. Ackyack here is being charged with violation of Town Ordinance three-oh-dash-seven—"

"Criminal untidiness," Ben said.

McDuff glared at him. "Then you don't deny you have made no effort to comply with the ordinance?"

"Don't you have anythin' better to do with your time?"

"I am sworn to uphold the law, sir," MacDuff said. "To which you have done nothing to comply…despite being warned of the serious consequences if you refused."

Jake broke through the throng and rushed forward with Lester at his heels. Jill pushed her way to the front of the crowd, ready to rush in and snatch Jake away if things got out of hand.

"Wait!" Jake shouted. "We can help you clean this up, Ben. We'll round up a bunch of guys and have this sucker lookin' like new."

A laugh rumbled through the crowd.

MacDuff held up his palm like an overdressed crossing guard. "I'm afraid it's too late for that, sonny. The law has been blatantly disregarded here. And the perpetrator is going to have to pay for his crime."

"No!" Jake scrunched up his face.

"Best you just stay out of it, son," Ben said.

Jake didn't respond, his mind in full gear.

"I'm afraid you have left us no choice in the matter, Mr. Ackyack." MacDuff gestured to Norbert.

Norbert ambled up to Ben and, in a voice bold enough to be heard at the back of the crowd, announced, "Benjamin Ackyack, I am placing you under arrest for the conspicuous violation of Town Ordinance three-oh-dash-seven-one-seven-fi—"

"Get to the point, Otto," MacDuff said.

"Right." Norbert pulled Ben's hands in front, handcuffed him, then slipped a dog-eared card from his uniform pocket, and read: "You have the right to remain silent. Anything you say can and will be used against you in a court of law..."

Jake pulled the lantern from his backpack.

Ben grimaced. "No, Jake, this ain't the time."

MacDuff flicked his wrist at Jake. "Move along, sonny. This is grown-up business. You and your little friend best go play some-where else."

Lester hooked Jake's arm. "C'mon, Jake, we gotta get outta here!"

Jill took a step forward but held back when she saw Lester pulling Jake off to the side. The boys stopped out of reach of the police. Jill could see they didn't intend to leave, but she figured they'd moved far enough away to keep out of trouble. She didn't like the fact that Jake seemed to be much more friendly with the old man than she expected. And where would he get an old lantern like that? Probably from Ackyack. A hot fist formed in her stomach. Something was very wrong here.

"Dude, think about what you're doing." Lester grabbed Jake's shoulder.

He brushed Lester aside. "I *am* thinkin' about it, Mr. Slade. This is a time to take action."

Lester recognized the Captain Hawke look on his friend's face. "Okay, Jake…it's your call."

"Just gimme a minute to think this whole thing through." Jake squeezed his eyes shut. After several seconds, Lester detected a nearly imperceptible smile forming at the corners of Jake's mouth. Jake began to slowly stroke the top of the lantern.

People noticed Jake rubbing the lantern, and snickers trickled through the crowd. Bethany gestured to Mike. "Oh, this is just too precious. Get the kid."

Jill had had enough. Now Jake was making himself a laughing stock. She headed toward him, intent on sending him home with a strong reprimand, which would include a demand he stay away from that old reprobate.

That's when all the laughter stopped.

Jill glanced back at the crowd. Everyone stared at the Old Addison Place. When she twisted back around to see for herself, her mouth fell open.

The mansion seemed to shake itself awake. Boards over the broken windows tumbled to the ground, revealing pristine windowpanes that sparkled in the afternoon sun. The building straightened itself with an audible groan. Its two huge crumbling chimneys rebuilt themselves and once again rose high above the sloping roof, as if the old building were stretching its arms toward heaven. The walls now shone bright sienna. Burnt yellow and dark brown hues highlighted the gingerbread trim, as well as the decorative window shutters and inlaid panels.

The collapsed second story balcony restored itself, its balusters springing one by one into place. The treacherously cantilevered porch that continued from the front door around the house to the side entrance now boasted its original burnt yellow color and was supported by sturdy, bright white pillars. Two spectacular stained glass windows enhanced the elaborate front door panels as well as the French doors on the side.

One of the onlookers standing on the edge of the lawn gave a squawk and leapt out of the way when sculpted shrubbery sprang up along the border. A fresh green carpet of lawn wove its way through elaborate flowerbeds and along brick-lined walkways.

Clusters of yellow, white and pink flowers bloomed in the freshly spaded beds alongside an English garden path. Vivid purple-red fuchsias cascaded from the many hanging baskets along the balcony and the porch. Alternating pink and white rosebushes popped up along the left side of the house and twined their way around to the back.

Almost hidden by the huge red and white rhododendron bushes near the front porch, a bronze plaque proclaimed the structure to be a California Historical Landmark. The Old Addison Place was now officially untouchable.

Friends tried to revive two women who had fainted. The rest of the stunned onlookers fixated on taking photos and video with their smartphones.

A few people pointed beyond the beautifully restored mansion to the Wood behind it. They could see a rush of movement in the lush green foliage as if a strong wind moved through the whole area. A flurry of startled birds shot from the trees. Clear enough, this miraculous transformation carried well beyond the old Victorian.

Officer Norbert glanced at Ben, who massaged his forehead, his eyes shut tight, as if he had a headache.

Charley Krock, as stunned as anyone, picked his way through the crowd to his car. Time to switch to Plan B. Except he didn't have a friggin' Plan B. Who the hell could plan a contingency for something like *this*?

Bethany DuVey finally regained her composure. Without taking her eyes off the mansion, she called back to her cameraman. "Jesus, Mike, you *better* be rolling on this!"

"You kidding? I got it all."

CHAPTER 20

Chief Broadcast Engineer José Ackerman reviewed the footage sent to NBC's New York studio by their small Northern California affiliate, KRUT. They'd gone through the video a couple dozen times frame by frame and still couldn't figure out the trick. But what they witnessed on the screen simply could not have happened.

Ackerman had even put in a call to the world-famous illusionist, Blake House, in the hope he could garner some insight into how someone could pull off a trick like this. House had established his reputation by making huge things disappear, like hippopotamuses and the Golden Gate Bridge. His staff admitted they really didn't have a clue how to make a building transform itself without using computer-generated graphics.

Sid Arthur, the producer of *NBC Evening News with Biff Everett*, trudged in wearing the anxious expression of a man foraging for a way to gain back market share. He offered a conspiratorial smirk to his Chief Engineer. "Okay, José, how'd they fake it?"

"I really don't know, Sid." Ackerman shook his head. "I've lost count of how many times we've been through the footage. We took it down to the individual pixels. There's absolutely no evidence of keys or mattes. As far as we can tell, this stuff has never been edited or altered in any way."

Arthur raised an eyebrow. "Come on, you're telling me you got nothing suspicious at all?"

"That's right. And given the state-of-the-art digital equipment we got, we should be able to detect anything that isn't kosher."

Arthur gestured to the video on the monitor. "So, you're telling me this is *real?*"

"All I can tell you for sure is we can't find evidence the feed has been altered." Ackerman glanced at his two assistants, who nodded agreement.

"The whole magic lantern thing? The kid? The mansion? None of it's a hoax?"

"I can't say that for sure either. Not for absolute one hundred percent certain." Ackerman focused on his feet. "What I'm trying to tell you is, we can't prove that this footage did or did not capture an event at the exact moment that it actually happened."

Everyone took a moment to unpack that statement.

Ackerman shrugged. "Anyway, we probably have people out there right now doing follow-up. Talking to real, live eyeball witnesses, right?"

"Oh yeah, our local fluff, Bethany DuVey, claims she can even get an exclusive with the kid who did it."

"Images of the event are already popping up all over the Internet," Ackerman said. "But it's all amateur stuff. We've got the only high-quality digital."

"So we have an exclusive on this video, but a fast-shrinking window to scoop the other networks, right?"

"Yep."

"Then run it!"

———◦◦◦———

Just as he did every night after dinner, Hank Cotter, an unemployed plumber's assistant, lay back in his genuine imitation Naugahyde lounger in front of the TV. Struggling to stay awake during the evening news constituted all the exercise Hank got these days, and he liked to maintain the regimen.

Then, right there on the screen, a broken-down Victorian seemed to be recreating itself. His mouth dropped open and he leaned forward, causing the chair, and Hank, to flip into an upright position. "Blanche! Hurry! You gotta see this. They're gonna show it again in super slo-mo just like football."

Blanche meandered into the living room, drying her hands on a dishtowel, ready to make one of her patented clever put-downs. But as soon as she saw the TV, the witty comment stuck in her throat.

This same scene played out in households across America and around the world. The people, the clothing, the furniture, and the setting varied, but nearly everyone with access to a TV had a similar reaction—they were all spellbound.

———◦◦◦———

Every newsreader delivered the breaking story with a great deal of authority. They all were paraphrasing from the initial NBC news release, but they didn't always credit the source.

Biff Everett was first with the story on NBC Evening News. "We lead off tonight's news with a fantastic tale that could have been ripped from the pages of *The Arabian Nights*. But it appears that *this* tale is no fable."

Jake's image appeared on the screen behind him.

"We now know that fourteen-year-old Jake Parker, from tiny

Santa Necia, California, has discovered an ancient ship's lantern that may actually be *magic*. And, like the legends of old, Jake has been granted three wishes." The segment included an exclusive interview with Jake, who fidgeted through questions thrown at him. Every cable, Internet, and network newscast showed the same interview.

The BBC newsreader: "What the world has now witnessed in the footage we've just shown you is the second of three wishes granted to the young lad."

TV Tokyo's news hostess: "There is every reason to believe that a third wish will be granted. But only to the American teenager, Jake Parker."

The Kenyan Broadcasting Corporation: "According to the elaborate lettering embossed on the top of the lantern itself, young Parker has complete control over the wishes he makes."

India's Doordarshan National Television: "The world anxiously follows this phenomenon to see what Jake Parker's final wish will be."

Canada's CBC Television news anchor: "It boggles the mind to try to even fathom the possibilities."

Fox News personality, Anita Frye, couldn't keep from embellishing the original release, concluding, "In a very real sense, fourteen-year-old Jake Parker now holds the fate of civilization as we know it in his hands."

Even the most casual observers couldn't miss the newspaper headlines online and in print:

The New York Times: THE MIRACLE ON MOZART STREET

The Washington Post: JAKE'S THIRD WISH STILL UNDECIDED

The Wall Street Journal: CAN JAKE SAVE US ALL?

USA Today: HOLLYWOOD CLEBS REVEAL THEIR PERSONAL 3 WISHES

Talk radio was abuzz with opinions about Jake and suggestions for making the perfect final wish. News sources tussled to scoop anything that would feed their audience's hunger for details about Jake Parker, although the accuracy of these details seemed not to matter.

The majority of the country—and the world—happily embraced a new cultural hero. And *this* one wasn't even associated with reality television. People everywhere looked upon a guaranteed bright future, if Jake Parker were to make the final wish they envisioned.

But not everyone was anxious to hop onto the Jake Parker bandwagon. In her weekly TV show, *A Closer Look,* feisty political commentator Heather-Anne Yahn offered her typical edgy take: "We have to raise the issue of whether or not Jake Parker legally *owns* the magic lantern. Our people on the scene have obtained evidence that the lantern might actually belong to Ben Ackyack, the man who stands to inherit the mansion Jake Parker has restored—the very place from which Jake appropriated the magic lantern *without* permission. Ackyack is adamant that the lantern belongs to young Parker. But he refuses to talk to us beyond that statement. In fact, Ackyack may have gone into hiding. I have to ask why.

"Legal issues aside, Jake Parker foolishly wasted his first wish on a Pluto's Super Colossal Pizza, and many are of the opinion he squandered his second priceless wish as well." She paused long enough for the camera to zoom in for her close-up. "So I pose this question to you, America. Given his age, his economically challenged background, single-parent lifestyle, and history of frivolous wishes…can Jake Parker be trusted to do the right thing for us all?"

Diehard conspiracy theorists, though, refused to be taken in by all the hype. They didn't acknowledge that a magic lantern even existed outside of children's fables—and if it did, it wouldn't be a common ship's lantern. They also dismissed the idea that a random fourteen-year-old could pull off such an elaborate hoax. Despite official statements to the contrary—or more likely because of those statements—those who sought government treachery behind every bush viewed the "miracle" as nothing more than a camera trick. But even the most adamant of the conspiracy theorists couldn't come up with a good reason why big government, or big business, or big-eyed aliens would perpetrate this particular scam. And nobody had been able to explain the dramatic televised trick. Jake's miracle had become the biggest boon to the conspiracy theory industry since 9/11.

Various right-wing Bible-belters, especially the leadership of the powerful Denizens of Decency, protested against the attention given to Jake Parker by the masses. As far as anyone could tell, Jake wasn't even born-again.

The loudest voices of protest came from extreme religious fundamentalists, such as the Right Reverend Tristram Choute: "Only God can perform miracles. Unfortunately, all this attention on Jake Parker's final wish suggests that too many of the faithful are now turning to Jake as if he might be some kind of *savior*. We all know there is only one of those."

Jake topped every search engine's list of trending topics no matter how much Google tweaked its algorithms. Hundreds of websites and Facebook pages sprung up like weeds overnight. He was a Snapchat star and memes about Jake and the wish blanketed the Internet. Twitter exploded with tweets about Jake and the Final Wish. It wasn't long before Jake Parker became more a symbol than a person—although no one could agree just what it was he symbolized.

His image showed up on television nightly and graced the covers of most popular magazines.

Time: AND A CHILD SHALL LEAD THEM

Rolling Stone: THE WISH WE ALL HOPE FOR

AARP: 25 THINGS JAKE MUST CONSIDER BEFORE THE FINAL WISH

Jake's face adorned the Pluto's Super Colossal Pizza box, now marketed as "Jake's First Wish." The image was a blowup of the absolute worst image of Jake—his high school yearbook photo; he cringed every time he saw it. Jill had second thoughts about making that deal, but at least Pluto's checks paid the major bills.

An avalanche of T-shirts and sweatshirts featuring Jake's likeness could be purchased online and everywhere from department stores to newly minted street-corner kiosks. Other pirated versions glutted foreign markets.

Once the word got out that the magic lantern had been discovered in an old house, garage, yard, and estate sales became a national pastime, second only to football, NASCAR, or pot farming, depending on the region. Swap meets weren't just for weekends anymore.

CHAPTER 21

In Washington, D.C., FBI Director Patrick Roberts called Special Agent Marvin Hacker to his office. A member of the Bureau's counterterrorism force, Hacker had a reputation for manhandling terrorism suspects—and sometimes being too rough on people who proved to be neither terrorists nor suspects. Recently he'd gone too far, and the public outcry had given the Bureau a black eye. Hacker figured he was facing yet another ass reaming from the top boss.

As it turned out, Patrick had something else in mind. "Hacker, you're one of our most effective anti-terror agents, but you've given the department one too many PR headaches."

Hacker didn't have a response.

"I'm getting pressure from above to pull you from the field for a while. But we've come up with a better option. The President is very interested in the final wish Jake Parker's going to make. He's worried that the kid might be in danger from what he calls 'the escalating terrorist threat.' His people agree."

Hacker pictured the synchronized bobble-headed response from the President's closest advisors. He swallowed a chuckle.

So you're going to head a special task force we've named the 'Genie Project.' The focus of this task force will be to protect the magic lantern...and the kid, from falling into the hands of terrorists, foreign or domestic."

Roberts waved off the protest before Hacker could open his mouth.

"That's our position as far as the public is concerned. But your actual assignment will be to make sure the kid doesn't make any wish other than the one the President's people choose. The best minds in the administration are working on what exactly that will be."

Hacker grimaced. "Sir, I know I've had some...*missteps* in the field lately. But are you sure an agent with my frontline experience is the right choice for this...this *babysitting* gig?"

Patrick stared him down. "Look, Hacker, I'm trying to do you a favor here. Trust me, this is the least painful of the alternatives suggested by the powers that be. You just have to make the best of this situation. Have I made myself clear?"

"Yes, sir."

"You're going to be in close proximity to an ordinary, white-bread American family, not some pod of crazies. And let me remind you that the whole damn world is following the kid's every move." He looked Hacker in the eye. "Clean up your act. No more dropping f-bombs, especially in front of the motherfuh ... the media. It makes us look bad. Your own team will be monitoring you for slip-ups, so I suggest you adopt a more family-friendly phrase to express your deepest feelings. You're supposed to be a sophisticated government agent. Act like one."

"Yes, sir."

"This may be your last chance to save your career." Patrick raised his upper lip in a sneer—as far as Hacker knew, this was the closest his boss ever came to a smile.

"I understand, sir." Hacker hustled to get to the door before his look of chagrin gave way to a sneer of his own. Jesus, how tough could it be? Okay, so he'd spend a few days keeping a close eye on the kid. The assignment sucked, but Marvin Hacker was confident he'd be back busting the heads of bad guys in no time.

The break might actually do him some good. The truth was, he needed one. Lately Hacker had been dealing with the cluster of sad memories that was his life. His greatest lament was letting his first wife go. Too much focus on the job; not enough focus on the woman who was still the love of his life. She dreamed of children and a normal life, but he wasn't ready to give up his budding career. Way too late, but if he could do it over, he'd do it her way.

CHAPTER 22

Ben slowed his pickup as he passed the Parker house. He'd driven by three times in the last few days, and this one was no different. TV crews kept their vigil, lusting after anything of interest. People milled around in front, most taking pictures of the house, hoping for a glimpse of Jake. And the usual bunch of crazies holding up signs. "Jesus is the Answer" glared at a young bearded guy who matched her step for step with "What's the Question?" "Mormonism: The One and Only True Church" glared at both of them. And "Keep America for Americans!" shot daggers at "One World Peace!"

Since Jake's spectacular transformation of the Old Addison Place, Ben had caught a glimpse of him only once, from a distance. Ben had a bad feeling about all this hoopla. It worried him that he had no way to know how Jake was handling the attention.

⎯⎯✺⎯⎯

At the moment, the latest of the parade of photographers was shooting Jake, Jill, and Kevin in the living room. Jill understood publicity couldn't be avoided, and there was no way she could stop this runaway train. But she wasn't comfortable with the limelight shining quite so brightly on her and the boys. Kevin blossomed under his celebrity status as the brother of the most famous person on the planet. And while Jake seemed to settle in to his superstar status at first, Jill now got the impression he wanted to escape from all the adulation. She resolved to do what she could to try to make it easier for him.

The photographer gestured Jill and Kevin aside. "Let's get some close-ups of Jake holding the lantern."

A perky female assistant pouted at Jake. "Now, let's see if we can coax a smile out of you, young man. We don't want the whole world to think Jake Parker is an ol' grumpy-puss, now do we? Ah, that's better."

To Jill, Jake's expression looked more like a grimace.

On the set of the wildly popular *Nighttime with Frank Lee Scarletti*, the host interviewed Bethany DuVey. Admiring her image on the huge monitor just out of camera range, Bethany had to admit that she looked fabulous in the new forest-green designer suit she'd bought for the occasion. Money well spent.

Scarletti clasped his hands in front of his chest. "So, Bethany, tell us how you happened to be in just the right place at the right time."

"Well, Frank Lee, it was one of those special times in our business when you realize *this* is going to be…well, the big one."

Scarletti nodded.

"I could feel it," Bethany said. "You see, I've always considered Jake Parker to be a unique young man."

"Oh?" Scarletti raised an eyebrow. "You mean you were already familiar with young Mr, Parker?"

Bethany offered a conspiratorial smile. "Santa Necia is a small town, Frank Lee. When you're a local celebrity as I am…well, let's just say I've become very close with the Parker family."

"So, Bethany, I understand you've brought us some additional footage."

"Yes, I have. I'm sure your audience has viewed our exclusive video of the magical transformation of our beloved Addison mansion into the beautiful historic landmark it is today." She nodded to the audience.

"Now that's what I'd call a pretty safe bet," Scarletti said.

The audience laughed in agreement.

"Well, now you're about to see something not many people have." She leaned in and lowered her voice for dramatic effect. "You see, Jake's wish was more expansive than we first thought. The forest behind the Addison mansion is known locally as The Wood. It was a neglected overgrown area…really, a serious blight on our community landscape. It turns out, Jake changed all that."

"I can't *wait* to see this," Scarletti said. "Let's roll that tape."

The video, shot from a helicopter flying low over the Old Addison Place and the two-mile-wide Wood behind it, revealed a number of restored hiking and biking trails. Two pristine soccer fields flanked a baseball-softball complex. Even with no games in progress, the infield dirt and the outfield grass of each field rivaled any major league venue. The new risers behind the backstop faced a majestic electronic scoreboard hovering above the center field fence.

"Wow, there must be a lot of happy people in Santa Necia these days," Scarletti said, as the screen went black.

"There certainly are. But I have to tell you, not everyone is enthusiastic about what Jake has done."

"Really?"

"Yes, in my prime-time newscast tomorrow evening, I'll reveal that Jake's miracle has destroyed plans for a retail-business complex in Santa Necia. That complex could have been a huge economic boost to the community."

"So, Bethany, do you think this new video offers us some clue as to what Jake's final wish might be?"

"I'm afraid only Jake knows the answer to *that* one."

CHAPTER 23

Jake peeked out from his bedroom window at the crowd across the street. Three black SUVs turned onto his street and glided to a stop in front of the house. He rubbed his forehead to ease the onslaught of a headache. "Now what?"

Ten minutes later, Kevin strolled into the room. "Hey, bro, a bunch of official-looking dudes are here. They want to see you in the Command Center."

"The what?"

"The Command Center. That's what they're calling the dining room. You should see what they're doing in there. It's totally awesome!"

"But who—?"

"Homeland Security, they said. They look like CIA or FBI to me. You know, like on TV. They never smile."

Jake hesitated at the entry to the dining room, studying the three clean-cut guys in dark gray suits. One guarded the door, and another stood at the window. Jake glanced over at his mom, who was scowling. He sprang back in alarm when the guard at the door moved to frisk him.

The oldest of the three stepped in. "That won't be necessary, Agent Bradley. Jake is on *our* side." He strode over and offered his hand to Jake, who shook it with some trepidation. "I'm Special Agent Marvin Hacker, Jake, FBI Anti-Terrorism." He gestured to the others. "And this is Agent Bradley…and over there is Agent Phelps. We represent the United States government. In fact, we're here at the direct request of Homeland Security and the President himself."

"I've heard of you guys." Jake looked to his mom for support. She was smiling, but her eyes looked worried. "But why are you here? I didn't break any laws."

"Of course you didn't, Jake." Hacker patted him on the back. "We're here to protect you and your family."

Jake looked back and forth between the agents. "Protect us from *what?*"

Hacker squatted to eye level. "You, Jake, are a very important young man. You have the power to make a wish that will…that *could* make a big difference for America and the entire free world."

Jake had trouble swallowing. Like that responsibility didn't already keep him awake at night.

"And there are lots of people who might want to do you harm. Bad, selfish people who want to make sure you wish for something *they* want."

Jake scowled. "Everybody wants that."

"Well, we're here to protect you and your family from these forces of evil." Hacker stood and placed his hand firmly on Jake's shoulder. He nodded to Agent Phelps, who was talking in hushed tones into a red satellite phone.

Phelps brought the phone over to them. "The line has been

secured. And he's on now, sir."

Hacker affected a much more official tone. "Jake, someone very important would like to talk to you."

Phelps handed the phone to Jake.

"Hello?" His eyes widened. "Thank you, sir. Um, but I didn't win anything. Yes, sir, I do. Yes, I mean, *no*, sir. Yes, sir, I will. I understand, sir. Good-bye." Jake handed the phone back to Phelps and turned to his mom. "That was the *President*."

"The President, huh." Jill squeezed her eyes shut and rubbed the bridge of her nose. "What did *he* want?"

"At first he congratulated me like I was a Super Bowl MVP or something. I guess maybe he starts all his phone calls like that."

Hacker closed his eyes, shook his head.

"Anyway, he asked me to hold off. I mean with the wish, you know? He's sending some people to talk to me. About the wish." *Damn, I was hoping to use the third wish to make us rich. Now what am I gonna do?*

Jill glared at Hacker. "And just who would these people be?"

"Experts in world affairs, Mrs. Parker. We can't really expect a fourteen-year-old to be well versed in the global political-economic climate."

"I'm almost fifteen." Jake stretched to his full height.

"Why should he be well versed in any of that?" Jill huffed. "What exactly does that have to do with anything?"

"It's just to assist Jake in making an informed decision."

Jill snorted a laugh. "Let me guess which way he'll be *informed*."

"Relax, Mrs. Parker." Hacker offered his best sincere expression. "Everything's going to be fine. We'll be here to protect the... to protect Jake and all of you from anyone who might pose a threat."

Jake slunk over next to his mom.

Hacker gave Jill a condescending wink. "Don't worry. Once we get everything set up, you won't even know we're here."

Jill took in the electronic debris cluttering the dining room and rolled her eyes.

Agent Bradley reacted to a knock on the door and talked in hushed tones to someone on the other side. Bradley gestured to Hacker.

Hacker nodded back. "I'm going to have to supervise the installation of some of our equipment, Mrs. Parker. Are there any other questions?"

"This is *our* home. Don't I have any say in this?"

"Of course, Mrs. Parker. We'll have a nice talk right after we secure the area."

"What does that mean?" Jill narrowed her eyes. "I'm not so sure I want my house turned into a bunker. We're not at war here."

"I'm afraid *that*, Mrs. Parker, is a matter of opinion."

She glared at Hacker. "Are you saying we've lost our rights and our privacy?"

"Look, Mrs. Parker, let me make things clear here. We are here at the behest of *your* government. We're here, in fact, at the direct request of the leader of the free world. Surely you're not saying that a little inconvenience is going to stand in the way of our country's national security, now are you?"

Jill clamped her mouth shut, spun around and stomped out of the room.

While the discussion went on in the Command Center below, Agent Donaldson stepped into Jake's room. He ferreted out

Jake's backpack stashed between the bed and a wall and removed the lantern from it. Setting the lantern on the desk, he proceeded to photograph it with a miniature digital camera, taking special pains to get close-ups of the details on top. He was about to flip the lantern over to shoot the bottom, when he heard the voice in his earpiece.

"Terminate immediately. The stairs are about to be compromised."

Donaldson settled the lantern back inside the backpack and stuffed the pack into its hiding place. Sliding the tiny camera into his jacket pocket, he slipped out the door.

CHAPTER 24

School life was out of control now for Jake Parker, International Celebrity. The fact FBI agents lurked in the hallways sure didn't hurt his status. Some students quickly adopted the pretense that they'd always admired Jake, and even Lester and Kevin. Others seemed content to adore Jake from afar, as if he were an untouchable luminary. Hundreds of selfies taken with Jake circulated online, and as many Snapchat images went viral. Lots of those images became memes—some cruel, some hilarious, some both.

In a video meme, Jake's image, substituted for Disney's Aladdin character, was dwarfed by the animated blue genie towering over him. Both the genie and Jake were the same color. The caption: "Little boy blue."

One cartoon meme featured a character drawn to look like Jake sitting at a table in a restaurant. A genie dressed as a waiter holds out a tiny plate of steaming fried chicken. The genie's speech bubble read, "The hot chick you wished for, sir."

In another, Jake's face was photoshopped onto the body of a little kid who had pulled out the waistband of his pants and was looking down at his crotch. The caption: "Not all wishes come true."

To Jake's surprise, Buster Flatt stopped tormenting him. In fact, these days Buster and the Tweedles could often be found on the fringes of the flock of admirers who followed Jake between classes. It was a little freaky, but Jake was too busy being a lightning rod of popularity to worry about Buster.

Not everyone treated Jake like a god, though. A few students were livid that Jake Parker, who had always been beneath their notice, had so quickly become a threat to their well-established place at the pinnacle of the Santa Necia High social order. It simply wasn't fair.

As Jake, Lester, and assorted followers headed down the hall toward their next classes, Jake noticed Carrie Cartwright and her matched set of disciples lounging against the lockers. He tossed her a friendly smile as he approached.

Carrie stepped in front of him. "I got news for you, Mr. Big-freakin'-shot, just because everyone else acts like you're so freakin' special now, don't think for one second that *I* could have even the teeniest interest in a dweeb like you."

Jake jerked his head back as if she'd slapped him. "No, Carrie...I...I don't think that at all. Honest, I was just bein' friendly." Jake stammered, wishing he wasn't blushing and sweating simply because this super-hot creature had spoken to him. Jake might be famous the world over, but that didn't mean he had any skills for dealing with the opposite sex—or any real social competence at all. He gulped, trying to regain some composure. "Besides, everybody knows you've been goin' with Buzz Kilgore since like forever."

She stepped closer to him. "That's right, Jakey boy, and don't you forget it! You might be a big deal now to some people, but once you make your silly little wish, you'll be right back to being *nothing*...you worthless little merp!" She gave Jake a condescending tweak on the cheek and swirled on her heel to make her dramatic exit.

"You oughta think twice about pissin' Jake off," a gruff voice from behind Jake called out.

Carrie spun back to see the huge form of Buster Flatt emerge from the group. She smirked. "I don't talk to overgrown retard-varks." She chuckled at her own cleverness, and her support staff harmonized in kind.

Buster was undaunted. "Hey, I'm just sayin'...if you're not careful, Jake just might use his final wish to make you as ugly on the outside as you are on the inside."

Jake heard what sounded like the whole group gasping in unison behind him.

Carrie stomped away. It wasn't clear whether the snickers from nearby students celebrated the mad cool diss of Carrie Cartwright or unexpected attack from lowly Buster Flatt.

Jake grinned at Buster. "Dude, that was freakin' epic. I didn't know you had it in you."

Buster looked down. "Yeah, well...um, she's a total bitch." A flush crept across his cheeks. "Look, Park...Jake, um...I thought you was just some wimpy little smart-ass. Guess I was wrong. I mean, now you got this freakin' mega-important choice to make...and you didn't just grab like a shitload a cash like most people woulda done. Like *I* woulda done. I gotta whole new respect for you, dude. You gotta chance to be somebody. A chance to do somethin' big."

"So does this mean you're gonna stop makin' my life miserable, like you've been doing for like six years?"

"Turns out you ain't the punk I always thought. I got no reason to mess with you anymore." Buster punched Jake softly on the shoulder. "Course you're *still* a smart-ass."

It was a long speech for Buster, and he'd run out of gas. He shuffled off down the hall, the Tweedles in tow.

Jake and Lester sat in the back seat of a black SUV, Agent Phelps at the wheel. Hacker no longer allowed Jake to ride his bike to and from school. Made him too vulnerable he said. The boys were silent. Jake stared out the window, enjoying the quiet.

Finally, Lester could no longer hold back. "Jesus, Jake, I thought we'd never get to PE in time. So many kids crowding around us, we barely got through the freakin' door before the bell rang."

Both boys noticed Agent Phelps watching them in the rearview mirror.

Jake lowered his voice a notch. "At least only *guys* could follow me into the locker room." Jake squeezed his eyes shut and rubbed his temples. "Kinda nice to escape for a while."

"Don't tell me you're complaining about the attention?" Lester said in a harsh whisper. "Especially from the chicks! Dude, Zoe and Juli almost got into a full-on fist fight to see who could be stand closest to you."

"Yeah, people are totally startin' to get more aggressive about hangin' with us."

"You mean hangin' with *you*," Lester said. "I'm just a sidekick."

"Just my best friend, you mean." Jake grinned and bopped

Lester on the back of the head. "Nobody else gets to ride home with me, y' know."

"But think about it, Jake. You've *made* it. You're a total chick magnet."

"Maybe. But all those girls crowding around makes me nervous...but kinda turned on at the same time." He grinned.

"*Deal* with it," Lester said, with a smirk.

Jake noticed that the face in the mirror had a similar smirk on its face. He slid closer to Lester. "But how do I tell if any of it's *real*?"

"C'mon, Jake, I know at least six freshman girls who would kill to go out with you. All you gotta do is ask."

"Yeah, they're comin' on pretty strong." Jake could feel his cheeks flush. "Seriously, it'd be the coolest thing ever to have a girlfriend. But..."

"But what?"

Jake rubbed his forehead. "How'm I supposed to know who really cares about me and who's just after me 'cause I'm famous now?"

Lester chuckled. "Dude, does it matter *why* you're a chick magnet? Run with it while you can."

"You're probably right." Jake shrugged.

"Man, remember how we always wished we could be *somebody*? Someone people would notice, look up to." Lester pointed his finger at Jake. "Now you're totally that guy."

"But it's nothin' like I thought it was gonna be. It's wearing me out, Les. I gotta be *on* all the time. And I'm pretty sure most of the people hanging with me don't really give a shit about the real Jake Parker. They're only looking for a thrill from being around the guy who's gonna make the damn Final Wish."

"Yeah, maybe being a big freakin' deal isn't as cool as it seems when you're dreamin' about it," Lester said.

"Being famous isn't what I imagined, and now that I've seen what it's like, it's sure as hell not what I *wanted*. I mean I know what it *looks* like to be a celebrity with fans all around and shit. But I never had a clue what that would *feel* like, you know?"

Lester winced. "Well, like they say, 'Be careful what you wish for.'"

"Dude, everybody's tellin' me that these days."

The boys glanced at the rearview mirror. Phelps smiled. Lester smiled back.

That night Jake crumpled into bed, so exhausted he drifted off to sleep in seconds.

Captain Hawke stands on the deck of his sleek black ship and peers through his spyglass at the shore of the lagoon. He signals First Mate Slade to have the crew furl the sails and prepare to drop anchor. It is just past dusk, so Captain Hawke cannot clearly see the people gathering on shore, but he knows they're there. It is the same in every port. Crowds of admirers gather at the shoreline to catch a glimpse of the famous adventurer.

Hawke is embarrassed by such enthusiastic displays, but there is really no choice. He signals for the longboat to be lowered. He steels himself against the emotional displays of gratitude from the throngs of worshipers. He understands that people are anxious to see the world-famous Captain Hawke. As the cheers from the crowd grow louder, he adjusts his watch cap, pulls up the collar of his leather jacket, and turns to Slade. "It is, I suppose, the price of fame."

CHAPTER 25

Inside Moby's, the trendy bar on the outskirts of Santa Necia, Cyndi fidgeted in her chair across the table from Steve, who studied his gin and tonic. "I mean, I'd wish for maybe a…a hundred million dollars." She twirled the stem of the little pink umbrella in her mai tai. "Promise you won't laugh."

She glanced across the table for a response, but Steve just stared into space and stirred his drink with his finger.

"Okay, here's the thing. I've always thought I could make it in the movies, you know?" Her voice trailed off and she disappeared into her thoughts. *I have the looks and, well, how hard can it be? After all, haven't I essentially been acting since I was fourteen? If you deal with men all the time you have to play the character they expect. You gotta be good at improvising. But guys never figure out you're making it up as you go along. Not even real smart ones. Like Steve.*

She watched him take a swallow of his drink; was he even listening? She took a sip and soldiered on. "I haven't got any formal training, so I might have to rely on my natural charms." She flipped a strand of hair from her forehead. "But I'll be a serious actress. I won't do any full frontal nudity. I mean…unless the director thinks the story calls for it. You know?"

She made a cute pouty face, but Steve focused on smoothing out his cocktail napkin. Then her eyes widened, "Y'know, maybe I'll just finance my own darn movies. I mean with all the money we'll have." She broke into a grin.

——————

Steve, lost in dreams of his own, had tuned Cyndi out long ago.

I can't wait to tell old man Herringbone he can take his damn job and shove it up his accounts receivable. Time to begin playing a major role in Jake's future. After all, I'm his father. Me and Jake, well, both boys…and Jill, of course…we all need to be a family again. Jake just needs to do the right thing and make the family richer than God. And, damn it, I deserve my rightful share. My old man never misses a chance to call me a loser. Now's my chance to show him…to show everybody Steve Parker is a goddamn winner.

He pounded his fist on the table.

Cyndi jumped. "Are you okay, baby? I don't have to do any nudity…I mean, if it bothers—"

"Things are just so complicated," Steve said to his gin and tonic. "There are some difficult decisions to make."

"I *know*. It's so hard for Jake to pick just one thing!"

Steve looked at her for the first time since they sat down. "Cyndi, I'm afraid it's over."

Cyndi slapped her hands to her cheeks. "Oh my *god*! Jake made the Final Wish? Wow, why didn't you *say* something? Geez, *tell* me. What was it?"

Steve noticed the agent who'd been monitoring them was now whispering into his wrist radio.

"What? No. I mean it's over between me and you."

She stared at him, mouth agape.

When he noticed the stricken look on Cyndi's face, he covered her trembling hand with his. "It's not your fault." He could see tears forming in the corners of her eyes. "It's—".

"Oh no you don't! Don't give me that it's-not-you-it's-me bullshit."

"It's just that I realize how much I miss the boys." He studied the intricate border pattern on his cocktail napkin.

"Oh sure. Now that Jake's a big ol' celebrity, you just all of a sudden—"

"I don't even know if Jill will take me back." He folded the corner of the napkin and creased it with his finger.

"You don't need her!" Cyndi's lower lip quivered. "We could still stay together, baby. We could have the boys over all the time if you want."

"What?" Steve squinted at her. "Oh, no, that's not what I mean. It's…well, I just don't think me and you have a future."

"But I…you…you said we were so good together." The tears welled up. "You said you loved me!"

"I know. I did love you. I still *do*." Steve grimaced. "But things are different now. It just wouldn't work out between us. I'm sorry, Cyndi."

She shuddered, caught her breath. "I thought you were different. But you know what? You're not. You're just another *bastard*. You're all only after one thing. You…you…oh, just *screw you!*"

Out of the corner of his eye, Steve saw two couples now blatantly watching them. Both wives reacted to Cyndi's outburst with "atta-girl" nods. Their husbands just ogled her.

Cyndi popped up from the table, picked up her drink, and tossed the contents in Steve's face, just like in the movies. Her act of bravado would have been a lot more effective, though, if the drink hadn't been almost empty.

She struck a pose, hands on hips. "Take a real good look at what you're giving up, mister! If you wanna go back to that skinny, saggy bitch, you go right ahead." She stomped toward the exit. At the door, she whirled back around. "I don't need you, Steve Parker. I don't need *anybody*."

Steve watched her backside disappear from view, absently removing the little pink umbrella from the damp collar of his shirt. He had to admit she got one thing right. He was going to miss that body.

CHAPTER 26

"This totally blows, dude," Jake told Lester on his new iPhone. "I never thought I'd miss going to class, but it's like a *prison* here. Besides, even though they got permission for me to stay home from school, I still gotta do all the freakin' homework." He glanced at the textbooks on his desk.

Lester's voice took on that whiney quality it did when he was sad and serious "Jake, I totally miss hangin' with you." He took a deep breath and eased it out. "And it sucks you don't even get to enjoy your own wicked cool popularity anymore, dude."

"Yeah, how's *that* fair?" Jake slid over and plopped down on the bed. "But you know, Les, Carrie's probably right. Once I make the wish, nobody's gonna even notice me anymore." He stretched out, his head sunk into the pillow. "I'll be nothin' again."

"Dunno about that, Jake. But everybody's still asking me and Kevin about you. All I can tell 'em is I don't know shit about what's happening…except you haven't made the Final Wish yet."

"It woulda been way better if I'd made all the damn wishes before everybody found out about it. Now they won't even freakin' let me have visitors."

"Seriously, dude, your house is on lockdown. Even *I* couldn't figure out a way to break in. And everybody knows I'm a total badass."

Jake laughed. It felt good. "Honest, Les, I asked 'em if you could come over...'cause we're totally best buds and all. They said it had to be this way 'cause of what they're calling Top Security Protocol. Nobody gets in who isn't officially cleared, and me and Kevin—even my mom—can't leave without being scanned like at the airport. I only get to leave for stuff like our ball game." Jake glanced at the half-opened door. "They're like followin' me all the freakin' time. I got a personal bodyguard, Agent Pirelli."

"C'mon, dude, it's gotta be awesome being part of a real-life FBI op."

"Y' ask me, it's all bullshit. I mean they're totally protecting me, but I think they're really just worried that as soon as I get out of sight, I'll make the wrong wish." Jake glanced up at the camera above the door to his room.

"Dude, everybody's afraid of that." Lester snickered.

Jake let go a snarky half-laugh. "Thanks a lot for the vote of confidence, Les. On the plus side, we got all these choice electronics now. There are like cameras everywhere, and they just gave me this cool iPhone for nothin'. You're the first person I called on it." He glanced up as Kevin strode into the room.

"Somebody here to see you, bro."

"Hey, Les, I gotta go."

"Okay, bye, Jake."

"Yeah, see ya at the game." Jake punched the off button and waited. He heard an unmistakable second disconnect. Of *course* they were monitoring his call. Some of the things he'd said would probably get him in trouble. He sat up and tossed the phone onto his desk. "Who is it, Kev?"

"You'll see." Kevin rolled his eyes. "He's right outside. I'm sup-posed to be like *announcing* him."

A tsunami of color and motion burst into the room. No more than five-foot-six and at least 250 pounds, his bulk was stuffed into a wide-shouldered, baby-blue pinstriped suit, with a bright yellow shirt and a flashy retro tie. His bald dome looked as if he'd just waxed it. To Jake, the only things missing were a red rubber nose and big floppy shoes. The guy pushed the door to shut it behind him, but Agent Pirelli caught it and stood in the open doorway.

"Jake Parker! It is a sincere, genuine pleasure to meet you! You, young man, are hot-hot-*hot*." The visitor extended his hand.

Jake shook it, biting his tongue to keep from laughing out loud.

"Forgive me. Of course, how would you know who I am? You don't read the trades." He bowed with a flair and presented his business card from somewhere in the folds of his outfit, like a magician pulling a fake flower out of his sleeve. "Dante Valentine, Star Maker Agency. You may not know *me*, but *everybody* knows my clients." Valentine registered Jake's lack of response. "Jake, are you aware of what an agent is?"

"I suppose you're not taking about the FBI. They're all over the house." Jake tilted his head toward Agent Pirelli.

"Oh, that's so *cute*." Valentine chuckled. "No, I'm a theatrical agent. I make *things happen* for important people like you, Jake!" He clasped his hands together as if in some kind of joyful prayer. "I'll establish the Jake Parker brand and protect you when prob-lems arise. And those problems *will* raise their ugly heads, Jake. Trust me."

Valentine laid a pudgy hand on Jake's shoulder, leaned in, and looked him in the eye.

"I'll be your connection to the possibilities and introduce you to the people who matter. I'll be your teacher and your advisor." Still clutching Jake's shoulder, Valentine shifted to theatrical sincerity. "You can count on me to be your *deeply* caring professional friend."

Jake glanced toward the door, mapping an escape route.

"Oh, Jake." Valentine's voice cracked as he pressed his hand to his heart. "I feel a strong emotional connection here." He smothered the boy in an enormous embrace.

Jake fought back a sneeze. The guy smelled like baby powder dipped in cherry cough syrup.

"I am truly, genuinely excited about this opportunity to launch you into the superstar stratosphere," Valentine slapped his hands together, then flung one into the air like a rocket taking off. "You're going to the biggest thing since the *Beatles*."

"The Beatles? Aren't most of them like dead?"

"You are absolutely *precious*." Valentine's hearty laugh caused his whole body to wiggle like he was made entirely of Jell-O. "The public is going to *love* you. I just have one *tiny* little suggestion." He backed off a step and stroked his chin while he appraised his newest client. "Can I level with you, Jake? Can we talk *mano a mano*?"

Jake glanced at his hands. He knew from Spanish class what "*mano*" meant. Jake sucked in a breath. In a half hour he'd have to change for the ball game. He didn't feel much like playing today, but he and his mom had spent nearly an hour yesterday trying to convince Hacker to let Jake play in the game. Hacker gave in, but only if Jake was joined by a full contingent of agents. Fine with Jake, he *really* needed to get the hell out of this freakin' madhouse.

CHAPTER 27

Standing in front of the dugout at the new baseball-softball complex in his green and white uniform, Jake took in the awesome facility. The outfield grass was pristine, not a chuckhole in sight. A huge electronic scoreboard loomed majestically over the bright green center field fence. A wire-mesh screen in front of the grandstand stretched all the way from first base to third.

Seats were filling fast for the last freshman game of the year. Families and classmates of the players, the curious from all around the area, some sign-carrying proponents of a particular Final Wish, and a scattering of media people either squirmed with excitement on the risers or paced nearby. Jill, along with Lester's mom, Vicky, and his sister, Angie, sat in the front row. Kevin and his two buddies commandeered a spot nearby. Dark suits and sunglasses could be seen everywhere, even in the dugouts, keeping an eye on the crowd.

Coach Michaels waved the team over into a huddle. "Okay, men, it may be our last game of the season, but it's our first in this great new ballpark. Let's christen it with a win!" He clapped his hands.

"Play ball!" the umpire shouted with a bit of extra flair.

Michaels nodded to Jake. "Come on, Jake, start us off with a base knock."

"What?" Jake looked up at his coach, eyes blank.

Michaels grinned. "Remember? We talked about it. You're batting leadoff."

"Oh, right." Jake pulled on a helmet, picked out a bat, and trudged up to the plate. The cheer rising from the spectators added more pressure than encouragement. Like he *needed* any more freakin' pressure.

He stepped into the batter's box and leaned toward the plate, his bat lying on his shoulder as if he were too tired to lift it. The first pitch sailed right down the middle. Jake didn't move.

"Ball!" the ump barked loud enough that no one in the crowd would miss his call.

The catcher glared at the umpire, but said nothing. Jake started to go for the next pitch, but he checked his swing. Not soon enough.

The ump pivoted to his right, raised his fist in the air, and slammed it down as if hammering a nail. "Stee-rike."

The next pitch got away from the pitcher and sailed high and inside. Jake dove out of the way at the last second, landing hard on the ground. The crowd rose up as one, with a collective gasp of horror.

The ump helped Jake to his feet, dusting off his uniform. "You all right, Jake?"

"Yeah, I'm fine."

The umpire pointed at the pitcher. "Let's be more careful out there!"

The pitcher shrugged.

Jake managed to make contact with the next pitch, trickling

a foul down the first base line. The next offering bounced in the dirt.

"Full count," the umpire shouted, holding up the appropriate fingers. "Three balls, two strikes."

Jake called time and stepped away from the plate. Several people in the crowd shouted encouragement, and his mom gave him a thumbs-up. Jake scanned the crowd for his dad. No such luck.

Just before he stepped back into the batter's box, Jake spotted Ben off to one side. Jake felt a catch in his throat as he nodded to Ben. He really missed the old guy. He hadn't seen him since the FBI invasion. Ben pantomimed a batting stance, twisting his hips, and flinging his wrists forward, as if throwing an invisible bat head. Jake nodded, took a deep breath, and stepped up to the plate.

This time, he concentrated on making the box shape with his arms and cocking his hips. As the ball left the pitcher's hand, Jake pivoted and thrust the bat head at the speeding ball, knocking it solidly over the pitcher's head into center field.

The crowd rose to cheer, then suddenly became deathly quiet. One of the women shouted what many feared. "Oh my god! He wouldn't waste our Final Wish for…" Her voice trailed off. Most of the spectators gawked at Jake in shocked silence.

He rounded first, stepped back to the bag and beamed at the spectators, but his proud grin quickly faded when he realized what they were all thinking. He flung his hands to the side, an unmistakable what's-wrong-with-you-people gesture.

His mind raced. *I just got my first solid hit of the season. And damn it felt good. Maybe the only thing on the minds of these idiots is the Final Wish, but this game has seven innings to go, and I'm gonna make the most of them.*

He studied the pitcher, and as soon as the guy made a move

toward home plate, Jake took off for second. He slid under the tag for a stolen base. *Screw it. Let 'em think I used the Final Wish for that one, too.* Two batters later Jake raced around third and scored on a single by Petey Barnum. His teammates high-fived him and patted him on the back. *This* was fun. Like baseball's supposed to be. And for a brief moment, Jake forgot about the stifling prison that used to be his home.

Off to the side of Wahdle's sprawling mansion, the councilman stood in front of his outsized backyard barbecue grill. He wielded a long handled fork like a saber and jabbed couple of thick steaks sizzling over the flame. Wahdle wore a chef's hat and an apron with "Feed me!" emblazoned in red on the front. To Krock, he resembled one of those fat Italian chefs on television—except for the Italian part...and the fact that the steaks on the grill were turning to charcoal.

"How 'bout a refill, Charley?" Wahdle asked, picking up the chilled pitcher of martinis and refilling his own glass.

"Sure." Krock held out his glass. "How can you stay so calm, sir? Montoya must be pretty upset."

"Oh, his goons paid me a visit all right."

"They did? Why didn't you tell me?"

Wahdle flipped his hand dismissively, as if swatting a pesky fly. "I handled it. Turns out the Parker kid's too high profile for them now. They prefer to stay out of the limelight." He chortled.

"I understand that. But why wouldn't they just—?"

"Ya know what Charley? Screw Montoya! I'm tired of all his tough-guy posturing. He's just blowing smoke. In fact, I'm gettin' the feeling that Montoya has lost his *cojones*, if you know what I mean." He reached under his huge gut in the general direction of his crotch in case Krock missed the reference.

"Fine, but what will you do now? You still owe him."

Wahdle reached into a bowl of taco chips on the slab next to the grill. He stuffed several into his mouth and nodded, the crumbs falling softly like spicy snowflakes onto one of his chins. He took a swig of his martini to wash down the chips. "That won't be a problem as soon as we're in a position to guarantee the kid makes the right wish."

"And just how—?"

"I don't know all the details yet. Jesus, Charley, that's *your* department. But I don't think we should have any trouble getting a fourteen-year-old punk to do what we tell him once we have him under wraps."

"You gotta be joking. *Kidnapping?*" He took a gulp of his martini and let it slowly coat his throat. "The kind of guy who could pull that off won't come cheap."

"Relax, Charley, money will be *no problemo* once we control that wish." Wahdle stabbed a badly charred steak with his barbeque fork as if trying to put it out of its misery.

CHAPTER 28

Jake slouched on the edge of his bed, changing out of his base-ball uniform. He tossed his soiled jersey at the clothes hamper. And missed.

Kevin rushed through the door, snatched the jersey in mid-air and slam-dunked it into the hamper. He brought his victory dance to an abrupt halt when he noticed Jake staring at the floor, expressionless. "Hey, bro."

Jake looked up.

"Dude, you were totally awesome in the game today. No way they woulda won without you." He walked over and plopped down next to his brother. "I've never seen you hit like that."

"That's 'cause I never have."

"Well, I gotta tell you, a double, two singles and a couple of runs scored wasn't what I expected to see from my little brother." Kevin gave Jake a playful shoulder chuck. "So you on steroids or something?"

Jake rolled his eyes and cracked a half smile. "Do I *look* like I'm on steroids?"

"Good point." Kevin laughed. "Okay, so why'd you suddenly

start playing like a stud?"

Jake shrugged, though about it. "Attitude, I guess." He looked away. "And a batting tip I picked up...from a friend."

"Too bad that was your last game of the season, huh?"

"Probably be my last game ever. I'll never make the summer travel squad, much less the JVs next year."

"C'mon, bro, the Jake Parker I saw whackin' the ball all over the field today is plenty good enough to be a *starter* on the JV team."

"Right now, Kev. Baseball is the furthest thing from my mind. I just want to take a really long shower."

"Gottcha. I just got a quick question, bro. So how does this whole wish thing work?" Kevin studied his well-worn Converse high-tops. "Like, could you totally change somebody forever? I mean, you know, transform a person physically?"

Jake managed a lopsided smile. "You mean like make some random short white kid, who shall remain nameless, the size of an NBA power forward?"

"Hey, I'm just askin' how it works.'"

"I know, Kev." Jake squeezed his eyes shut and concentrated on the thoughts whirling around his brain. *Jesus, it feels like I'm turning my back on my family. I was gonna use the Final Wish to give us a better life, but now...now I'm supposed to wish for whatever the President of the freakin' United States tells me to. He's supposed to be all about family values, but there's not a chance in hell he gives a shit about my family.*

"You okay, Jake?"

"What?" He noticed Kevin's look of concern. "Yeah, just really tired. If I could just get away from all this...*pressure.*" Jake scrubbed his face with his hands. "I haven't done anything on my own in like *forever.* It's getting hard to even breathe around here."

He grimaced. "It's like they're holdin' me hostage. I didn't commit any crime, but I'm still a freakin' prisoner in my own house."

Kevin patted Jake on the shoulder and hopped to his feet. "You'll feel better after your shower." He stopped at the door and pointed at the video game controllers next to Jake's TV. "Later maybe we can blow up some zombies."

Jake nodded, and Kevin disappeared into the hallway.

He pulled a clean T-shirt and a change of underwear and socks from the top drawer of his bureau and grabbed his jeans and sneakers from the floor. Eying the camera, perched like a hungry, one-eyed vulture on the windowsill, he let out an audible sigh. At least they didn't put any cameras in the bathroom.

Heading home after her evening shift at Clarke's, Jill checked her rearview mirror. Yep, there it was, the black sedan two cars behind her. Well, they couldn't hear her thoughts. In quiet times like this, she allowed herself to think about what it might be like if Jake used his wish to turn their lives around. She was fed up with barely scraping by paycheck-to-paycheck. Living in fear that one of the boys might need braces or an impossibly expensive hospital stay. And alone in the car, away from the prying eyes of Hacker's agents and the general public, she could say it out loud: "We deserve a better life. We deserve our *share*."

Jill had no idea how she'd frame the Final Wish if she were in Jake's shoes. She understood the challenges, especially if Jake chose to benefit mankind. But the pundits made sure everyone understood that even the most charitable acts could hurt more people than they would help. Poor Jake faced an impossible task. He wouldn't talk about it, but trying to come up with the right

Final Wish had to be tearing him up inside. Jill remembered what high school was like. Teenaged angst is debilitating enough for any kid, but all the notoriety and the pressure of the Final Wish was suffocating Jake. Maybe it would be best, after all, for Jake to go ahead and wish for personal wealth and happiness and then take the heat for being selfish. That's what most people would do anyway. "Christ, I just hope we all get through this intact."

Jake murmured in his sleep, his hands balled into fists, his legs tangled in the sheets, and the bedspread half on the floor.

Inside the huge meeting hall, the line of people winds back and forth on itself like a queue at Disneyland. The stream of people leads to a raised platform, where Captain Hawke sits on a wooden chair. Each supplicant approaches in turn, pleading his or her case to the pirate hero as if he were a rich and powerful ruler.

Hawke slumps forward and tries to massage life back into his eyes. He is determined to make the best of the situation, but he has been enduring the pleas of the needy and the greedy for much too long.

"I ask only for the sake of my family and my people." The man raises his eyes to Hawke. "So we might once again have bountiful crops for our village."

"Granted." Hawke dismisses the man with a wave of his hand.

A middle-aged couple approaches. They are each covered with well-worn, ripped coats, but glimpses of fine clothing can be seen through the holes in the cloth.

"Please, most benevolent one," the man begins, affecting a pained, forlorn expression. "My poor wife and I request only that you grant us a portion of your vast treasure." He pulls his wife to him. "We are but humble people who have never had enough—"

"You are but humble liars." Hawke has seen too many imposters to muster any real anger for the likes of these two. "Take them away!"

Mr. Slade signals a crewmember to usher them out.

A young woman and her crippled child shuffle forward. Tears well up in Hawke's eyes as he witnesses the child's halting progress. The boy drags his badly deformed leg behind, supporting himself with a homemade crutch as best he can. Hawke is reminded of Dickens' Tiny Tim.

The woman's face is streaked with tears. "I ask nothing for myself. It is my poor innocent son—"

Hawke stops her with a raised hand. "Granted." He doesn't have the energy to hear explanations or offer condolences.

Astonished, the child lays aside his crude crutch and takes a few tentative steps. His grin is nearly too broad for his tiny face.

The woman shouts, "It's a miracle! Bless you, Captain Hawke!"

She follows her beaming child, as the boy skips and dances through the hopeful crowd. At the door, they pass a tall, cloaked figure who motions the boy and his mother through. The guard's cloak falls open, and he quickly pulls it closed. But not before revealing his dusky gray suit, white shirt and tie. He is wearing dark sunglasses.

CHAPTER 29

Jill felt the morning sun on her face as she stood just outside the kitchen door, cradling her first morning cup of coffee. She slowly released a deep breath and scanned the array of construction tools, rolls of cable, and mystifying collection of electronic devices strewn around her driveway. It looked like a Good Buys Elecronix warehouse had exploded next to the house. Workmen in government-issue coveralls were everywhere, connecting cables, installing exterior security cameras, and reinforcing locks on doors and windows. She glared at Agent Bradley and heaved her arms up in disgust. "Really? Don't you think this is overkill?"

"We have our orders, Mrs. Parker. We've been told to enhance perimeter security."

She rolled her eyes. "Oh yeah, I get it about your orders. But this is *my* house! I'd appreciate it if—"

"Trust me, Mrs. Parker, it's for your own safety."

About to respond, she noticed Agent Cohen striding up the driveway with someone in tow ... oh shit. *Steve*. Jill growled under her breath, "Great! That's all I need."

Steve dropped his duffel onto the ground next to her. "Honey,

I'm *hooome*." He added a sheepish grin.

Jill stared, mouth agape, trying to recall when she found that grin endearing. "I thought you guys were supposed to protect us from deadbeat jerks."

Agent Bradley swooped up Steve's bag and headed for the house.

Steve started after him. "Hey, where you goin' with my stuff?"

Bradley waved him back. "Just procedure, sir. You'll get it back after we clear it."

Cohen turned his attention back to Jill. "This man claims to be your husband, Mrs. Parker. His ID checks out."

"Ex. This intruder has in fact moved out on his family to live with some sex puppet. He's about to become my *ex*-husband. You can just take him back to whatever rock you found him under." She pivoted around and stormed inside.

Steve followed her into the cluttered kitchen. "Please, Jill, can't we at least talk?"

She spun around and glared at Steve, causing him to back up a step. "*Talk*? What exactly do you think we have to talk about, Steve?"

Kevin crept into the kitchen, eyes wide, looking from his mom to his dad and back again. "Dad, so you're back?"

"Well, that'll depend on your mother, Kevin."

They both turned to Jill.

Jill narrowed her eyes. "How can I put this?" She shot Steve a withering scowl. "No…effin'…way!"

Steve sighed. "Well, Kev, as you can tell, she's not all that happy to see me."

"Can you blame me?" Jill's eyes blazed. "After all you've put me … *us* through?"

Jake burst into the kitchen and slid to a halt, quickly gauging the mood of the room. He probably should give his dad a hug, but he wasn't sure he wanted to. "Dad? Um, you gonna stay?"

Steve gave the boys his patented thousand-watt smile. "Great to be back home. I really missed you guys. But your mother is the one who has to make that decision."

Jill turned to Jake. "Oh, *honey*, it's just too late for that. Too much has happened…we can't just pretend it hasn't." She sucked in a breath through clenched teeth. "It's just too late to pretend your dad and I could ever be together again."

Steve stepped forward, but Jill shut him down with a ferocious glare.

Jake sidled over next to his brother, out of the line of fire.

"Jill, I understand you're upset," Steve said. 'I'm just offering to chip in is all." Steve studied the cracked linoleum beneath his feet before he made eye contact with Jill again. "It's gotta be a madhouse around here."

"Ya *think*?" Jill rolled her eyes at the rat's nest of electronics surrounding them.

Hacker strode into the kitchen. "Ah, Mr. Parker, I see you have decided to pay us a little visit."

"I've come back home…to lend a hand."

"Not *his* decision," Jill said.

Hacker frowned at Jake.

Jake glanced from one adult to another. "*What?*"

Hacker stayed focused on Jake. "Exactly what caused your father to return home all of a sudden?"

"Well, I, ah…I missed the boys." Steve stepped over and mussed Jake's hair. "And *Jill*, of course. Plus I thought maybe I could do something to make things go a little easier around here. You know with all that's happening because of the Final Wish."

"Really?" Hacker never took his eyes off Jake, who began to

squirm. "You just, *out of the blue*, decided that now is the time to return home and rejoin your happy little family."

"Well…sorta, yeah. I mean I broke it off with my, um—"

Hacker peered over at Steve. "Yes, Mr. Parker, we're well aware of your recent activities regarding Ms. Parfay."

Steve's eyes widened. "You are?"

Hacker cut his eyes at Jake. "Do you have anything to tell us, young man? You *did* make a promise to the President himself."

"Yeah, I *know*." Jake's eyes darted between Hacker, Jill, and Kevin, grasping for some clue to what he'd done wrong.

"Can I tell the President that you have kept your sacred oath to him and to your country, then?"

Jill stepped in; she'd had enough. "Quit treating him like a criminal. What exactly are you driving at, Agent Hacker?"

Hacker kept his eyes on Jake. "Oh, I think Jake knows exactly what I'm asking him."

"Oh!" Jake nodded. "*No*, I didn't use my wish to make this happen. Honest." He stepped over to Jill. "I promise, Mom, I *didn't*."

Jill pulled Jake to her. "I believe you, sweetie. That's one wish that would have no chance of coming true anyway."

Steve shook his head. "Totally *my* decision to come back."

"Once again, not your decision to make," Jill said.

"Come on, Jill, I'm their father. I have a right—"

Hacker cut off Jill's response. "Actually, Mrs. Parker, "we think it would be best if we kept the family unit intact until this situation is resolved. For security reasons."

Jill sneered. "You mean so Jake won't be tempted to use his wish to make us all one big happy family again?"

Jake hopped up next to Kevin sitting on the edge of the kitchen table. When Jill raised her eyebrows at them, they leapt down in sync.

"Mrs. Parker, our orders are to protect your son…to protect *all* of you from anyone who might be lying in the bushes for a chance to force Jake to do something we'd all regret."

Jill's gaze could have burned a hole through Hacker's navy-blue tie. "So you're saying his *own mother* doesn't really have a say in the matter."

"What I'm *saying*, Mrs. Parker, is that we believe it's in every-one's best interest to have you all together in one place."

Jill swallowed hard. "In other words you've already decided he's staying."

Hacker slapped his hands together. "Good. So it's settled then."

Jill closed her eyes and kneaded her forehead. "As soon as this is over, he's gone. Which I hope is very soon."

"That all depends on the timing of the Final Wish," Hacker said. "And we're not ready for that to happen just yet."

Jill scowled at Hacker. "What do you mean, *you're* not ready?"

Steve's mouth dropped open. "Wait. What the hell do you guys have to do with the wish?"

"It's a matter of national security, Mr. Parker."

"What? That's crazy!" Steve gasped. "You guys don't have any-thing to do with it. It's *our* wish, not yours."

"*Our* wish?" Jill smirked. "No, Steve, it's *Jake's* wish. Not theirs. Not ours. Jake's."

"Right. That's what I meant."

"You're sleeping in the guest room. Don't even think about—"

"We have a guest room?" Kevin and Jake asked in unison.

Jill nodded to the boys. "Yes, we do. It's old, faded, and green. We sit on it when we watch TV."

Steve nodded. "Oh, right…the couch is fine with me."

"We'll return your suitcase, Mr. Parker, as soon as we finish our scan and search." Hacker took hold of Steve's elbow. "Since you'll be joining us, you and I need to have a little talk."

"Why? What kind of talk?"

"They call it a 'debriefing,' Dad," Kevin said. "It's no big deal."

"We just need to be absolutely sure that you understand the rules, Mr. Parker." Hacker placed a meaty hand on Steve's shoulder and maneuvered him into the Command Center.

That night, as Jake muttered in his sleep, Agent Donaldson slid into Jake's room. Donaldson slowed his breathing, adjusting to the dark until he established the location of discarded shoes, textbooks, and other debris that littered the floor between him and the bed. One stumble could give him away. Keeping his body between Jake and the camera on the windowsill, Donaldson made his way to the side of the bed. He pulled a replica lantern from his shoulder bag, leaned down, eased the original out from the crook of Jake's arm, and replaced it with the fake in one smooth motion. He slipped the original into his bag and stood stock still a few more seconds to be sure the kid didn't wake up. Jake rolled over to face the wall, clutching the faux lantern tight to his chest. Donaldson grinned. Like taking candy from a baby.

Back in the Command Center, Donaldson handed the original lantern to Hacker as if it were a piece of delicate china. "Operation completed without incident, sir."

Hacker studied the ship's lantern. "Well, don't just stand there. Get the hell outta here and call for the courier so we can get the f-f…fricassee'n thing to Washington."

Donaldson reached for the lantern, but Hacker waved him away. "I'm sure I'll be able to keep the thing safe, Donaldson. Just tell 'em to make it quick."

Hacker's eyes darted around the room to ensure no one lurked in the shadows. Satisfied, he closed his eyes and dragged his palm across the surface of the lantern. As soon as he opened them, the bemused smile faded. No beautiful wife, no kids, no normal life. No second chances. He glanced down at the lantern. Guess it really did only work for the kid. Shit.

Hacker marched over to the corner of the room, where he settled the lantern into the precisely molded interior of the black metal container, closed it, and engaged the electronic lock. Now it was someone else's problem.

CHAPTER 30

Ben paused outside Moby's Bar and peered under the neon Bud Light sign at a group of patrons; all eyes were fixed on the big-screen TV. He shuffled inside as Bradley Rupp, another of the horde of late night talk show hosts, introduced Jake. Tonight's other guests—an up-and-coming blonde starlet and an aging comic, known more for his penchant for alcohol than his witty comebacks—lounged on either side of Jake, who clutched the lantern protectively to his chest.

"Welcome." Rupp smiled at Jake. "I must say *you* are a very lucky young man."

Jake avoided eye contact and fiddled with the lantern's window latch. "I don't know, sir. It's not really that cool. Sometimes I wish—"

"Whoa there, cowboy." Rupp laughed. "You better choose your words more carefully."

The audience chuckled.

Jake tried to explain. "No, um, see I have to be rubbing the lantern when I—"

"You're just sooo adorable." The actress reached over and

patted his shoulder with her fingertips.

Jake cringed.

"I gotta tell ya, I know what *I'd* be wishing for." The comic wiggled his eyebrows. "Say, Jake, can I borrow the lantern for the weekend?"

"I can't lend it to—" Jake's words were swallowed up by the raucous laughter from the audience.

Ben shook his head and marched outside. Why couldn't they just leave Jake alone? How did his wish become everybody's business?

The next afternoon, Jake perched on the edge of an over-stuffed chair, this time next to Lydia Breeze for the taping of her hugely popular daytime talk show, *Lydia Live!* The predominately female audience hung on her every word.

After some generic questions about how he was dealing with his meteoric celebrity status, Lydia reached over and rested her hand on Jake's shoulder. "Now, young man, suppose you tell us about these wonderful high seas fantasies of yours."

Jake scrunched up his face. "Wait. What?"

Lydia winked at him. "Come on, Jake, let us in on your fascination with seafaring adventures."

Jake blanched, his voice barely above a whisper, "How do you even *know* about that?" He glanced off stage, where his dad gave him a thumbs-up. Jake squeezed his eyes shut. Why would his dad do this to him?

"Come on now, show us that Captain Hawke watch cap."

"Naw, that's okay. Besides, I didn't—"

"How about it?" Lydia stood and gestured to the audience.

"Let's give Jake a little encouragement."

The audience erupted in applause—Dante Valentine's cue to swoop in wearing a yellow-and-red striped suit and a bright red watch cap covering the top of his glossy dome. He waved two more red caps like a princess in a homecoming parade.

Lydia gestured to Valentine. "Please welcome Jake's tireless agent and personal manager, Dante Valentine!"

The audience responded enthusiastically as Valentine presented watch caps to Lydia and Jake.

Jake examined the cap. The trademarked logo on the front featured a small ship with the name "Hawke" on its side. *Jesus.* For a second Jake considered using the Final Wish to disappear.

"Don't worry, we have Hawke Hats for everyone," Lydia said.

Ushers rushed in from the wings and began to distribute red watch caps to the studio audience

Hawke Hats? Great, now everybody in the freakin' universe knows about Captain Hawke. Jesus, it's like I've been stripped buck naked in front of the whole world.

The Hawke Hat became an instant sensation. Big box stores featured huge displays of watch caps with the Hawke logo in nearly every color imaginable. They flew off the shelves so quickly stores had to keep waiting lists. Chinese and Tijuana knock-offs appeared at corner gas stations and freeway off ramps. Children, teens, rap artists, construction workers, street punks, chemo patients, people just trying to look hip, and anyone with a shaved head now favored Hawke Hats. Women of all ages, who bought them at malls and upscale boutiques, sported watch caps at a jaunty angle as fashion accessories.

The Hawke watch cap sensation, though, was only the beginning. Overnight plastic replicas of the famous lantern flooded the market. Sea-captain heroes became a thing, cropping up in comics and cartoons, and versions of "Captain Hawke's Adventure" were the hottest sellers for PlayStations and Xboxes. Studios rushed to be first in the theatres with swashbuckling sea captain movies. Television producers worked into the night to develop the hottest lost-at-sea reality show.

Valentine often lamented the fact he couldn't make Halloween come a few months earlier this year. Other than that, his timing had been perfect. Riding the Jake Parker craze, he'd be flush for the rest of his life, already banking plenty in kickbacks and enjoying a considerable share of the profits from sales—the standard fifteen percent agent's cut was for amateurs. And given his shrewdly engineered licensing agreements and residual deals, the money kept pouring in. Valentine had easily convinced Jake and his parents they could expect no more than a small amount in the early stages.

He figured Jill would spend too much time on the fine print, which would have completely fouled up Valentine's scheme. Steve was the one with dollar signs in his eyes and big-ass dreams, so he regaled Steve with vague promises of big payoffs down the road while glossing over the details about percentages and rights. Steve made sure Valentine understood just how determined he was to get his share. But just as Valentine suspected, Steve made no effort to read the contract. When Valentine presented an estimate of how much cash might be coming to the Parkers, Steve looked at him as if he'd just won the lottery.

Dishonest? Valentine didn't see it that way. He was an agent, not a financial advisor.

CHAPTER 31

Charley Krock strolled into a picnic area adjacent to the new playground at the edge of the Wood. He tried to maintain a casual air as he ambled past small children frolicking on slides that resembled famous cartoon characters. Their mothers chatted away nearby keeping an eye on the cartoon mouth that continually spat out squealing toddlers.

The women pivoted in unison and stared at this lone adult male who suddenly appeared at the playground for no apparent reason. Krock offered a non-threatening smile. It didn't work. They monitored Krock's departure with a collective sigh of relief. Once again, they had successfully protected their adorable little OshKosh-B'gosh-clad future sports heroes and political leaders from a sicko pervert. Before he was out of sight, every cell phone had his picture.

Krock strode over to a concrete table in a picnic area out of sight, where a hulk in a gray jacket and a black baseball cap seemed to be engrossed in a newspaper. Krock slouched down across from him, casting furtive glances around the area. The hulk didn't acknowledge him.

"So…you must be Roarke." Krock offered his hand. "Charley Krock."

Roarke ignored him.

Krock pulled back his hand and rested it on his lap. "You come highly recommended."

Still no response.

"Not that I've been talking to a lot of people." Krock's attempt at a laugh came off more like a whine with a question mark at the end.

Roarke didn't take his eyes from the paper. "Got the money?"

Krock extracted a fat envelope from his jacket pocket and passed it under the table. Roarke seized the envelope, pocketed without giving it a glance.

"Half the money up front. Just like—"

"Better be."

Krock fidgeted in his seat. "So you're gonna contact us as soon as you nab him, right?"

Roarke glared at him over the paper. "Friggin' amateurs." He stood, glowered like a ravenous grizzly, and lumbered away.

Krock rubbed his eyes. He wondered what the hell happened to his career. He came here as a respected political consultant, but the truth was, he was little more than an errand boy for an asshole felon. And now he had to deal with this rude thug with the conversational skills of a sedated slug. He'd been willing to stretch moral and legal boundaries, after all that was essentially the job description for a consultant. But what Wahdle had him involved in this time could get him arrested, if not killed.

As soon as this whole mess ended, Krock resolved to haul himself out of this hick town for good.

CHAPTER 32

At Stan's Superette, Kevin absently flipped grocery items into bags. The checker waited for an elderly woman to complete her forage for loose change in her purse. Stan's teemed with curiosity seekers, who far outnumbered the regulars, as they had since Jake's second wish. Given Kevin's connection with the most famous person on the planet, management had posted signs at each register requesting that customers refrain from asking store employees for autographs. Today, Kevin wore a T-shirt that announced, "No *#^ idea what the Final Wish will be." Even so, the queue at Kevin's checkout stand far outnumbered any of the others.

He chuckled to himself as he noticed his buddy and fellow courtesy boy, Max, bobbing his head to the beat of one of the popular raps he kept in his head. Kevin envied Max's ability to escape the real world. For Kevin, that world was always in his face.

The magazine racks at each checkout stand overflowed with the latest tabloids and pop culture magazines, many of which showed signs of wear and tear from constant casual perusal.

The tabloid headlines shouted for attention:

National Inquirer: IS JAKE THE SECOND COMING? NEW EVIDENCE!

The Weekly World News: ASTROLOGERS: TIME RUNNING OUT FOR WISH!

Star: JAKE SEEN WITH ALIENS! SHOCKING PHOTOS INSIDE!

The Globe: SCIENTIFIC PROOF MAGIC LANTERN A HOAX!

Many of the women in Kevin's checkout line wore versions of the Hawke Hat. In fact, each member of a family of five in his line wore matching Hawke watch caps, including an infant in a baby carrier on its father's back.

"God, I hate those things," Kevin muttered.

Max slid up behind Kevin and nudged him. Kevin caught on as soon as he spied Angie and Lester Woo approaching the checkout stand Max had just vacated. Kevin felt so lightheaded he had to hold onto the counter for support.

"Man, she is so *tight*," Max whispered. "Dude, you oughta go for—"

Kevin tossed Max his half-filled bag and bolted over to the check stand as Angie and Lester arrived at the head of the queue. It took all of Kevin's reserve not to gawk at her. He didn't notice that the bulk of the customers had moved in tandem with him and now lined up behind Angie and Lester.

"Hey, Kevin." Angie beamed at him while their groceries slid along the belt.

Kevin glanced up as if he'd just noticed her, but he couldn't stop the flush crawling up his cheeks. "Oh, um, hi. So…um, plaper or pastic?"

"Well, normally I'd choose plaper." Angie chuckled. "But I think we'll go with the tote bag we brought with us." She handed the cloth bag to Kevin.

Kevin managed to wrestle the few items into the bag.

Lester stepped around his sister. "Jesus, I haven't seen Jake in like *forever*. I guess now they won't even let him like text or nothin'. That sucks."

Kevin couldn't take his eyes off Angie. It took all his concentration to keep his breathing near normal.

Lester waved a hand in front of Jake's face. "Dude! Hello? How's Jake doin' anyway?"

"What? Oh, um...Jake's having kind of a tough time these days, Les."

"Yeah. I figured."

Kevin cradled the small cloth bag. "Can I give you a hand with this?"

Angie grinned as she eased the bag from his grasp. "I think we can handle it."

"Tell Jake 'Hi' for me, okay?"

"Sure, Les."

As Angie and Lester headed for the exit, Kevin froze, hypnotized. Shaking himself, he called forth every molecule of courage he could muster. "Angie!"

She and Lester swung back to face Kevin as he rushed up to them.

"I was wondering..." Kevin studied his shoelaces. "Well... do you think, maybe, I could, ah...you know, like, um, give you a call or something...sometime?" He looked back up at her and shrugged. Something did a backflip in his stomach. "I mean, if you're not...*you* know—"

"I'd like that." Angie gave him the sweetest smile he'd ever seen in his life. "And I'm not...*you* know."

As Angie and Lester reached the exit, Kevin stared after her, his gaze moving past the agent stationed at the door. For his protection. Or so Hacker claimed. The stupid grin on Kevin's face might well have become permanent if Max hadn't ambled over to give Kevin a congratulatory punch on the shoulder.

"You are one smooth-talkin' dude." Then, as Angie left the store, Max added a subdued "Woohoo!"

The cashier called out, "Kevin?"

Kevin floated over to the groceries piling up on the counter.

Agents Cohen and Donaldson sifted through several large cartons in the Parker driveway. They had pulled out a huge plasma TV, a few state-of-the-art sound systems, three new computers, and some high-tech kitchen appliances.

Hacker ambled through the kitchen door and stood next to Jill. "Kind of extravagant, don't you think?"

Jill glared at him, hands on hips "I didn't order any of this."

"Really?" Hacker raised an eyebrow.

"Really. And when your goons are through trying to ferret out bombs and secret messages from evildoers, they can just pack up all this crap and take it back."

"But if you didn't order this, Mrs. Parker, then who? Oh *no*, that little fu…finger-licker better not have—"

Three short blasts on a car horn cut his comment short. Jill and Hacker peered down the driveway at a red BMW convertible, top down, Steve at the wheel.

"Beauty, huh?" Steve hopped out and patted the glistening finish. "The last red one they had."

Jill gaped at Steve. "What do you think you're doing?"

"Relax, it's all good. See, with all of Jake's TV and endorsement deals coming up, we've got a *ton* of credit. We don't even need cash. I worked it all out with Valentine. He says there could be a huge movie deal too. We're going to be filthy rich!"

"Ah, I see, Mr. Parker," Hacker said. "So it was *you* who ordered all the electronics."

"Hey, it's only fair that we get something outta this too." He appealed to Cohen and Pirelli standing nearby. "Isn't it?"

They both shrugged.

Steve gestured toward the two agents. "See?"

"At least it's not as if you squandered it all on something completely frivolous." Jill stomped back inside.

"Jesus, it's only a four series. It's not even the top of the line!"

———— ⟳ ————

Jake arranged the speakers on his bureau while Kevin knelt on the floor and connected the last speaker wire.

Kevin whacked the power button. A rock anthem exploded into the room. "All right! Let's crank this puppy up!"

Jake bobbed his head to the music. Then stopped.

"Everything all right, bro?"

Jake waved his hand toward the speakers. "Could you just turn it off?"

Kevin switched off the player. "What's the matter?" He checked the CD case. "Don't you like these guys?"

Jake buried his face in his hands. "You know? I guess I'd rather have some quiet."

Kevin joined his brother on the edge of the bed. "I know it's tough."

"It's not *tough*. Tough is having to tell your teacher you didn't finish your homework. This is…this is freakin' *impossible*."

"Can I help?"

Jake rubbed his eyes with his the heels of his hands. "Nobody can help."

Kevin stood. "Okay, Jake. I'll be in my room if you need anything."

Jake collapsed face-first into his pillow.

CHAPTER 33

The unmarked gray van parked halfway down the block had become a neighborhood fixture. Once hidden behind crowds of onlookers, now it stood out, blocked from view only by a few sign-toting fanatics and the occasional curiosity seeker who braved the night air.

Inside the van, two FBI agents in headsets monitored conversations in the Parker house. One of them thumbed through the latest issue of *Playboy*—the cover of which featured a beaming Cyndi Parfay, wearing a gold Hawke Hat and little else. A banner across a corner proclaimed this to be the SPECIAL JAKE ISSUE, its features listed below: "Father's Former Mistress in Sizzling Pictorial"; "The Playboy Interview—Bethany DuVey's Insider's View of Jake's Mind and Motivations"; "Playmate Fantasy: The Call of the Wild Girls!"

───※───

Hacker stepped out into the driveway and watched Jill back out her Fiesta and head off to a hastily called late evening conference with Walt Staley. He wanted to discuss her possible new role with the agency. She had no idea Hacker had strongly "recommended" the meeting to Staley. The time had finally come to take care of business, and things would go a lot smoother without the kid's mother questioning everyone's motives and generally being a pain in the ass.

As soon as Jill turned the corner, a black Lincoln Town Car sped down the street from the opposite end and pulled up in front of the Parker house. Special Agents Jack Bundy and Ann Berkowitz stepped out and nodded to Hacker.

Jake and Steve lounged on the couch in the family room pretending interest in a *Friends* rerun. The agents stationed at the entry stepped aside for Bundy and Berkowitz, who glided into the room like visiting royalty. They introduced themselves and announced they were there at the specific request of the President of the United States.

"I really don't think we need such a big crowd," Bundy said. "We're just going to have a friendly little chat with Jake." He carried a small, black cardboard box.

Taking their cue, the other agents vacated the room. Berkowitz caught Steve's eye and nodded toward the door.

Steve pushed himself off the couch. "Oh, you mean *everyone*."

"It'll be a lot more comfortable for Jake." She flashed a practiced smile.

Bundy offered an identical expression. "I'm sure you understand, Mr. Parker."

Jake got that all this smiling was meant to make everyone feel at ease, but it gave him the creeps.

Steve hesitated at the door. "Jake's a minor. Isn't he supposed to have an adult present?"

Berkowitz offered a broad smile. "Come on, Mr. Parker. This isn't an interrogation. It's just a friendly chat. We're sworn representatives of your government. Are you suggesting we can't be trusted?"

"Well...no, I didn't mean to imply—"

"Good." Berkowitz gestured to the door, and Steve fled the room like an escaping felon.

Berkowitz and Bundy plopped down on either side of Jake.

"There, that's better." Bundy loosened his tie.

Jake glanced back and forth between them. He didn't trust either one.

"Hey, take it easy, buddy," Berkowitz said. "We're the good guys."

Jake knew these two were here to spell out the actual wish the government had decided on. Pretty damn likely it would be one he didn't want to make.

Bundy laid his hand on Jake's shoulder. "So, Jake, things have been a little hectic lately, huh?"

"Yeah, no sh...kidding." Jake shook Bundy's hand off.

"Seems like a lot is riding on this last wish of yours," Berkowitz said.

Jake stared at her. Had she been living in a freakin' cave or something?

"Too bad you had to use up your other wishes so quickly," Bundy said.

"I *know*." Jesus, everyone in the whole world thought the same thing. He hugged his backpack, feeling the comforting corner of the lantern pressed against his chest.

"I'm just curious, Jake," Berkowitz said. "Why did you... squander your second wish on this Ben Ackyack character?"

Jake glared at her. "I didn't squander anything! He's my friend, and he was in trouble."

"So who *is* he, anyway?" Bundy asked. "Where'd he come from?"

"I don't know. He's just a guy who showed up one day."

"You've spent quite a lot of time with him," Berkowitz said.

"Not really. We went to a ball game once. He helped me with my swing a little."

"Has he ever…touched you?" Berkowitz's expression dripped with sincerity. "You know…inappropriately?"

"No!" Jake leapt off the couch and began to pace. What the hell was the matter with these people?

"Relax, buddy," Bundy said.

Jake took a few more steps toward the window. "Ben's not like that! He's just a nice old guy." He stopped and spun back around. "Why would you even *think* that?"

"It's okay, honey. Come sit back down." Berkowitz patted the couch beside her. "We understand. Children often feel they need to protect their abusers."

Jake rolled his eyes, heat flashing through his body. "I told you already! He's never done *anything*."

"Okay, okay." Berkowitz held up her hand and nodded. "I can see you're upset about…what Mr. Ackyack may have done. Why don't we save that for another time."

Bundy rested his arm on the back of the couch. "Believe me, we're well aware there's been a lot of pressure on you lately."

"We're here to give you some relief," Berkowitz said.

Jake massaged his forehead. If this was their idea of providing relief, they totally sucked at it.

"And to prove that we're on your side, sport, we have something very special for you." Bundy produced the cardboard box and gestured for Jake to rejoin them on the couch.

Jake cut his eyes at both of them as he dropped back down on the couch, and Bundy set the box in his lap. Jake lifted the lid and stared at a clone of the lantern in his backpack. He spun around to face Berkowitz. "Seriously? You're giving me one of those cheap replicas? They're like *everywhere*."

"No, no!" Berkowitz said. "This is the original ship's lantern you discovered, Jake. Some very bad people…terrorists…sneaked in and stole it from you when you were sleeping."

Jake didn't blink.

"We suspect they were ISIS operatives," Bundy said. "Our people recaptured the lamp in a daring midnight raid on their base camp in Afghanistan."

Jake scrunched up his face. "Lemme get this straight. You're sayin' some terrorists managed to get by all the security cameras and FBI agents in the house…agents who are here specifically to keep *out* the terrorists…and the bad guys just walked out of here with my lantern? Seriously?"

Bundy and Berkowitz nodded.

Jake closed his eyes and rubbed the bridge of his nose. How stupid did they think he was? Jesus, if anybody managed to get in here and take the lantern, they'da had to be freakin' invisible. Jake yanked the lantern from his backpack. "So then, what's this?"

"My guess is the terrorists left a fake to replace the one they stole," Berkowitz said.

Bundy took the lantern from Jake's hand and gave examined it. "Looks to me like a pretty darn good copy of your original lantern."

"Lemme see that." Jake took back the lantern from Bundy and turned them both upside down in his lap.

"Crap, it *is* a fake." Jake tossed the bogus lantern back to Bundy, and wiped the bottom of the original with his sleeve.

"Yeah, the one I found has the smiley face on the bottom."

"Smiley face?" Berkowitz furrowed her brow.

"Not really a smiley face." Jake held the real lantern out for Berkowitz to see. "More like some kinda symbol…maybe a signature of the guy who made the lantern or somethin'."

Both agents made quick mental notes for the ass-kicking they'd administer later.

"Sooo…anyhow, I'm sure you recall the President's request that you delay the Final Wish."

"Course, I remember." A hot dagger twisted in Jake's gut.

Berkowitz clasped her hands together. "Well, the President's decided you've waited long enough, Jake. You can just go ahead and wish for whatever *you* feel is right."

Jake rechecked the symbol on the bottom, shoved the authentic lantern into his backpack, and sank back into the couch. A cautious sense of calm washed over him. He really wanted to believe them. "But it's so hard to pick just one thing."

"Trust us, sweetie, we understand how difficult this is." Berkowitz pulled out the latest issue of *Newsweek* and handed it to him.

The cover featured Jake with a worried expression. The headline read: "The Top 50 Problems the Final Wish Could Solve—and 50 It Could Cause!"

"I'm sure you're aware of the polls," Berkowitz said. She showed him a recent copy of *Cosmopolitan*. Next to the standard cleavage shot, the cover displayed a list of featured articles, topped by one entitled "The Most Popular Final Wish Revealed: The Results of the Latest Cosmo Readers' Poll."

"Yeah," Jake said. "Those surveys are like everywhere. There's a ton on Twitter and Facebook. That blog, 'Wishful Thinking,' has a new poll like every week!"

"Well, you can forget about all those people and their selfish little opinions, Jake." Berkowitz grinned and gestured with the magazine. "That's *all* they are, sweetie…just opinions."

"Yeah, but there are a lot of good ideas about—"

"Don't you worry, sport," Bundy said. "We're here to eliminate all this silliness for you." He snatched the *Newsweek* from Jake.

Bundy and Berkowitz tossed the magazines across the room with a flair.

"No pressure, Jake. We're not asking you to do it right this *minute*." Bundy grinned. "We've scheduled a media event for three days from now. A perfect time for you to announce to the world that the Final Wish has been made."

"It's *your* wish." Berkowitz removed a manila envelope from her courier bag and clutched it to her chest. "What the President's people have come up with here is a…a *suggestion* of a wish that won't, you know, turn out to be a terrible mistake. Like your first two."

A bolt of electricity raced through Jake's body. If he had an extra wish at that moment, he'd make them both explode.

Bundy looked Jake in the eye. "You love America, don't you, buddy?"

"Well, sure I—"

"Good. That's very good," Berkowitz said. "Because, well, frankly, Jake, America needs you to step up to the plate."

Were they finally being straight with him?

"Jake," Bundy said, "let's pretend just for a minute that you are…oh, I don't know, let's say…a *sea captain*."

"A *good* sea captain," Berkowitz said. "A hero. A *patriot*."

Okay, now they were actually treating him like a damn five-year-old.

"And let's pretend that America is your beautiful ship," Berkowitz said. "A ship that is carrying all your family and friends to a wonderful, safe place. But, Jake, that magnificent ship and all its innocent passengers are in danger of being viciously attacked...maybe even dismembered or *worse*...by evil terrorists."

Jake shut his eyes tight. If he didn't look at them, maybe he wouldn't break out laughing.

Bundy lowered his voice. "Jake, we're going to let you in on some top-secret information."

That got his attention. This might at least give him some bragging rights.

Berkowitz whispered in his ear. "You have to absolutely promise to never, *ever* tell anyone."

Jake rubbed his forehead and glanced over at Bundy. "Fine."

"I'm sure you remember back when those cruel, despicable terrorists savagely attacked America," Bundy said.

"So many innocent, brave American heroes were murdered in cold blood." Berkowitz paused, placing her hand over her heart as if she were too choked up to continue.

"You know, back when those beautiful twin towers were destroyed," Bundy said.

Jake nodded. "Yeah, we read about it in school."

"That assault by the forces of evil was only the tip of the iceberg, buddy," Bundy glanced around the room as if to assure himself no one was within earshot.

Jake stifled a laugh. Did this guy really not know the whole place was bugged?

Berkowitz handed the envelope to Jake. "So, Jake, the President would like you to look over this top-secret document that has been prepared for *your eyes only*." She pointed to the word "Classified" stamped in red on the envelope. "*We* don't even know what's inside this sealed envelope."

Bundy leaned in. "We know that you're probably a little

worried about what will happen to your family. You know, if you don't use the Final Wish to make your lives better."

Jake's heart jumped.

"We're not asking you to give up that dream," Berkowitz said.

Jake looked at her, then back at Bundy.

Bundy glanced furtively around the room. "Jake, once you've kept your promise to the President and followed the suggestion in the envelope for the Final Wish…your family will be well taken care of."

"*Very* well taken care of," Berkowitz said.

Jake looked away. *I may be a kid, but I know a bribe when I hear one. It would be great to be able to make sure the whole family was really well off. If there was a chance in hell I could trust them to go through with it.*

Bundy gestured to the envelope in Jake's hand. "Take your time. Look it over carefully…I'm sure that you, as a loyal American patriot, will do what's best for all of us in this great country of ours."

Berkowitz reached over and laid her hand on Jake's shoulder. "Of course, you understand that if for some reason you choose not to honor your President's request, there could be…*consequences* for everyone involved. Dire consequences." She wasn't smiling.

Jake's heartbeat raced. He could feel the color drain from his face.

Both agents rose. "Jake, we need you to stand."

Jake managed to get to his feet, but his knees felt so wobbly he wasn't sure they'd hold him.

"Now raise your right hand and repeat after me. I, Jacob Daniel Parker, as a citizen in good standing of the United States of America, do swear and avow…"

CHAPTER 34

As soon as Jake got back to his room, he pulled the printed document from the envelope. It was a whole page long, and he didn't understand half the damn words on it. It was obvious Bundy and Berkowitz expected him to memorize the whole freakin' thing; one wrong word might screw up their whole plan. He tried reading it again, but the words melted into each other and kind of dripped off the page. Jake switched on his new clock radio and tried to concentrate on the talk show, but he couldn't keep his eyes open. The paper slipped from his fingers to the floor.

Hawke is alone in the frozen north. An icy blanket of white covers everything. It is nearly impossible to see the trail in front of him, and there is nothing visible behind him but his own footprints sunken deep into the snow. He can see no living thing, but he has heard the savage beasts howling ever closer in the night, their red eyes glowing in the darkness. His team of huskies has been attacked and killed one by one. Each dog hauled off into the night to be devoured by the pack of wolves that remains always within striking distance. Hawke

is running out of time to reach civilization, such as it is here in the Yukon.

He has gone without food for three days, or is it four? Time has little meaning in this unforgiving land where nights and days are often indiscernible from one another. He has used the stars as his guide, and if his eyes have not failed him, he is no more than a few hours from the safety of a mining camp. Hawke's legs throb with pain, but he cannot stop, even to rest, for he has no more ammunition and has burned his snowshoes and the last few pieces of his sled. The fires are the only hope of keeping the wolves at bay after dark.

The beasts become bolder. They allow themselves to be seen on the trail. First one, the alpha male, then another…and another, until it is difficult for him to accurately guess their number. It is not, however, difficult to understand their bared fangs.

Even though he can no longer feel his legs, only the pain, Hawke tries to put distance between himself and his pursuers. But the wolf pack matches his pace. Ahead is a clearing in the trees, and the flat surface beyond them means he is approaching a frozen lake. It is too wide for him to stay to the shoreline, and that would bring him dangerously close to the trees. He has only one choice.

He knows it would be best to crawl onto the ice, testing for weaknesses, but the beasts would be on him in a flash. He steps out onto the ice and shuffles along as quickly as he is able. The wolves seem hesitant to go onto the ice, but he knows their reluctance will be short-lived. He is focused on keeping his balance when the silence is broken by a "crack." He hears another, then several more close at hand.

The ice beneath his feet gives way, and he plunges deep into the icy water. Fighting with all his strength, Hawke forces himself up and breaks through the surface for a desperate gasp of air. His breath freezes in his throat, but he manages to utter a single frantic scream only the wolves will hear.

—⟋⟍⟍—

Jake bolted upright in bed, his T-shirt soaked with sweat. The low droning voices on the clock radio reminded him he'd drifted off during a call-in show. The voices buzzed around his head like angry wasps.

"Well, you're entitled to your opinion, no matter how stupid it is," the popular radio host, Marty Grass, said. "Next caller. Greetings, you're on Night Talk."

"It's not that simple," the caller said. "So Jake provides enough food for all the starving people in the world, right? Well, who's gonna distribute it? Who decides who receives what? Can we trust 'em to do what they're supposed to do with it? Who's gonna watchdog the whole thing if it's worldwide?"

"Okay, we take your point," Grass said. "Most intelligent people understand that a better way to deal with world hunger is to teach folks how to grow their own crops and give them animals to raise for food. But that, too, is complicated."

"Yeah, that only works until the first dry spell or bad weather in the middle of growing season. Not to mention diseases that could wipe out crops and livestock."

"In which case, the Final Wish would be wasted. Yes, we get it. Next caller. Greetings, you're on Night Talk."

"If he gives a bunch of money to the poor or to the homeless, they're just gonna squander it on booze and crack, and they'll be right back where they started. What a waste!"

"Thanks for the jaded point of view. Some of us would like to think people are better than that, but you might be right," Grass said. "Greetings, you're on Night Talk."

"If he would simply wish for all of us to find the only true salvation in our Lord Jesus Christ—"

"Thanks for that enlightened perspective. Let's go to line seven."

"I heard that Jake's really hurting existing charities, 'cause people are holding back their donations to see what he does. I mean, how is anyone supposed to figure out who will receive aid and who won't?" the caller asked.

"Apparently people figure Jake's wish will take care of every-thing," Grass said. "A little naïve if you want this man's opinion… and you *do*!"

"The point is…the longer the kid stalls making his damn wish, the more he hurts some really good causes."

"Thanks for that. Okay, let's take another call," Grass said. "Greetings, you're on Night Talk."

"If he wished for like a zillion dollars, wouldn't the taxes on that alone wipe out the national debt?"

"Did you sleep through math class?" Grass moaned. "A glut like that would most certainly render the dollar worthless. Think about what that would do to—."

Jake jabbed the OFF button, rolled over, and stared at the wall. He was so over people and their freakin' opinions about what he should do. So what if there wasn't really any perfect fi-nal wish. Didn't matter anyway, now. The President sure as hell wasn't thinking about making the world a better place. And that was the wish he was stuck with.

He wiped his damp face on the sheet and released a long, ex-hausted sigh. Squeezing his dreary eyes shut, he tried once again to give in to sleep, clutching the lantern in the crook of his arm like a pointy-edged teddy bear.

CHAPTER 35

Lester wheeled down the street, hung a sharp right into the Parker driveway, and dropped his bike on the ground.

"Hold it." Agent Donaldson stood in front of him, hand raised like a stop sign.

Lester winced. "But they said I could come over."

"Right," Donaldson said. "We're allowing this visit as a special favor to Jake; he asked for you personally. But I'm still going to have to frisk you. Standard protocol in a high-security area."

Lester scowled, affecting the look of a movie tough guy. But that image faded as soon as Donaldson began the pat down. On TV frisking didn't seem as creepy as it felt. Donaldson straightened up, nodded.

Lester darted off to Jake and Kevin, who had been following the whole thing from under the basketball hoop. While Kevin idly shot baskets, Jake and Lester slid off to the side of the driveway.

Jake curbed his instinct to hug his friend; not a guy thing to do. He settled for a fist bump and lowered his voice for effect.

"Thanks for coming over, Les."

"I sure missed you, Jake." Lester gave him a friendly punch on the arm.

"Missed you, too. It's been totally outta control around here." He looked away. "I could use a friend."

"Dude, how can you be lonely? You're like on TV all the time, and you're the hottest thing going on social media. C'mon, man, you're a freakin' superstar. Everybody knows Jake Parker. Besides, your house is like full of people."

"Trust me, I know. But I'm telling you, Les, these people are *not* my friends. They treat me like a little kid—when they're not actin' like I'm some kinda hard-core gangster. Christ, Les, I'm lucky if I get to take a whiz without one of those guys spyin' on me."

Agent Pirelli, who'd been checking for suspicious activity on the street, pivoted back toward the boys.

"I don't think I could handle a situation like this as good as you," Lester said.

Jake's shoulders slumped. "That's the reason I asked if you could come over. I'm not really handling it that good. Seriously, dude, I *hate* this. I don't think I can take much more."

Lester squinted at Pirelli, who came to an abrupt halt, suddenly concerned with the condition of his cuticles. "Yeah, I can kinda see what you mean."

Jake checked to be sure neither agent was near enough to hear. "And now they're really pressing me to make a certain wish."

"Yeah? So what do they want you to wish for?"

"Dude, I can't tell you. I can't tell *anybody*. Remember? If I tell what I wish for, it'll be like erased."

"Course I do, it says that right on top of the lantern."

"Besides, I had to swear like an official government oath. The wish they want is freakin' complex though. It's like they jammed at least sixteen wishes in it."

Lester raised an eyebrow. "Guess they don't get that it's one wish at a time."

"Not only that. It's like a whole page long. I don't think I could even memorize the whole thing. Dude, at the Giants game, I couldn't even remember the all words to the National Anthem. And I hear them before just about every single game in every single sport. I had to fake it."

Lester laughed. "Doesn't everybody?" He scrunched up his face. "This huge freakin' wish they want you to do sounds like that saying—a camel is a horse designed by a committee. Somethin' like that. Anyway, I thought it was just the President doing it."

"Naw, I don't think he wrote any of it by himself. Except at the bottom, there are some wishes just for him, personally. Those he wrote for sure."

Both boys looked over at Agent Donaldson, who was heading their way. Kevin threw the basketball hard against the backboard, and it bounced out into the driveway near Donaldson. The agent hopped over and retrieved it. He eyed the hoop and lifted the ball, as if about to launch a shot. Instead, he tossed a bounce pass back to Kevin.

Lester leaned closer to Jake. "Jesus, how's that supposed to work? Besides, if you wish what they tell you, they'll already know what the wish is...and it won't come true. Don't they understand the 'recant' part?"

Jake narrowed his eyes at Donaldson, who came to a standstill several feet away and swung around to make a quick street-check again. Jake had to be extra careful—the President's final wish request was supposed to be top secret.

"Guess they think they've figured out some kinda technicality that lets them work around that. They got a ton of lawyers, and maybe they assume if I don't actually *tell* anyone whether or not I wished for what they told me to, then it's the same as if they don't know…or somethin'."

Lester chuckled. "Dude, I don't even understand what you just said. But I still don't think that's the way it works."

"I know, right? But these guys play by different rules than the rest of us." Jake puffed out a breath. "And you'll never guess what else they did."

Lester's eyes widened.

"Bastards jacked my lantern."

"No way!"

"Way. They gave it back, but the one I been carryin' around was a freakin' *fake*."

"Can't you report 'em?"

"Who to, dude? They're the FBI and they're working directly for the President. Anyway, they fed me some bullshit about ninja terrorists sneaking in at night and switching the lanterns. But I know who really took it." Jake looked over at Donaldson and Pirelli talking in hushed tones off to the side. "I guess the FBI big shots thought I was gonna be so freakin' grateful they rescued my lantern from the bad guys, I'd use the wish for anything they wanted. Stupid." He shook his head.

Lester nudged Jake, who glanced at Pirelli, now close enough to overhear them.

"You are *not* gonna believe what Heather Hogan said to ol' man Grimsby in history yesterday." Both turned their heads toward Pirelli. Lester bit his lip and Jake scrunched up his face, doing their best to imply this juicy information wasn't something they wanted to share with an adult. They cruised over to the side of the driveway, where they dropped down onto the ground.

Lester made a subtle check of the agents' locations. "Cool, it worked." He looked Jake in the eye. "So, you gonna make the wish they're expectin' you to?"

"I don't want to, but they said there'd be serious consequences if I didn't."

"Dude, they no-shit *threatened* you?"

"Sure as hell did."

"That…that's just *wrong*." Lester's voice broke. He took a second to collect himself. "We didn't cover everything in civics class, but I'm sure the government isn't supposed to work like that. Can they really get away with anything they want?"

Jake shrugged. "Seems like it. Oh, and now that they finally figured out exactly what they want me to wish for, they're super anxious. They got some big event planned for day after tomorrow. They're expecting me to make their wish by then so they can announce to the whole world that Jake Freakin' Parker has made the Final Freakin' Wish."

"Wait. I thought you were supposed to be able to wish for anything you wanted."

"That's what I thought, too." Jake's voice wavered. "But they promised me and Mom and Kev would secretly get like a *ton* of money if I make the wish the way they wrote it out."

"Dude, bribery's not legal."

"Don't think that matters, Les."

"This whole thing so sucks! No wonder you seem beat down, man."

"Jake took in a deep breath and released it slowly. "I don't even know what's happened to Ben. I really miss *him* too."

"Oh my god, I almost forgot. I was riding by his ol' wacked trailer yesterday and he was outside…so I hung out and talked with him for a little while."

Jake broke into a grin. "Yeah? Is he okay?"

"Yeah. He said they hauled him in on some bogus charge, asked him a ton of questions about who he was and shit. They even took a blood sample. They're probably checking his DNA, like they do on the cop shows. Anyway, he asked me how you were handling all the pressure. He's worried about you." Lester offered a half smile. "Jake, we *all* are."

"Tell him 'hi' for me next time you see him." Jake rubbed his eyes. "Havin' to go through all this crap is hard, Les. Too hard. Sometimes I just want it all to go away."

As Agent Pirelli took a couple more steps toward Lester and Jake, Kevin dribbled over in front of the agent, stopping Pirelli in his tracks. Kevin nodded to him. "So, you play any hoops when you were a kid?"

"What? Oh, not really. I played a little football in high school, though."

"Really? What position?"

Lester studied his best friend. Jake had those dark circles under his eyes you get when you don't get enough sleep. And he was all slumped over like he didn't even have the strength to hold himself up—like somebody had sucked all the energy…all the *fun* out of him. Lester had to do something. And soon.

Jake closed his eyes and shook his head. "If I could just get away from all this." He waved his arm toward the house. "Even if it was only for like an hour or two…maybe I could think straight."

"What if we tricked 'em, so you could get outta here for a while?"

"No way, dude. These guys are like combat-trained and all

high tech and shit."

"Yeah, but they still think like adults." Lester, tongue between his teeth, stared out into the distance, lost in thought. Then he broke into a grin so big that creases formed at the corners of his eyes.

"Okay, what's spinning around in that brain of yours this time?" Jake asked.

Lester leaned over and whispered in Jake's ear.

Both agents closed in on them.

Jake's eyes lit up.

Lester could tell. Captain Hawke was back!

Kevin halted the agents' progress by dribbling up to them and taking a jumper over their heads. "Nothin' but net."

Jake and Lester leapt to their feet.

"Carry on, Mr. Slade," Jake commanded with a brisk salute.

"Aye, Cap'n." Lester returned the salute, then snatched the basketball as it came off the backboard. He passed the ball to Jake, who took a couple of shots, while Lester spoke rapidly to Kevin.

Lester saluted Pirelli and Donaldson, ran over, and hopped on his bike.

Once Lester had sped around the street corner, Jake dashed over and plucked the basketball from his brother's hands. "How 'bout a game of horse, Kev? Feel like havin' your butt kicked?"

As Lester picked up speed around the corner, a tan Taurus pulled out from a cross street. Roarke kept just far enough behind so the kid wouldn't notice.

In spite of his assurances to Krock, Roarke's plan to snatch

the Parker kid had smacked into a wall. Too damn many government spooks lurking around the place. Roarke understood how
they operated, how thorough they could be. Hell, he used to be
one of them. But Roarke hadn't yet been able to figure out a back
door—a way to get past the kid's army of protectors. When Lester
zipped into an alley, Roarke face-palmed. Christ, why hadn't he
thought of it before? The Woo kid was his best shot at Jake. He
just had to keep Lester in his sights.

CHAPTER 36

Inside the Command Center, Hacker leaned over Cohen's shoulder and scrutinized the data rolling across the computer screen. The data probe ceased: NO INFORMATION ACQUIRED.

Hacker pounded his fist into his palm. "Damn it. The guy *exists*, for Christ's sake."

"'Ackyack' is probably an alias, sir."

"No shit, Sherlock." Hacker rolled his eyes. "It sounds Arabic to me."

"We've tried 'Ackeeact,' 'Actyack,' 'Hacieact,' 'Hackysac'…every logical ethnic variation of 'Ackyack' and 'Akiak' through our U.S., Middle Eastern, European, and Asian data bases, sir," Cohen said. "Doesn't seem to be Australian Aboriginal either. One of our recruits back at Quantico thought it might have an obscure origin—like Inuit or Lapp—so they checked." He shrugged. "Came up with nothing."

"And we're told there's no DNA match, right?"

"Right," Cohen said. "And he isn't showing up on any known sex offenders list either?"

"Yeah, he's just a kindly old fart from nowhere who likes to hang out with young boys," Hacker said. "What about facial recognition?"

"Even with image-morphing technology, we're still coming up with zilch."

"I'm betting he's had extensive plastic surgery."

"You're not implying that he had surgery to give him the appearance of an *old man*, are you, sir?"

"That's exactly what I'm saying, Cohen. Oh, he's one slippery son of a bitch all right. Otherwise, we'd have nailed his real identity by now."

"We're working with the most sophisticated computer network in the world, sir."

"So use it, Agent! Scour the whole damn universe and every database that exists. I want to know who this fu…fudge-head is!"

Hacker paced. This Ben Ackyack, or whatever the hell his real name was, had to be up to something. But it seemed the old man—if he really *was* an old man—had shown up in Santa Necia before anybody had even heard about the Final Wish. So how did Ackyack fit into all this? There had to be some nefarious reason the kid wasted his second wish to save the old guy's ass. Damn it. Nothing in this assignment added up.

"Sir? You should see this."

Hacker whirled back around to the screen: ALL SOURCES PROBED. NO INFORMATION ACQUIRED.

Cohen threw up his hands. "It's as if he never existed…or like he's from another planet."

"The guy's f-froot-loopin' diabolical, I'll give you that." Hacker stared at the monitor. "But we're gonna nail his butt. Count on it!"

That evening Angie paid Kevin a visit at Stan's Superette. She pulled him aside, away from the agent who was keeping an eye on them.

Conscious of being watched, Angie shuffled her feet and avoided looking Kevin in the eye, making sure this looked like no more than the awkward beginnings of a teen romance. Kevin grinned awkwardly and stared at her starry-eyed. He wasn't acting. But they didn't spend much time with small talk. Angie described the plan Lester had come up with. "Kevin, you'll have to write the details down so can Jake read it. It'll be too dangerous to talk about it out loud in a place with zero privacy."

Angie pulled him in for a hug. "Now tell me the plan so I can be sure you got it all." Even though Kevin felt a little dizzy and disoriented from the warm-soft sensation of her body pressed against him and the intoxicating scent of her hair, he managed to whisper the plan details and promised to destroy the note as soon as Jake read it.

CHAPTER 37

Agent Donaldson kept a wary eye on the street from the Parker driveway, and Agent Pirelli watched Jake and Kevin, who were crouched next to Kevin's bike. The boys huddled together as if focusing on some perplexing mechanical problem. In fact, Kevin was loosening the front wheel.

Kevin called out to the agents. "Hey, you guys know anything about bikes?"

"What's to know?" Pirelli headed over. "Got a problem?"

"I dunno." Kevin twisted the wheel bolt one last time to the left. "I think the flange deflector socket is slipping."

Donaldson joined them as Pirelli crouched down next to the boys.

"See? Right here." Kevin pointed to the gear assemblage.

Pirelli shook his head. "Man, these bikes are a lot more complicated than the ones I had as a kid."

Donaldson reached down, picked up an x-type crank arm, and turned it over in his hand. "I don't even know what this is."

Pirelli laughed. "Looks like a miniature battle-ax to me."

Kevin tilted his head toward Jake. "Looks like we're gonna

need the double-sided phalanx wrench, bro."

"No problem." Jake bounced to his feet. "I'll get it."

Both agents watched Jake disappear into the dark garage.

"So…didn't you guys have gears like this on your bikes back in the day?"

Pirelli and Donaldson shifted their focus back to Kevin.

Pirelli shrugged. "Well, sure…but not quite this com—"

Jake charged out of the garage on his bike, swerved around the agents, made a sharp left at the end of the driveway, and tore off down the street. He was wearing dark sunglasses and a red Hawke Hat under the cowl of the most popular black hoodie—the one with Jake's smiling image and "He's Magic!" emblazoned in white on the front.

"Shit!" Pirelli sprang to his feet.

Donaldson grabbed his walkie-talkie. "All units! The pigeon has taken wing! I repeat, the pigeon has taken wing!"

Pirelli snatched Kevin's bike off the ground, hopped on, and started after Jake.

Kevin stood. "Wait! I wouldn't—"

As Pirelli picked up speed, the front wheel came off, sending him head first into the plastic garbage bins at the curb.

Kevin broke into a grin. "Never mind."

Two unmarked SUVs materialized out of nowhere and sped off after Jake, Hacker in the lead vehicle.

Kevin slipped away unnoticed.

Three blocks from the Parker house, with the lead pursuit vehicle closing fast, Jake zipped into an alley. The driver screeched around the corner right behind him. Hacker smirked when he saw Jake swerve into an open garage halfway down the alley.

"We got him now!" Hacker said. The Lincoln Navigator skidded to a stop in front of the garage.

Lester and nineteen other high school kids—all dressed in the same black "He's Magic!" hoodies, red Hawke Hats, and dark sunglasses—spewed out of the garage. The riders swerved around Hacker's car. Half the bikes took off for one end of the alley; half shot for the other.

Hacker grabbed the first one he could reach who was small enough to be Jake, and pulled him off his bike. He squeezed the kid from behind, harder than necessary, but damn it, he had a point to make. Jake had no idea how much danger he was in without FBI protection.

Hacker spun his captive around to face him. "You need to be a lot smarter than this to—"

"Let go of me, you *pervert*," she screamed.

Hacker threw his hands out to the side, palms out.

The young girl straightened her Hawke Hat, pulled the hoodie back over her head, and picked up her bike. As she rode off, she shouted back at Hacker. "You're a real sicko, mister! Seriously? You should seek professional help!"

At the ends of the alley, the bikes took off in different directions. Agents chased on foot, and the second black SUV took up the pursuit.

Hacker scanned the dark garage. Empty. He whipped out his walkie-talkie. "We have a Code Three situation here! I repeat. A Code *Three* situation!" He leapt back into the vehicle and slammed the door.

The agent at the wheel waited for instructions.

Hacker glared at him. "Just drive! Follow somebody! Anybody!" Hacker shouted into his walkie-talkie. "Snatch every one of these smart-ass *accomplices* you can find. Somebody knows something about what the kid's planning. Arrest them…for obstructing justice…not wearing a helmet…*anything*, just find that farking Pucker kid!"

At the sound of screeching tires, Angie emerged from behind the same garage the Jake impersonators had just poured out of. She checked the surroundings and signaled for Jake to come out.

"You gotta be freakin' *kidding* me!" Jake whispered from the shadows. "I don't think I can do this, Angie."

"C'mon, Jake, it's not that bad."

A young girl in horn-rimmed glasses, blue T-shirt, and a denim skirt stepped out into the sunlight. With one hand, Jake adjusted his blonde wig to fit more comfortably. With the other he clutched a backpack, the lantern inside resting on a cushion of a red T-shirt, jeans, and a nondescript gray hoodie. "When Les said I needed a disguise, I sure as hell wasn't expecting *this*." He glanced down at his skirt and shook his head. "I'm gonna take so much crap for this."

Angie reached over and tucked a couple of rebel strands of Jake's dark brown hair back under the wig. "Just go with it, Jake. They won't be looking for a girl. Trust me, this is gonna work." When they reached the end of the alley, Angie pulled him behind her as a tan Taurus drove slowly past the alley entrance. She checked around the corner. "All clear, Jake." She gestured to the familiar blue Honda Accord parked at the curb. "I promised my mom I'd be back in time to pick her up from work."

Once he settled in the passenger seat, Jake slumped down so only the top of his wig could be seen from the outside. "Okay.

Where we goin'?"

Angie grinned. "The mall. Who would ever expect Jake Parker in a place as crowded as the mall when he's trying to hide out? We're not gonna be there long. Kevin'll meet us with the guys, and you'll all split right away. When I call in a few Jake sightings at the mall, FBI Agents will cover the place like crazed fire ants. And you'll be long gone."

News crews from all the major TV networks and online agencies swarmed in front of the Parker house. Vans topped with elaborate antenna arrays parked wherever they could find space, like confused, giant mutant scorpions. Their occupants leapt out with all the intensity of a SWAT team. Most of the on-camera reporters would have to add their lead-ins later, but the CNN correspondent decided to rush through it. "This is Warren Watson *on the scene.* We have just received a report that Jake Parker, the young man who holds the fate of the world in his hands, is *missing!* We take you live to the Parker home for an official statement."

Hacker winced at the phalanx in front of him thrusting microphones in his face. "Ladies and gentlemen, given the highly sensitive nature of the situation, I cannot give you any details at this time, except to confirm that Jake Parker is unaccounted for."

"Was he taken?" Bethany DuVey shouted.

"There is a possibility that we may be dealing with a kidnapping. But we have only sketchy information at this time." Hacker's eyes darted back and forth among the crowd as if staking out an escape route. He pointed to Chris Payne, CBS News.

Payne asked, "Do you have any suspects?"

"I cannot comment on that at this time. There may be several people involved." He pointed to ABC's Marci Bowe.

"Terrorists?" Bowe asked.

"We are considering that possibility, but we can't share any information as yet…as I'm sure you all understand." Hacker gestured pleadingly with both hands. "The President has pledged every means at our disposal to keep the Final Wish from…to bring Jake back safely."

"So you're saying the magic lantern is missing too?" Noah Vale, from Reuters, yelled just before he tripped over the foot of PBS's Howard Case and crumpled to a knee.

"We cannot confirm whether or not the lantern is still inside the Parker house."

Questions flew at Hacker like angry bees from a ruptured hive.

"Was there a ransom note?"

"What clues do you have?"

"What's your strategy?"

"When did you last see Jake?"

"Any evidence of foul play?"

Hacker waved off the barrage. "That's all I can tell you at this time. Now, if you'll excuse me, I have work to do." He slipped back inside the house, leaving the scrambled mass of TV personalities, cameramen, and technicians to untangle themselves and race to scoop the story.

CHAPTER 38

Jake's eyes darted back and forth as he assessed the situation at the West Valley Mall.

"Relax." Angie checked her watch. "Kevin'll be here any minute, and you'll be outta here."

When they passed a display window, Jake cringed at his reflection. "Come on, Angie, at least I gotta put my jeans back on."

"Okay, but make it quick."

Jake strode toward the door with the international male symbol, just like he'd done his whole life.

Angie grabbed his arm. "Wait!" She pointed to the female symbol on the door a few feet away. "Sorry, but if you really want to change out of that skirt without blowing your cover, it's your only choice."

Jake scrunched up his face.

"Okay, I'll go in first and make sure no one is in there."

"Thanks."

She came back out. "Empty. I'll keep an eye on the door, but I have to stay out here so Kevin can find us as soon as he gets here."

—◦◦◦—

Like most guys, Jake had always wondered what the inside of the girls' bathroom looked like. To his surprise this one turned out to be pretty much a boys' room with more stalls and no urinals. Just as messy, but it smelled a little better. The closest of the three stalls was bigger and had the international disabled symbol on the door. Jake hurried to the back wall. Not sure what laws of man or nature he might be breaking.

He tore off the skirt and reached down and took off his hightops so he could pull on his jeans. Shit, now he was standing there in his tighty-whities and socks—with a girl's wig on his head. He grabbed his jeans from his backpack and froze. Voices! At the door! Jake kicked his sneakers into the nearest stall and dove inside.

Once he could breathe normally again, he dropped to his knees and peered under the door. Two women jabbered and primped in front of the wall-length mirror. That's when he spotted his backpack still outside the stall. Reaching under the door, Jake worked the backpack toward him, but it was too tall to slip under the door. The pack was unzipped. If he flipped it on its side, the lantern and his regular clothes might spill out. The women would sure as hell notice, and he'd be exposed as a male intruder, dressed half in girl's clothes, in the women's bathroom. He'd probably be arrested.

He was about to straighten back up, when he heard a childish giggle. He peered into the face of a drooling, wide-eyed toddler in a stroller parked in front of his stall. Jake jerked back out of sight, praying the freakin' kid wouldn't give him away. He yanked on his jeans, laced up his sneakers, and waited, heart pounding.

Then he heard the door open again.

Angie quickly assessed the situation inside the bathroom. The stroller, toddler inside, was parked in front of the last stall. She spied Jake's backpack jammed against the same stall door. So that's where he was. Good, maybe they hadn't seen him.

One of the women turned and glanced at Angie. Probably wondering why she was standing in the middle of the room like an idiot. Angie smiled a greeting and casually strolled over to the middle stall, closing the door behind her. She and Jake would just have to hang until the women left.

As soon as Angie heard the door open and close, she flushed the toilet and opened the stall. She could stall at the sink if she needed to. Nobody there.

Angie rapped on Jake's stall. "Come on out, Jake, the coast is clear."

"Angie?" Jake pushed open the door slowly to avoid knocking over his back-pack. "Jesus, I thought they had me."

"Me, too. Let's get outta...hold on." She checked her cell phone. "Kevin. Damn, he's running late."

Jake checked his image in the huge mirror. Same as before, but at least the blonde girl in the blue top frowning back at him was now wearing jeans. When he hefted his pack his heart started pounding. He looked inside. The lantern was *gone*. "Shit! That stupid kid musta grabbed my lantern. We gotta get it back!"

Jake tore out of the bathroom, Angie right behind him.

The women were nowhere in sight.

A beat-up '72 Plymouth Barracuda reached the edge of the mall lot and shimmied into a parking spot. The engine wheezed and died. Kevin, Brian, and Max tumbled out. Kevin now wore a black baseball cap, sunglasses, and a fake mustache.

"Just great!" Kevin glowered at the steam spewing out from under the Barracuda's hood. "Now how the hell am I supposed to get Jake to the—"

"Chill, dude." Max raised the hood, releasing a gush of steam and smoke. "She probably just needs a little adjustment. Brian, grab my tools from the trunk."

Brian called back over his shoulder as he went. "Don't worry, Kev, the 'Cuda will get you out of here just like Lester planned it."

Kevin shot him an incredulous look and took off toward the mall entrance.

Brian handed Max the toolbox and watched Kevin sprint away. "Seriously? Kevin's mustache is totally bogus." Brian smirked and ran a finger over the hint of genuine fuzz on his upper lip.

Jake rushed through an explanation of the crisis for his brother. "There were two of them...and the little kid, a boy, in the stroller. We can't find 'em *anywhere*."

Angie scanned the crowd. "We'll get it back, Jake."

"Okay, let's spread out," Kevin said. "Jake, just don't do anything to call attention to yourself."

Jake took off to the left. Kevin moved right.

"Kevin?"

He spun back around.

Angie chuckled. "Lose the mustache."

"But I don't wanna be recognized. If the cops see me, they might figure Jake's nearby. Besides, it makes me look older."

"Actually, it makes you look like Snidley Whiplash." She

dazzled him with one of her brilliant smiles.

Kevin tore off the mustache, wiped his lip, and watched Angie dash into Macy's.

Just outside the food court, the toddler's mother noticed for the first time her little boy was sucking away happily on the edge of an old lantern.

"Yuck." She pulled the lantern away and stuffed a pacifier into the child's mouth in one smooth motion. "These damn replica lanterns are everywhere these days. God knows where this one has been."

"Oh my god, Liz, Joshua must have picked it up from the floor of the restroom when we went in to freshen up," her sister said. "It's the last place we stopped."

"Ew!" The mother grabbed the lantern by the handle with two fingers, carried it to a nearby trash can, and dropped it as if it were a dead sewer rat. Plucking a baby wipe from the diaper bag, she cleaned her son's face and then wiped her hands thoroughly. "We're definitely going to have to give you a bath when we get home, sweetie."

CHAPTER 39

Kevin rushed up to Angie, his face in full grimace. "Damn it, I couldn't find them anywhere. What'll we *do*?"

"I didn't see them either." Angie shook her head. "Maybe we should check the parking lot. A toddler would probably put up a fuss if they kept him out very long."

"Okay."

They headed for the mall exit.

"Wait." Angie pointed. "There!"

Two women with the stroller came out of Gap Kids, with Jake closing in on them fast. The mother pulled the stroller protectively behind her.

A security guard, sensing a problem, aimed his Segway toward Jake and the women.

Kevin grabbed Angie's arm. "We need a diversion."

Angie let out a scream, followed by some body-shaking sobs. She draped herself onto Kevin.

Once he got over the sensation of her body so close, Kevin got into the act. Pretending to comfort her, he put his arm around her and patted her on the back.

The security guard spun his Segway around and sped to her. "Is something wrong, miss?"

"It's…it's…it's…" Angie sobbed.

"Take a deep breath, miss. Tell me what happened."

"My brand-new iPhone…it's gone…my mom is gonna kill me!"

Jake did his best to explain to the two women who he was and why he needed to locate the lamp right away. "See, that's why I'm disguised as a girl."

They just stared at him.

Frustrated, Jake raised the blonde wig and quickly smashed it down askew. Something in his stomach was doing full-on somersaults.

"Oh my God!" Liz's eyes widened. "You really are Jake Parker!"

"Yes, ma'am." Jake stepped closer and lowered his voice. "Do you have my lantern?"

Her sister, Gloria, squinted at Jake. "Hold on a minute. Weren't you kidnapped or something?"

"Um, not really, ma'am."

"Oh yes you *were*," Gloria admonished. "There's a statewide Amber Alert and everything. It was on the radio. We heard it on the way over."

"Did you escape?" Liz asked.

Jake shook his head. "Um, it's kind of a long story."

Liz looked him in the eye. "Do you need help?"

"No, ma'am. But please may I have my lantern back? Seriously, I'm in a super hurry."

Gloria grabbed her sister's arm. "Oh my God. Liz! He's saying you actually touched his magic lantern? The *real* one?"

Jake nodded. "Yes, ma'am, and I really need it back."

"We don't have it anymore," Liz said.

Jake's heart dropped into his stomach. "Oh my god, what did you do with it?"

Liz raised her hand to her cheek. "I am so sorry. We just assumed it was one of those replicas they're selling on the Internet. We thought my little Joshua had just picked up one of those fakes from the floor—"

"Of a public *restroom*," Gloria said.

Liz nodded. "Plus, I was afraid Joshua might hurt himself. It had sharp edges, you know? So I dropped it into a trash can at the food court."

"Damn it! Sorry...um, which trash can?"

"The first one when you walk in," her friend offered. "By that Asian place that gives you those meat-on-a-stick things."

Jake spun around toward the food court.

"Wait," Gloria yelled after him, pulling a Hawke Hat from her purse.

Jake stopped and looked back at the women.

"Would you sign this for me?" She dug through her purse. "I'm sure I have a Sharpie in here somewhere."

Jake flung his hands out, palms up, shrugged and took off.

Liz called after him, "I hope you find it...and good luck with your wish!" She rolled her eyes at her sister. "You were kidding about that autograph, right?"

Gloria grimaced. "Guess I wasn't thinking."

Angie pulled Kevin closer to get a better view of Jake and the women.

"Let's go to the mall office," the guard said. "Someone coulda picked up an iPhone and turned it in."

"Do you really think so?" Angie rummaged in her purse as if searching for a tissue. "Wait." She held up the cell. "Found it." She hiked her purse strap onto her shoulder and strode off.

Kevin shrugged an apology.

The guard shook his head. "Women."

By the time Angie and Kevin caught up with Jake, he'd yanked open the door of the first trash kiosk and pulled out the can. "It's empty! Damn it, they said the *first* one."

"Look." Kevin pointed to a gangly young guy in a brown mall-maintenance uniform. "He looks kinda familiar. I think he was a couple years ahead of us in school."

They all rushed toward the guy, who emptied the trash bag of the next kiosk into a large container on his rolling cart.

"Well, well, what do we have here?" He grinned at Angie. He didn't seem to notice Kevin or Jake.

"Hi ..." Angie glanced at his name tag, "Karl." Big smile. "We seem to have misplaced something that might be in one of those trash bags you just picked up. A small ship's lantern? Red glass windows? Looks like brass? You think you could—"

"You mean something like this?" Karl reached into a compartment on the cart and pulled out the lantern.

"Yes! That's my lantern. Thanks, man." Jake reached for it.

Karl pulled it back. "I look stupid to you?" When no one responded, he gestured with the lamp. "This sorta looks like the one that Jake Parker kid is supposed to save the world or some shit."

Jake started to raise his wig. "But *I'm*—"

"Stay calm, Stephie." Angie patted Jake on the head, settling the wig back in place.

Kevin stepped in. "Look, Karl, obviously there are replica lamps like this one all over the freakin' place, ever since the media made such a big deal out of the Parker kid."

"Then it won't be too hard to get another one, will it? I kinda got attached to this one."

"No!" Jake pointed to the lantern, "Um, this is like a special present for my grandma. She's totally into stuff like this."

Angie winked at Karl. "Come on, Karl. Do you really think it's possible this could be that famous lamp? I hear the FBI never lets the real one out of their sight."

"Good point." Karl grinned. "But I oughta get a little sumpin-sumpin for it, you know?" He raised an eyebrow.

Kevin pulled out his wallet. "I only got seven bucks on me, but it's yours."

Karl's leered at Angie. "I'd be more interested in a show of gratitude from the little lady here."

"Okay." Jake rushed in and locked Karl in a bear hug. "I really appreciate this. Thank you *so much*."

Jake's maneuver startled Karl enough that he didn't notice Kevin slip the lantern from his hand and run. Jake let go and took off after Kevin and Angie.

"Come on, that's not what I..." Karl glanced down at his now-empty hand. "Hey!"

CHAPTER 40

Max had the Barracuda running again. The engine still knocked and groaned as if in pain, but at least smoke didn't belch from the tailpipe anymore—reason enough for Max to stand back and admire his work.

Brian shook his head. "I just hope this heap holds together long enough for us to get the hell out of here."

"Yeah? If you're so worried about it you can take the freakin' bus."

Brian nodded toward the mall entrance. "Here they come."

Doing their best to look casual, Jake, Angie, and Kevin strode toward the car. Once they arrived, everybody but Angie piled in.

Brian grinned at Jake. "Nice outfit, sugar pie."

Jake flipped off Brian and peeked out of the window, expecting to see a battalion of security guards on their tail.

"Okay, time to call in a few Jake sightings here at the mall," Angie said. You guys better bounce. This place is going to be swarming with government agents, police, and god knows what else in a few minutes."

"Um, I think I kinda blew my cover," Jake said. "I had to tell those ladies who I was."

"All the better for my credibility." Angie marched back to the mall, punching in a phone number.

"Let's rock and roll." Max stepped on the accelerator. The car chugged forward, belching and sputtering as if it were its last gasp.

It was.

Max looked over at Kevin. "Sorry, dude, I guess that used carburetor wasn't as primo as the guy said."

Jake tumbled out of the backseat with Kevin right behind him.

"We're screwed!" Jake said. "We gotta find another way out of here, fast." He scoped the parking lot, the knot in his stomach tightening into a hot fist.

Kevin grimaced. "Okay, look. I'll run in and find Angie. She can drive us."

"You gotta be kiddin' me!" Jake pointed at an awesome midnight blue 2008 Camaro Super Sport one row over. Buster Flatt was behind the wheel. "Come on, Kev. Buster'll give us a ride."

"But I thought he was the dickweed who—"

"Not anymore." Jake sprinted toward the Camaro.

When Buster spied Jake running up to the driver's side window, he broke into a laugh and shook his head. "Dude, you better have a freakin' good explanation for tryin' to look like a chick."

"I'll explain it all later. What are you doin' here, anyway?"

"I was gonna do the bike thing, but Lester sent me over in case you needed backup." Buster glanced over at Max and Brian staring into the smoking engine of the Barracuda. "Guess he was right."

"I gotta get to the Wood without the FBI and cops seein' me."

"You got it, dude. I'm always willin' to help a guy avoid five-oh."

Jake dove into the backseat and dropped to the floor out of sight.

Kevin slid into the front passenger seat, leaned out, and yelled over to Max and Brian, "You guys meet me at Bonzo's like we planned…if you can get that thing going again."

Max and Brian stared at Buster's Camaro. "Sick ride, dude," Max shouted.

Buster nodded and headed for the exit.

"So you really *do* have a hot Camaro," Jake said. "Guess I shoulda believed you."

"Dude, nobody believes me about nothin'."

"So why don't you ever drive it to school?"

"My old man won't let me unless I get at least a 'C' average." Buster let out a sigh. "So it don't look like I'm gonna be showin' up at school in this baby any time soon."

In less than two minutes the Camaro had left the parking lot far behind. Jake felt safe enough to sit up straight.

Buster glanced at Jake in the rearview mirror. "This is so freakin' awesome, dude. You got a chance to do somethin' special… somethin' nobody else can. You're *somebody*, Jake. People are totally gonna remember you, dude…like for-freakin'-ever. Guys like me, we get forgot real easy. But you ain't like me, Jake. You ain't like *anybody* else."

Agent Cohen lifted his headset and faced Hacker. "He's at the West Valley Mall…over in Crowne Pointe."

Hacker seethed. "Cohen, you stay here and monitor the phone. I want everybody *else* on this. We have to get that lantern back now!"

"But why would he be at a mall?" Pirelli asked.

"Who flippin' cares?" Hacker said. "He's a kid. He's probably gonna waste the damn wish on skateboards and hip-hop CDs!"

"He's smarter than that," Cohen said.

"Okay, okay, you're right," Hacker closed his eyes. "But if the Final Wish falls into the wrong hands because of that smart-ass—"

"He may actually be in danger, sir," Donaldson said.

"I know that! Let's just find the kid before anything happens to him."

The agents stampeded out, nearly knocking over Steve and Jill, eavesdropping just outside the door.

"What's going on here?" Steve demanded.

"This doesn't concern you." Hacker brushed him aside. "This is official government business—"

"It sure as hell *does* concern us," Jill said through clenched teeth. "It's our *son* you're talking about."

"Yeah, she's right." Steve seized Hacker's arm.

"I haven't got time for this crap." Hacker tore his arm free of Steve's grasp and sprinted out the door.

After checking to make sure Agent Cohen was focused on his computer, Jill whispered, "I imagine that Beemer can haul ass."

———✺———

Once Buster dropped off Jake at the Wood, he drove Kevin over to Bonzo's Burgers. The fast growing crowd—liberally sprinkled with people in red watch caps and "He's Magic!" hoodies—already pushed beyond Bonzo's, past Starbucks, and now threatened parking spaces in front of Stan's Superette.

Kevin hopped out of the car and glanced back at Buster, who seemed frozen in place. "Dude, come on. The bigger the crowd, the better."

Buster climbed out. "I don't know, man. Guy like me don't really belong in this crowd."

"You sure as hell do." Kevin pulled Buster along with him. "Besides, we need lots of bodies so the cops and Hacker's goon squad will be sure to check us out. This massive party'll be a perfect decoy. They're totally gonna come looking for him in a crowd like this."

"Yeah, that's how cops think, all right."

"It'll take the FBI awhile to figure out Jake isn't here."

Buster grinned. "Even if they don't come lookin' for him here, if this mob gets big enough, somebody'll sure as hell call the cops…and that'll keep 'em busy doin' somethin' besides chasing down Jake."

In seconds the crowd swallowed them up.

CHAPTER 41

After Buster dropped him at Vivaldi Street next to the Wood, Jake strolled casually along the edge of the foliage. Still in disguise, he searched for the partially concealed hiking trail. He found it—right where Lester said it would be. One last glance back at the street, and he sprinted down the trail. After a couple of minutes, he veered off and hunched down behind a clump of manzanita bushes. No one in sight.

The dappled sunlight warmed him, but the shadows from the tallest oaks and redwoods were already shrouding the underbrush. Jake tore off the wig and blue top and buried them deep in his backpack. He pulled the red T-shirt and gray hoodie from the pack and put them on. Slipping his old watch cap into the front pocket of his sweatshirt, Jake jumped to his feet and took off deeper into the Wood.

He didn't stop until he reached the laurel patch at the base of the huge oak that housed *The Snark*. Pushing his way through the tall brush, he checked once more to make sure he was alone. All clear. He bolted up the makeshift ladder onto the platform, slumped onto his knees, and dropped his pack next to him.

Stretching out on the bare boards, Jake eased out a breath. Here, out of sight from below, he was safe. Lester was the only other person who knew about *The Snark*. Jake had never been so worn out in his life, but he didn't want to waste even a second of his freedom. It was his chance to think. To try to decide what he should do with the final wish—with nobody messing with his head.

Just as he was about to lose the battle with exhaustion, he heard rustling below. Lester was early. He peeked over the edge of the platform and spotted the Brooklyn Dodgers cap above a tall laurel bush. A bolt of adrenaline shot through him. "*Ben?* Oh my god! How'd you find this place?"

"Lester come by my place and tole me how t' get here. Even drew me a map." Ben patted a pocket of his bib overalls. "He thought ya might wanna talk." He glanced at the rickety ladder and winced.

"Hold on. I'm comin' down." Jake plucked the red-flagged rope from the railing and swung easily to the ground. "Man, I've really missed you." He raced over, gave Ben a quick hug, then stepped back and scanned the area. No sign Ben had been followed. Even so, best not to stay out in the open like this.

He maneuvered the old man out of the foliage. "Watch your step." He nodded to an innocent looking patch of dead grass. "Me and Lester set up a few hidden surprises."

The two of them headed down the trail that led to the pond at the center of the Wood. Jake blew out a sigh.

Ben glanced over. "What ya frettin' about, Jake?"

Jake checked behind them. "I'd be better off if I'd never found that freak … stupid ship's lantern," Jake said through clenched teeth.

"Now why would you say a thing like that, son?"

"Seriously? If I didn't have the wishes, my life wouldn't have gotten so *out of control*." The familiar hot fist formed in Jake's stomach.

"Then maybe you oughta just keep it simple."

"If only. Hardly simple when everybody's pressuring me—including the President—to make the wish they want." He ran his fingers through his hair. "Even if I don't make the wish the President's people told me to, how am I supposed to pick the right thing?"

"Just choose somethin' you're really pining for."

"But how can I do that? Everyone's counting on me to do something important…like for the whole world. Or at least for *The United States of America*." Jake added the air quotes, then headed down the trail.

"You don't have to—"

"Seems like there's a ton of bad stuff that could happen even if I wish for something that could really…you know, help all of mankind!"

"Jake, you ain't responsible for the whole danged world."

"Well, I am now! Guess you don't watch TV or hear what everybody's saying online." Jake shot Ben a look that would have come off a lot more sarcastic if it weren't for the tears welling in his eyes.

"Shoot, this ain't the way it's s'posed to happen," Ben stared at the dirt beneath his feet.

Jake snatched a broken laurel branch from the ground. "Yeah, I'm supposed to know what to do, and then just freakin' *do* it." He flung the branch into the bushes. He noticed Ben's anxious expression. Had he somehow hurt the old guy's feelings? Maybe Ben was disgusted with him for being such a wimp. "Well, at least you inherited a super cool house."

Ben paused at a bend in the trail. Shot glances around the area, as if making sure they wouldn't be overheard. "I'm really not s'posed to be tellin' you any of this." He leaned in close to Jake. "Thing is, son, I'm not here because of Charlotte Addison's will."

"Wait. You're not?"

"Nope. I'm here because you rubbed the ship's lantern."

"Yeah, right, you're some kinda *genie*." Jake chuckled. "I am *so* sure."

"Somethin' like that."

The crooked smile on Jake's face faded. He studied the old man for signs he was kidding. There weren't any. Jake shook his head, trying to clear it. "Come on. You couldn't be. I mean you're…well, you know, you're not—"

"Lemme guess. You was expectin' some young, oversized hulk in a turban, big fat clown pants, and a pair of those really uncomfortable purple pointy-up shoes?" Ben raised an eyebrow.

"Well, I…yeah, kinda."

"Afraid that stuff only happens in fairy tales. The truth is I'm more like a…*facilitator*. I got the power to do whatever it takes to grant three wishes to whoever possesses the magic talisman. I'm allowed to interpret the wishes however I see fit, but that's pretty much it."

Jake squinted at him.

"Come on, Jake, think about it. You didn't know all them little details of what Charlotte Addison's place looked like way back when it was a real showplace, now did you?"

"No, not really."

"But *I* did. I's here back then. I seen it in all its glory. So I just kinda interpreted your wish and embellished it a bit."

"I guess that makes sense." Jake's laugh was high-pitched, nervous. "But you gotta have some kinda superpowers, right?"

"Not exactly. I ain't able to transform myself into an animal or a piece a furniture. I don't have superhuman strength. Can't shoot lightnin' bolts outta my sleeves. Can't fly. Don't have a magic carpet to zip around on. Can't make myself invisible. Did I leave anythin' out?"

"Guess not."

"Jake, I have enough dern trouble just gettin' around on foot these days, especially when my arthritis is actin' up." He grimaced. "One a them magic carpets'd sure come in handy."

Jake checked behind them. "We're almost to the pond. You can rest there for a while."

"Really, I'm just an old fart who's tryin' his best t' do his job." Ben headed down the trail. "And I sure ain't doin' it very well."

Jake followed along, doing his best to make sense of what Ben was telling him. "But what about old lady...umm, Mrs. Addison's will?"

"She musta been all alone at the end." Ben shook his head. "Her husband picked up the lantern when he was overseas with the Navy. Came t' Charlotte with her husband's remains. She was devastated when she got the news that he'd died in that awful, awful war. She gathered up the things the Navy sent home and made a kind of shrine to her beloved Desmond. She polished and dusted that shrine every day. 'Course when she rubbed the lantern, I showed up."

Jake opened his mouth to respond, but he didn't know what to say.

Ben took off his cap and rubbed the top of his bald head. "Charlotte was so lonely...she just needed someone t' talk to. We'd go on long strolls together. It wasn't like courtin' or anythin', but we got to be pretty good friends. I couldn't tell her who I was, but I tried to drop a hint now and again. It dang near killed me to see her suffer so. If only she woulda took advantage of the lantern and made the dern wishes, she coulda got Desmond back. She coulda been *happy* again." He shrugged. "But she never made any wish at all. And one day she just stopped polishin'…and stopped dreamin'." Ben cleared his throat and looked away.

"So you've just been hanging around here in Santa Necia all this time?" Jake asked.

"Nope, been all over the place. Had a few assignments along the way. Got me some great memories and some not-so-good ones." He paused. "But after a while, I wasn't called to grant no more wishes at all…until you brought me back by rubbin' that old ship's lantern."

"Jeez, where've you been all this time?"

"Kinda hard to explain. You might say I been in a state of limbo for a spell." Ben stepped into the underbrush and snapped off a long piece of a fallen oak branch.

"Limbo's a state? Man, I really suck at geography."

"Limbo ain't really a place so much as a kinda dream." Ben tested the branch to make sure it was sturdy enough for a walking stick. "It's like being frozen in time. Only you keep gettin' older. Pretty bad deal if ya ask me." He leaned heavily on the stick. "There ain't much call for old fart facilitators like me…except when we got ourselves some unfinished business—like with the ship's lantern you found."

Jake shook his head. "I never suspected that the old beat-up ship's lantern was…well, magic."

"You're thinkin' the whole three wishes shebang only happens with one a them ancient oil lamps. Like the Aladdin story."

"Guess so." Jake shrugged.

"Nope. The magic talisman could be just about anythin' a guy can easily carry. Anything bigger is likely t' cause problems." He groaned as he kept pace with Jake. "It ain't so much the actual object that calls a facilitator. It don't mean nothin' until someone chooses it and rubs it with some care, some respect."

Jake nodded. "Oh yeah, I wiped off the dust when I found it. Forgot about that."

"Yep. Lemme tell you a story. It happened 'bout ten years or so after I finally left Charlotte." Ben slowed to a stop and pulled off his baseball cap; he dusted it off with his sleeve. "I got this here ball cap as a gift. See, there was this Brooklyn Dodgers clubhouse boy who loved his team more than anythin'. They was pretty dang successful. They played in the World Series plenty of times, but they never once managed to win one."

Ben began to trudge along the trail again. "The kid was polishin' up a certain trophy and wishin' with all his might that his beloved Dodgers could finally win it all. That's when I showed up. Course I couldn't tell him nothin' about why I was there, but we became pretty good friends."

"Kinda like me, huh?"

Ben nodded. "This all happened back in nineteen and fifty-five...the one and *only* time the Brooklyn Dodgers ever won the World Series. That trophy he was polishin' turned out to work just fine as a magic talisman. So you see? It ain't really got nothin' to do with them silly lookin' oil lamps."

"So the talis...object isn't magical or nothin' until somebody comes along and treats it like it was special?"

Ben grinned. "As good a explanation as any, Jake. Anyway, grantin' the wishes of that kid in Brooklyn was the last assignment I got, and I'd kinda given up hope of ever gettin' back into action." He shook his head. "I figured the lantern would just lay there with those wishes unused 'til long after I's gone. But you changed all that."

Jake squeezed his eyes shut; all of the things he'd just learned crashed around in his brain like a bunch of outta control bumper cars. The pond was just around the next bend. He could use the rest, too.

CHAPTER 42

Lester slowed as he pedaled past the Wood. He continued a half block past it, pulled over and watched a few cars speed by. He checked his watch: four o'clock. If all went according to plan, Jake should be at *The Snark* by now. Maybe Ben, too, if the old guy was able to follow the crude map Lester scratched out for him. Satisfied he hadn't been followed, Lester zipped across the street, hopped the curb, and headed down the hidden trail.

A tan Taurus pulled up to the curb. Roarke smirked. Clever kid, using an out-of- the way trail instead of the main gate. But not clever enough. Roarke stalked his prey down the same trail, punching keys on his cell phone as he went.

At a bend in the path, Lester checked behind him. Still nobody. He stashed his bike in the bushes, glanced back one more time, and, seeing no one, sprinted deeper into the trees.

—⟨∂∂∂⟩—

The late afternoon sun made the clearing around the pond bright, in sharp contrast to the shadows on the trail among the trees. Jake led Ben to the shade of an ancient willow, leaned back against the trunk and slid down to the grass.

Ben eased himself down onto a bench nearby and smiled.

Jake scrunched up his face. "What?"

"Got me a strong feelin' you'll be makin' that wish right soon."

"But if I make the wish…will you have to go back to that limbo place?"

"Not this time. Thing is, son, there ain't no more wishes in that old lantern after your last one."

"Seriously?"

"Yep. All any talisman's good for is the three wishes. Charlotte shoulda finished 'em off, but she never did. Now it's up to you to end this thing. Soon's you make your third wish, all this wish grantin' will pretty much be over for me."

"You mean…you're gonna *die*?"

"Let's just say I'm gonna be gettin' outta the facilitator business." Heavy sigh. "And I tell ya, son, I'm ready."

"So, I'll never see you again?"

"Now you're just stallin', Jake. Stop makin' this thing bigger'n it is."

"But it *is* big, bigger than anything I've ever—"

Ben held up his palm. "Most a the time this whole dang thing is real predictable. The person who finds the magic talisman usually does somethin' stupid and blows the whole deal, or else he goes for the big three…fame, fortune and love. And it hardly ever ends the way they figured. But you—"

"I have a chance to do something really important."

"Quit tryin' to save the whole dang world, Jake. Folks gotta take care a theirselves."

Jake stretched out on his back, hands behind his head. The cool grass was soft, soothing. "Yeah, I know. I don't mean I can like eliminate world hunger or end wars forever. I've heard all those experts talking about how trying to do anything like that will make things worse than doing nothin' at all."

"Everybody's got their opinion, son. Don't mean you gotta pay attention to 'em."

"But I might be able to wish for something way more basic, more…I dunno, like to get people to act better…crap! I just want to do something that'll be important enough to last, you know?"

"It'll last, Jake, long's it's a wish from here." He patted his chest with an open palm. "You cotton to what other people want, and that wish'll wither away in no time. Don't underestimate the ability of humans to twist somethin' good into a load a horse manure."

Jake rose up, rested on an elbow. "But don't I have to try to make things better?"

Ben leaned down and looked him in the eye. "It really is okay to do somethin' just for yourself."

"Maybe it is, but if I don't try to make a difference in the world, who will?"

The old man sat back, shook his head. "Jake, you're putting too big a responsibility on yourself. In the end, this is somethin' you gotta decide without everybody pesterin' you to do what *they're* hopin' for."

Jake groaned, rubbed his forehead.

"Just relax, son. The right wish'll come to ya."

Jake lay back in the grass. "Yeah, well, how will I recognize it?"

"It'll be whatever *you* really want, Jake. Don't worry, you'll know."

The willow fronds danced in the light breezes off the pond. Maybe Ben was right. Maybe he ought to just wish for something he really wanted—and forget about the rest of the freakin' world. Through the branches of the willow, he spied a hawk circling in lazy, swooping spirals almost as high as the puffy white clouds. For the first time in months, Jake felt he had the freedom to think.

At the Crowne Pointe Mall, a cadre of FBI Agents gathered around Hacker's vehicle in parking lot. No sign of the kid. Lots of people had claimed they'd spotted Jake, but the descriptions varied so much none proved credible. A couple of women even said they'd spotted him dressed as a girl. Once again, Hacker's opinion of eyewitness accounts held true: worthless as balls on a taco.

Hacker glared into the blank faces of his agents. "Come on, I gotta have *something* to feed the media. We're in full CYA mode here! Somebody give me a bone to throw those vultures."

Agent Donaldson flipped open a folder to reveal Ben's photo on top of a stack of computer printouts. Hacker glanced at the photo. A smile formed at the corners of his mouth.

CHAPTER 43

Lester scampered up the ladder to *The Snark* and popped through the trapdoor. He couldn't shake the feeling that he'd been followed. His heart was beating like mad, same as when he was a little kid and had to race to the bed and dive under the covers before the monster in the closet could grab him. He peered over the edge of the platform. No one.

Lester dropped down on the planks and picked up Jake's backpack. The lantern was inside. So where was Jake? Something was wrong! Did the FBI catch him? Lester had been sure his plan would work. He thought for a bit, remembering he'd sent Ben here, too. Maybe Jake and Ben went farther into the Wood to stay out of sight.

Then he heard it. Someone charging up the ladder! Someone heavy. Not Jake, that's for sure. And certainly not Ben. No old man would be bolting up the ladder that fast. Just as the trapdoor began to open, Lester leapt on top of it. Each thrust from beneath propelled Lester's body several inches into the air. He snapped up the backpack and dashed over to seize the rope and swing to the ground. There was only one. Beware the blue flag, mate.

Lester spun around and stared wide-eyed at the trapdoor as it flew up, and the head and arm of a large, mean-looking dude burst through. The gun he pointed at Lester's head seemed as big as a bazooka.

"Where's the Parker kid?" Roarke growled.

"Who?"

"Don't screw with me, smart-ass."

"How should I know where he is? Look around." Lester waved his arm over the deck. "Sure doesn't look like he's here, does it?"

"Well, then, I guess me and you'll just have to hang out here until he shows up."

Roarke tried to force his body through to the platform, but the opening proved much too small for his frame. He'd scraped a shoulder busting through the goddamn hole, but now he'd jammed himself tight. "Friggin' kids."

With no other way out of the tree house, Lester stood by help-lessly as the guy bashed the butt of his gun against the weathered boards. Several ruptured, sending shattered fragments of wood crashing to the ground. Sucking in his stomach as best he could, Roarke inched his way up and finally pulled himself through, demolishing a few more boards in the process.

Lester figured that had to hurt. Great. He hugged Jake's pack to his chest and backed away searching for something he could use to defend himself. Not even a big stick. Even if there were one, though, it'd be no match for that huge-ass gun.

Jake awoke and rubbed his eyes. He was sure he couldn't have slept more than a couple of minutes, but the shadows from the trees now stretched out more than he expected. Anyway, he felt more relaxed and rested than he had in months. Rising to a sitting position, he stretched out the kinks, and twisted toward Ben.

He wasn't there! Jake reached for his backpack. Gone! He leapt to his feet, his eyes darting everywhere in a panic. Oh my God! Did Ben take...? No. Calm down. *Think.* He'd been so anxious to talk to the old guy he'd forgotten to grab his backpack when he swung down from *The Snark*. Stupid! He had to get back there as fast as he could.

Lester would have snagged it for sure. Unless somebody else beat him to it. Jake took off down the path, stumbled twice, but kept going hard.

Why would Ben desert him like that? He'd trusted him, especially since he learned the old man's true identity, but something felt weird. He checked his watch. Crap. He was supposed to have met Les at *The Snark* an hour ago. Les would be worried. Jesus, what about his mom? She'd be totally freakin' out. Maybe they should have thought things through a little more. Naw, it would all work out. Les would be waiting at *The Snark*, and he'd know what to do. Captain Hawke could always count on First Mate Slade.

Charley Krock slowed his pace now that he could see the tree house Roarke had told him to look for. Krock had already ruined his custom Italian shoes trudging through the dirt and under-brush, and he was sweating like a fat man on a treadmill. Damn it, he hadn't signed up for this physical crap.

Krock saw Roarke peering down at him, his beefy arm clutching Lester to him.

"What took you so long?" Roarke growled.

"Sorry. I couldn't find that damn trail you mentioned. Had to come in through the Wood's main gate. Parked in the lot." Krock took in a breath. "Had to locate you by the GPS on your phone."

Roarke closed his eyes, groaned.

"Okay, so now I'm here. But I don't understand why the hell you insisted I come out to this godforsaken place. I am *not* supposed to be involved in this at all. Thought I made it very clear you were *not* to associate me or Wahd…or anyone else with this thing."

"Like I told *you*, the plans have changed. Now that everyone thinks the kid's been kidnapped, it'd be too friggin' easy for you to roll over on me."

"I told you we would never double-cross you."

"You sure as hell won't *now*." Roarke smirked. "You're up to your crotch in this. Turn on me, and you're goin' down too."

"Yeah, well, you got the wrong person anyway."

"The Woo kid here's an insurance policy. I know what I'm doin'."

"I hope so. But, somehow, I doubt your *plan* included a witness." He nodded toward Lester.

"I'll eliminate that little problem once we grab the Final Wish."

Lester turned pale.

"That wasn't part of the deal, Roarke," Krock said.

"What part of *change of plans* don't you understand?"

Krock glanced around. "How can you be so sure the Parker kid is anywhere near here?"

"He can't be too far away." Roarke held up the lantern for Krock to see, then dropped it into the backpack. He released his grip on Lester and shoved him hard to the deck of the tree house.

Lester massaged his elbow. "Jesus, take it easy."

"Hey, no need to hurt anybody," Krock said.

Roarke scowled. "You complainin'?"

"No...it's just that your methods are—"

"We do it my way, Krock. That's the deal."

Lester looked from Krock to Roarke. "You guys are obviously not FBI. So who are you?"

Roarke raised his arm, poised to slap Lester. "Shut your mouth. And stay *down*. You're lucky I haven't snuffed you already."

"Don't just stand there like an idiot, Krock," Roarke said. "Keep out of sight. When he shows up for the lantern, we'll nab him. Here, in case you need some help persuading him." He tossed a small revolver to Krock, who jumped out of the way. The gun hit the ground with a thud. Krock picked it up by the handle with his thumb and index finger, as if it might blow up in his hand. He held the gun at the ready like the cops on TV, then stuffed the revolver in his belt. Finally, he put it in his pocket.

Krock looked up to see Roarke shaking his head in disgust.

After running in spurts along the hiking trail and forcing a couple of shortcuts through the dense underbrush, Jake finally approached the familiar laurel bushes near *The Snark*.

He slowed his pace as soon as he heard voices. Something was wrong. He recognized Lester's voice, but who was he talking to? Unless Ben had... Naw, it didn't sound like him either. He crept closer to *The Snark*, dropped flat on the ground, and crawled forward, concealed from above by the heavy foliage. Rising to his knees behind a tall bush, he brushed off the dirt and leaves and assessed the situation. Jake spied dirt-covered dress shoes just visible beneath a bush about twenty feet away, and he could hardly miss the huge guy up on *The Snark*. They sure as hell weren't FBI.

Jake knew he should be scared out of his wits, but he wasn't. His heart pounded like crazy, but he was a lot more excited than afraid. Everything snapped into focus; he knew what he had to do. He crouched down in the underbrush, slipped his watch cap from his hoodie pocket, jammed it down tight on his head. Almost dark. He took a slow deep breath. Time for the Hawke to strike.

CHAPTER 44

Patrons paid little attention to the huge TV on the wall at Fuggstrutter's, a popular watering hole in upscale Crowne Pointe. It was Friday, Happy Hour, and their focus was on hunting and gathering. That changed when the bartender turned the volume high enough to be heard over the slurred pick-up lines and forced laughter of the bar's mating-game participants. Conversations died mid-innuendo when Jake's face appeared on the screen behind Fox News' Anita Frye.

"We interrupt our regular programming to bring you this special news bulletin. We have learned that Jake Parker has been kidnapped. Our exclusive sources tell us the magic lantern is also missing. No demand for ransom has been received, but authorities have revealed that they have a suspect in custody."

Ben's picture filled the screen.

"Early reports indicate that *this* man, a transient who goes by the name of Ben Ackyack, may have ties to a militant terrorist group. Ackyack's origins are still unclear. However, speculation is strong that he may hail from somewhere in the Middle East or Asia. Officials would neither deny nor confirm Ackyack's connection with ISIS or Al Qaeda. As this recent photo illustrates, Ackyack is usually seen wearing an old Brooklyn Dodgers baseball cap, suggesting that he may not be aware that the team relocated to Los Angeles several decades ago. It's doubtful that someone who has been in this country for long would make that mistake."

Most of the bar patrons now stared at the screen. Talk about a buzzkill.

"As always, you can count on Fox News to be on top of this fast-breaking story. Stay tuned for further developments."

For what felt like hours, Officers Patt and Norbert had been cruising the streets of Santa Necia looking for suspicious activity. When they happened upon a lone tan Taurus parked in a red-curb zone near the Wood, Patt pulled in behind it. While Norbert called in the license number, Patt rolled out and began to hunt for clues along a nearby trail.

Norbert joined Patt. "It's a rental. To a John Smith." He provided air quotes.

Patt rolled his eyes. "I'm guessing whatever Mr. Smith was after is down this trail."

"I'll call for backup." Norbert reached for the radio on his shoulder.

"Can it, Otto. First of all, we don't even know if this guy has anything to do with the Parker kid's disappearance. Second, there's no one to back us up. Everybody else is searching the town for Jake. Just call in our position."

"Right. Gotcha."

Anxious, but determined, they hurried down the nearby trail.

—ↄﾉﾉↄ—

At the Santa Necia police station, Ben slumped against the back of a metal chair in the stark gray room. Special Agents Brett Malloy and Hal James paced in shirtsleeves.

James came to an abrupt halt in front of the old man and leaned down, his face inches from Ben's. "I'm gonna ask you *one…more…time*. Why'd he take off like that?"

"I'm gonna tell you *one…more…time*. I. Don't. Know."

"Sure you do, old man," Malloy said. "And we're gettin' pretty damned tired of your attitude."

"Well, if I's Jake, I'd sure have been lookin' for any chance to clear outta that cage you had me in."

"We've been ordered by the *President* to protect the kid, for Christ's sake," Malloy said.

"*Protect* him? Ha! That's a load a steamin' cow manure. You'd most likely be treatin' him same way you're treatin' me."

James pointed a finger at Ben. "You don't know shit about our agenda."

"Don't I? It's pretty dern obvious you fellas're tryin' to steal the wish from him. You don't give a fig about Jake."

"Quit tryin' to change the subject, gramps," Malloy said.

James slammed his hand down on the back of Ben's chair. "You're *gonna* talk. You aren't movin' outta this room 'til you tell us the *truth*."

"We don't care how well trained you are, Ackyack." Malloy leaned in. "We've broken terrorists a lot tougher than you."

"Don't amount to a hill a beans, since I ain't no terrorist."

"Yeah?" James sneered. "Don't think you're gonna be able to hold on to that lie much longer."

Ben shrugged. "Guess the truth don't mean nothin' to you

guys anyways."

Malloy spit out a laugh.

"Then why don't you give us your opinion...as a non-terrorist who doesn't know any of the facts?" James smirked. "Why do you *think* the kid took off like that?"

Ben twisted his neck to relieve some of the tension. "He's a kid. Remember what that's like? He couldn't stand bein' cooped up. He prob'ly escaped that stiflin' prison of a house to give his-self a chance for some freedom...maybe even a little adventure."

"Well, he's playin' a pretty dangerous game," Malloy said.

"And he's playin' it with our lantern," James said.

"*Your* lantern?" Ben shook his head.

"Maybe you should let me talk to him for a few minutes... alone," James said. "I think it's about time we got a lot more persuasive on his ass."

Malloy moved in front of Ben. "Ackyack, I'm telling you, you don't want that."

"Got that right. 'Specially since you know dern well you ain't got nothin' on me. I ain't done nothin' wrong."

James slapped Ben hard on the back of the head. "Don't screw with me, old man. Trust me, I'm not afraid to leave bruises."

Ben squeezed his eyes shut, and felt the pain in his head to begin to subside. He could hold on a little longer. That was all he'd need.

CHAPTER 45

"Where the hell *is* the kid?" Krock shouted. "It's getting dark!"

"Shut up and stay out of sight. He'll be here all right." Roarke glared at Lester, who sat hunched up against the tree, his knees pulled up to his chest. Roarke lumbered over to the edge of the platform and checked the underbrush for signs of movement. For damn sure the Parker kid wouldn't abandon his buddy, and he'd sure as hell come back for the lantern. Unless the feds already nabbed him. That would be a real turd sandwich. Naw, Roarke knew Marvin Hacker too well. If Hacker had grabbed the kid, he'd have taken the lantern too.

The area was now bathed in semi-darkness. Jake took a deep breath and eased it out slowly. Time for the Hawke to make his move. He tossed a rock well off to the left of the guy who was barely concealed in the bushes.

The guy spun around, crouched down, and waved the gun in the general direction of the sound. "Who's there?" he shouted.

Roarke dropped to a knee and peered over the side.

"Time to face the music, scumbags!" Jake yelled, affecting as deep and raspy a voice as he could. "Toss down your weapons, and we might go easy on ya!"

Lester swallowed a grin and rose to his knees, eyeing the back-pack at Roarke's feet.

Jake sprang into view, grinning, and sauntered over to a spot a few feet in front of an innocent looking pile of dry grass.

"Grab him!" Roarke yelled.

Krock took off in awkward pursuit. Jake didn't move. Two steps before he reached Jake, Krock stepped into a camouflaged snare that yanked him upside down into the air. He let out a sur-prisingly high-pitched scream and dropped the gun.

"Yes!" Jake pumped his fist in the air.

<hr/>

Patt and Norbert, still foraging for clues along the bike path, swung around toward the scream in the distance. Patt called in their position and told dispatch they were investigating a possible distress call in the Wood, as they ran off in the direction of the scream.

<hr/>

Jake darted over, snatched Krock's gun, and heaved it as far as he could into the brush.

Roarke aimed his revolver at Jake's head. "Hold it right there, smart-ass."

"Think again, dude." Jake grinned. "Without me, there's no wish."

Roarke knew the little punk was right. Even if he just wound-ed the kid, he might not be in any shape to make the wish. "Yeah, but I can sure as hell waste your little bud—"

Lester swung Jake's backpack hard against the back of the big man's head, knocking him off balance. Roarke clutched the makeshift railing, which began to give way. By the time Roarke righted himself, Lester had hoisted the remains of the trapdoor, dropped the backpack through, and scrambled down the ladder after it.

Roarke plunged toward the trapdoor but stopped short. Should he try to force his bulky frame through that friggin' hole again or just leap the twenty feet to the ground and risk shattering a leg?

"Step lively, Mr. Slade," Jake shouted. "Before he swings down on the rope!"

Roarke snickered, stuffed the gun in his belt, and seized the blue-flagged rope next to him.

Lester tossed the backpack to Jake.

"Beware the blue flag, matey," the boys said in unison as they barreled down the trail.

Roarke gripped the rope firmly and swung over the side. At the height of his arc, the rope gave way, sending him crashing to the ground. Roarke groaned in pain as he righted himself, and limped after the boys. "We'll see how funny it is when I get a hold of you little pricks!"

"Hey, what about me?" Krock asked, his face already red from the rush of blood to his head.

"Screw you! Now I'm *pissed.* That little asshole is gonna pay for this!"

As the boys disappeared around the first corner of the hiking trail, Roarke fired a warning shot over their heads.

Hacker and four agents assembled at the edge of the Wood, where they'd just discovered the Santa Necia police cruiser and Roarke's Taurus. Their heads shot into the air like a family of startled meerkats when they heard the gunshot.

"Spread out," Hacker ordered. "And find the kid before it's too late!"

The agents dispersed in different directions.

Flushed with adrenaline, Jake and Lester tore into a trail intersection. Their confidence soared when Patt and Norbert, guns drawn, came running toward them. Roarke hobbled around the bend and stumbled to a halt when he spotted the police.

Patt and Norbert aimed their weapons. "Stop! Police!" Patt shouted. "Drop your weapon! Boys, get down!" They couldn't risk a shot with Jake and Lester in the line of fire.

Roarke had no such qualms. A bullet ripped through Norbert's shoulder.

Jake and Lester dropped to their knees and crawled toward the underbrush at the side of the trail.

With Patt focused on pulling Norbert out of range, Roarke took the opportunity to lunge toward the boys, firing a shot that grazed the cowl of Jake's hoodie and ricocheted off a large rock inches from them. "Stay where you are or the next one won't be a warning shot!" Roarke snarled.

Patt yelled, "Boys, go! Now!" He fired at Roarke to cover their escape.

Roarke winced in pain and grabbed his thigh.

Jake shoved Lester forward, and they rolled down an incline to a small pocket of safety.

Hacker's voice rang out behind Roarke. "Federal Agent! Drop your weapon!"

Roarke lurched toward the sound, managing to get off a wild shot at Hacker, who returned fire. Roarke tumbled to the ground, clutching his chest. He twitched once and slipped into silence.

Jake righted himself. "Jesus, that one almost freakin' hit us."

"That'll teach 'em to…mess with…Cap'n Hawke."

"You okay, Mr. Slade?"

"Yeah…just feeling a little…funny, Cap'n."

Jake reached under his friend to help him sit up. When Lester grimaced in pain, Jake pulled his hand back. It was covered in blood.

"Oh my god, Les! You…you've been hit!"

Lester tried to respond, but couldn't. When Jake attempted to shift his buddy into a more comfortable position, he saw it—the whole side of Lester's sweatshirt soaked with blood. Jake raised Lester's shirt. "Oh god! No!"

Lester's eyes glazed over; he coughed once, and passed out.

"You *can't* die, Les!" Jake pleaded. "Please!" He buried his face in his bloodied hands and tried to think, but his mind was a thick black cloud. He screamed into the dark. "You goddamn sons-a-*bitches*!"

The straps on Jake's backpack felt unbearably confining. In a rage, he ripped it from his body and slammed it to the ground so hard it clanked against a boulder.

CHAPTER 46

A flashlight glare blinded Jake and Lester as they rose to their feet.

Hacker diverted the light. "Damn it! You did it, didn't you? You wasted the wish."

Jake glanced at him as if he were no more than an irritating gnat. Lester rubbed his hands along his shirt, then stared at his palms.

Patt rushed up behind Hacker. "You boys all right?"

Hacker waved Patt away with a flick of his wrist. "I got this." Hacker scowled at Jake. "Well?"

"Well what?" Jake nodded to Lester, and the boys climbed the small incline back to the trail.

"Did you or did you not waste the damn Final Wish making sure we'd get here in time to save your sorry ass from the bad guys?"

Jake stopped beside Hacker. "If and when I make any wish, I can't reveal the details to anybody." He rejoined Lester on the path, and called back, "Anyway, you'd be the last person I'd tell if I did."

Hacker whacked the flashlight against his open palm and stomped off to lead the boys out of the Wood.

In a makeshift triage area near the street, paramedics did their best to staunch the blood flow from Officer Norbert's gunshot wound, then rushed him off in the ambulance. Roarke's body was bagged and loaded into a coroner's van. Agent Donaldson tucked Krock, hands cuffed behind his back, into a waiting government SUV.

Unnoticed, a beat-up green pickup towing an old Airstream slowed as it passed the flurry of activity at the edge of the Wood. Then it rounded a corner and vanished.

Paramedics finished treating Jake and Lester for minor scrapes and bruises. The boys hopped off the back of the ambulance just as Jill, Steve, and Vicky Woo, rushed to the scene. Steve ruffled Jake's hair. Jill hugged him so hard, he had trouble catching his breath. Vicky planted several kisses on Lester's face, and he bravely refrained from wiping them off or cringing. Kevin and Angie sat together close by.

Off to one side, Bethany DuVey stood next to Sergeant Patt, as her sound engineer held aloft a light in one hand and counted down with his fingers with the other.

"This is Bethany DuVey, Channel Six On-The-Scene, with Santa Necia Police Sergeant Stanley Patt." She nodded to Patt. "Sergeant Patt, when did you first realize you would play such a dramatic role in this dangerous turn of events?"

"Y'know, it was a little strange. I mean it was like this, this *voice* just came to me." Patt rambled on, milking his moment of celebrity. "And so we just took off as fast as we could to…"

Bethany stopped listening when she saw CBS's Chris Payne heading for Jake and Lester—disregarding Hacker's demand that there be no interviews of either of the boys.

DuVey gritted her teeth. Damn it, why didn't she go right to Jake? The hell with Hacker. She scowled at her crew. "That press conference tomorrow is *mine*! You can bet your ass on it."

———⁂———

As Payne approached, camera crew in tow, Jill unwrapped herself from Jake and moved a few feet away. Vicky joined her. They kept a close eye on the scene, a couple of tiger moms.

"This is Chris Payne, with a special CBS News *live* report. I'm here with Jake Parker, the boy who holds the fate of the world in his hands, near the scene of the violent gun battle that just ended with one person dead and another seriously wounded." Payne shifted his gaze to Jake. "Well, Jake, looks like you've had a very close call!"

"Yeah, I guess so." Jake clutched his backpack to his chest.

"Thankfully, you and your friend—"

"Lester," Jake said through clenched teeth. "His name is Lester Woo."

"Right. Thank God, you and Lester appear to have survived relatively unscathed."

"Yeah, we were real lucky, I guess." Jake said.

Payne addressed the camera. "Well, I think I speak for the whole world when I say we're all very thankful that Jake Parker… and Lester Woo…are safe and sound."

Hacker swooped in and used his palm to block the camera

lens. "I said *no* interviews with Jake."

"This is Special Agent Heckler. He has been entrusted with protecting young Mr. Parker." Payne turned to Hacker. "Agent Heckler, would you tell our viewers how this horrible turn of events happened on *your* watch?"

"No comment. There is a major press conference scheduled for tomorrow, at which time you will get the details. And it's *Hacker*, not Heckler."

"Sorry, my error." Payne wedged himself between Jake and Hacker. "I see, Jake, through all this turmoil and horror, you have managed to protect the famous magic lantern." Payne nodded toward the partially closed backpack in which a corner of the lantern could be seen, and on cue, the cameraman zoomed in on the lantern.

Jake hugged the backpack, and Hacker elbowed Payne out of the way.

Payne clasped his hand to his heart as he swiveled around for his close-up. "What a brave young man! You have just seen an exclusive CBS News live interview with the boy of the hour, Jake Parker. This is Chris Payne reporting."

Hacker began to lead the boys away.

Jill started after them. "Hold on! Where are you taking them? And why?"

"We just have to debrief the boys after all that's happened. Nothin' to worry about."

"Wait just a damn minute!" Jill glared at Hacker. "You can't interrogate a minor without an adult present."

"Actually we can, but relax, it's *not* an interrogation." He forced a smile. "We just need them to give us a few details, so we can solidify our case against the kidnappers. Standard procedure. We'll bring them back home right afterward." He hurried the boys to separate unmarked black sedans.

CHAPTER 47

The debriefing Hacker mentioned turned out to be a two-hour grilling of Jake by FBI interrogators. Jake squirmed on a metal chair in the middle of a small, cold room—with three, sometimes four agents hurling questions at him from all directions. At first, he was scared shitless. The questions came so fast he sometimes didn't get a chance to respond to the first one before he was slapped with another. Who else was involved besides Lester? Ben? Kevin? Angie Woo? What was his relationship with Ben? Who is Ben? Did he make the Final Wish or not? Who planned the escape? Did Ben help him breakout? Why this? Why that? Why everything all over again.

Jake had seen plenty of cop shows, so he wasn't surprised when they kept throwing the same questions at him. But after a while, those questions felt more like gut punches. He wasn't sure if they were trying to catch him in a lie or make him say something that wasn't true. Probably both. Eventually, the agents simply ran out of questions and energy. Didn't matter. The only thing Jake cared about was that it was over. He couldn't recall exactly what he'd said. But he was sure of one thing, he'd refused to tell them whether or not he'd made the Final Wish. No matter *what* they did to him, he would never tell.

Jake and Lester sat in the back seat of the black SUV, so exhausted they didn't have the strength to talk. After Agent Pirelli dropped off Lester at the Woo house, he delivered Jake.

Jill, Steve, and Kevin were outside in the driveway when the SUV drove in. Jill rushed to Jake and hugged him so long he started to squirm. Luckily the two FBI Agents stationed nearby were more interested in watching out for bad guys on the street than this family reunion.

At first, all the balloons in the family room confused Jake. He thought it was a welcome-home thing, until he saw the Happy Birthday banner. In all the chaos he'd had to slog through, Jake had completely forgotten his birthday.

He felt a hell of a lot older than fifteen.

Slumped between Jill and Steve on the couch, he picked at a piece of birthday cake. Kevin, sprawled on the floor, finished his second piece. They all watched the late-night news, but Jake had trouble concentrating.

"With the surprise arrest of Santa Necia Town Councilman James Claude Wahdle, 56, at Bubba's All-You-Can-Eat Barbeque earlier this evening, the authorities now have two men in custody," NBC's Biff Everett reported. "Wahdle is the alleged mastermind behind the plot to grab Jake Parker and force him to make an as-yet-unrevealed final wish. Under questioning, Wahdle's chief aide, Charles Mayfield Krock, 33, alerted authorities to his boss's role in the kidnapping scheme. Krock was arrested at the site of tonight's fatal gun battle. Dead at the scene was the third man involved in the attempted kidnapping, Nathan Allan Roarke, 45, whom NBC News has discovered is a former FBI operative who left the Agency under undisclosed, but suspicious circumstances six years ago."

Jill pulled Jake to her. "It's okay, honey. You're safe now." She rocked him a little, and he let her.

"They're going to put those bastards away for a long time," Steve said. "Things will get back to normal around here."

"Like things will *ever* be freakin' normal again," Jake said.

"There is speculation," Everett said, "that Jake Parker may in fact have used the Final Wish to alert the authorities to his whereabouts…or at least to aid him and his young friend, Lester Woo, in escaping from their assailants. I must emphasize that this information has not yet been confirmed. In the end, only Jake Parker knows for sure what—if anything—happened with the Final Wish during tonight's harrowing sequence of events. We'll be back after these messages."

All three Parkers stared at Jake.

"Seriously? You know I can't say *anything*. I've told everybody like a thousand times already. I can't say whether or not I made any wish, and I can't reveal the details of any wish I make. If I *do* it'll be recanted. Remember?"

"It's okay if you did." Jill put her arm around him.

"Aw, come on, son. Surely you can give us a little hint."

"No! I *can't*!"

"We understand, honey," Jill said.

Kevin rolled his eyes. "Come on, Dad, the place is bugged, remember? Besides…" He tilted his head toward Agent Pirelli standing in the doorway.

Steve glanced at the agent and leaned toward Jake. "Of course," he whispered, "if you haven't really made the Final Wish, you could do it now and no one would be the wiser."

Jake gave his father a look that conveyed some annoyance—but mostly disappointment.

"Whaaat?" Steve glanced at Jill, then back at Jake. "I'm just sayin' if our lifestyle, you know, kind of gradually improved, no one would think anything of it."

Jill glared at Steve. "For Christ's sake, you just don't get it, do you?

"I'm just trying to watch out for our best interests. What's so wrong with—"

The ring of the cordless phone next to the couch startled them.

"Probably for me," Kevin said.

But Steve snatched the phone from its docking station. "Hello? No! What are? No comment!" He threw the phone onto the floor, barely missing Kevin. "I've had enough of those damn media vultures." He yanked the phone cord from the wall.

Jill shook her head. "Nice, Steve. You could have just turned the damn thing off." She squeezed Jake's shoulder. "Listen, sweetie, you've been through a lot. You look exhausted. Maybe you should try to get some sleep. Besides, you have that big meeting tomorrow."

Jake cringed. "Almost forgot about that. I don't know what's gonna happen at that meeting, but it's not gonna be fun." He forced himself up from the couch.

Jill, Steve and Kevin watched him shuffle out the door, with Agent Pirelli following at a respectful distance.

The three Parkers focused on the television again, as Biff Everett reappeared.

"We've taken our cameras out into the streets of New York to gather reactions from average Americans to the possibility that Jake Parker may have—justifiably or not—made the Final Wish."

"Hey, I'm not sure what I would have done," a well-dressed businessman said. "If he did it, it's just too bad it had to turn out like this."

"I'm sure he felt he had no choice," an older woman said. She turned to the camera. "But then neither do the thousands of children around the world who are now going to starve to death."

"I dunno," a young girl said, "he probably had to do what he did. I mean, if he really did it."

"From the beginning none of this was handled right," a casually dressed man said. "So much could have been done. But now we're right back where we started. We got nothin' out of this."

A young man in a crimson Harvard sweatshirt shrugged. "Maybe he did it. Maybe he didn't. When did the kid become answerable to all of us for the Final Wish? It was always *his* wish to make."

A scraggly-bearded thirty-something guy looked directly into the camera. "Why can't you people see what's really going on here? There never was any *magic lantern*." Air quotes. "This is just another hoax manufactured by the government and rich fat cats to distract us from their real agenda…and, once again, their well-orchestrated ruse has worked!"

"I admit I was hoping for a lot more," a young mother holding an infant said. "There's just so *much* that still cries out to be done. I really hope it's not over yet."

A middle-aged man scowled. "Serves us right. People expected too much. Our *big hero* has been exposed for what he really is… just an ignorant, immature kid."

Jill buried her face in her hands. Steve balled his fists, ready to punch whoever appeared on the screen next. Kevin leapt to his feet. "This is bullshit!" He glanced over at Jill. "Sorry, Mom, but these people don't have a freakin' *clue* what Jake's been through." He stomped out of the room, texting Angie as he went.

CHAPTER 48

Bethany DuVey assessed the crowd now straining the confines of Santa Necia's largest venue, the high school gymnasium. This press conference, scheduled for ten, was about to start. The conference was originally supposed to be a brief announcement by government officials that Jake had made the Final Wish. But given yesterday's gun battle and rampant speculation about the wish, she wasn't sure what this would turn out to be. Every major network and independent news source was on hand, but Bethany had wangled a prime spot in the cordoned-off press area in front of the gym's small stage.

On a folding chair in the middle of the stage, Jake fidgeted between Special Agents Bundy and Berkowitz. Chief MacDuff, in full dress blues, hunkered next to Berkowitz. Bethany could see Jake's family in the wings next to Lester and his mom and sister. FBI agents, curly white wires protruding from their earpieces, were everywhere. Nothing new about that, but the California National Guard troops stationed at every entrance and around the perimeter of the building? *That* was new.

Bethany waited for the signal from her video tech, brushed

back a strand of hair, and wet her lips. Showtime.

The tech counted down on his fingers, then pointed to her.

"This is Bethany DuVey, Channel Six, *live*, at the Santa Necia High School gymnasium. We are about to hear an official statement regarding the rumors surrounding Jake Parker and the Final Wish."

Her intro complete, she switched off her mic. The camera zoomed in on a middle-aged man in an expensive charcoal pinstriped suit who approached the battery of microphones. Bethany didn't recognize this guy, and surprises always made her uncomfortable. She shot her crew a questioning glance, got only shrugs in return.

"Ladies and gentlemen," Pinstripes said, "for those of you who may not know me, I am Hugo Furst, Special Presidential Advisor, and I'm here this afternoon as an envoy of the leader of the most powerful country in the world."

While some people in the crowd expressed surprise, most turned a skeptical eye toward the stage.

"I won't take much of your time," Furst said. "As you can plainly see, Jake Parker is now safe." Furst gestured toward Jake, who squirmed on the edge of his chair, backpack in his lap.

"I would like to offer my heartfelt thanks to the heroic FBI agents and to the brave Santa Necia Police officers for their efforts to keep the Final Wish out of the hands of terrorists. But I think we would all concur, especially given the circumstances of the last twenty-four hours, those efforts have left something to be desired. As a result, Special Agent Hacker has been reassigned."

Nervous laughter from the assembly.

"I am aware that unsubstantiated rumors have surfaced regarding the events of yesterday evening, but we cannot comment at this time. Those details are still classified."

"Why?" someone shouted. "We have a right to know what's going on."

"Please, if you will have the courtesy to let me finish," Furst said, "I will entertain a few questions after my prepared statement." He cleared his throat and furrowed his brow—an expression meant to convey the full weight of his authority. It didn't work. He raised his voice so he could be heard over the grumbling of the attendees. "The decision has been made to place Jake Parker and the magic ship's lantern in protective custody at a secure, undisclosed location, until such time as it is safe for him to return."

"You mean until he makes the Final Wish!" a woman screamed.

"You can't control the Final Wish!" bellowed a booming voice from the middle of the crowd.

"You can't force Jake to make the wish *you* choose," another woman yelled.

Furst held up his hand. "I'm quite sure most reasonable people would acknowledge that this is not a decision that can be left to a...a rather naïve young man." Furst cut his eyes at Jake.

Voices erupted from the crowd.

"The Final Wish should be for humanity, not for politics!"

"Yeah, what about all the starving children?"

"How about giving us affordable health care!"

"You politicians don't give a crap about what the *people* want!"

"As if we'd ever be able to count on *this* administration doing anything worthwhile...like ending the destruction of our environment!"

Furst pulled a handkerchief from his coat pocket and patted

his forehead. "You can rest assured the President and his advisors will consider all the options before he decides—"

"Yeah, like he's considered the plight of the little guy in this country," shouted a bearded young man near the stage.

A man in a white tank top featuring an American flag raised a fist. "Stuff it up your ass, you bleeding-heart liberal crybaby."

"The Final Wish should be used to eliminate the problems that have forced millions of people to live in the streets!" shouted a woman in a tattered overcoat.

"Get a job, you lazy bitch!" an overweight guy with a severe crew cut yelled back.

People shoved each other. Shouts of derision volleyed back and forth, rising in volume and intensity. Fights broke out, and soon the whole throng became a punching, kicking, out-of-control mob; the combatants striking out at anyone within reach. National Guard troops waded into the melee, none of them sure how much force was called for.

Jake stared wide-eyed at the riot unfolding in front of him. Agent Bundy clutched Jake's arm and led him toward the wings. Senator Furst fled for safety, shoving Jake aside and causing Bundy to loosen his grip. Jake broke for the microphones.

"Everybody just *shut up*!" Jake screamed at the combatants, his voice cracking.

They all froze and gaped at the boy who was supposed to be their salvation. Bundy seized Jake's arm again, and as Jake struggled to shake loose, he lost his grip on the backpack. The pack fell to the ground, and the lantern tumbled out onto the stage. A collective gasp rose from the crowd.

"Let Jake speak," someone near the stage shouted.

"Yeah, we want to hear what Jake has to say," an older man yelled, while massaging a bruise forming on his cheek.

Bundy assessed the situation, released Jake and backed away a safe distance. Jake seized the battered lantern, and winced at the signs of wear—several scratches, a large dent in the top, and a crack in the red glass window. It would have to do.

"Just *look* at yourselves...at what you're doing to each other. What is the *matter* with you people?" All eyes on him. "I wish...I wish we could end all this stupid, *selfish* arguing and fighting... and just...just show some *respect* for each other for a change."

Jake squeezed his eyes shut, and pent-up tears rolled down his cheeks. He rubbed the top of the lantern and held his breath as long as he could. Finally, he blinked, as if awakening from a trance.

A cloud of silence engulfed the room. All looked wide-eyed at Jake.

"Oh my god!" a woman screamed. "The Final Wish! He made the Final Wish!"

Someone flung open the main doors to the gymnasium, triggering a mass exodus as people rushed out to spread the news.

———✦———

Bethany DuVey, turned on her mic and nudged her cameraman, who swung back around to focus on her. "We have just witnessed one of the greatest moments in our collective cultural history." She paused for dramatic effect. "After all the hesitation, after all the speculation, after all the debate...the wait is finally over."

She glanced up at Jake, who had joined his family. The camera followed her gaze. Jake showed no concern when Bundy snatched the lantern from his grasp and handed it to another agent who slunk away with the prize.

DuVey faced the camera. "The drama that has held the world entranced for eighty-seven days has ended spectacularly, right here in tiny Santa Necia, California, where it all began." The camera zoomed in for her close-up. "So all our hopes and dreams of what might have been...have ended. And we are left with a vague appeal that we all show *respect* for one another. What that will mean is anyone's guess. It is now up to each and every one of us. Jake Parker has made the Final Wish."

CHAPTER 49

Nine o'clock the next morning, Jill and Jake Parker sat across the desk from Mallory Jameson, the acclaimed San Francisco attorney known for taking on corporate bullies and government agencies.

Jill shifted in her seat. "I'm hoping you will be willing to go after Dante Valentine, Ms. Jameson. I'm sure he stole most of the money made from Jake's notoriety." She looked the other woman in the eye. "I don't want it all, just our fair share."

Mallory scanned the documents Steve had signed and shook her head. She looked at Jill and Jake. "Well, he's set up a proper blocked trust account for Jake in which fifteen percent of all the money made from Jake's celebrity status is to be invested and only available to Jake when he turns eighteen."

"Valentine never mentioned that."

"He had no choice. It's a California law—the Coogan Law—designed to protect child performers from unscrupulous relatives and other adults who might want to grab the child's money."

Jill grinned at Jake. "Good law."

"But the rest of this," Mallory tossed the papers across her desk, "is complete crap. Valentine has taken way more than he's entitled to, and it looks like he's shifted most of it into a couple of shell companies. As Jake's agent, he's certainly entitled to his share—but not to anywhere near as much as he's expropriated."

Jill grimaced. "But Steve is still legally my husband, and he signed the contract! Although I doubt he even glanced at the fine print." She took in a breath. "Since he and I are separated, how binding is this contract?"

"Your husband was acting as Jake's representative, but we can probably get around that. I'm sure Valentine misled him about the details. If that's the case, we can invalidate the contract. I'll handle Valentine. He knows what he's done, and when we hit him with the threat of a very public lawsuit, he'll do whatever he has to do to save his reputation. Don't worry, we'll get your money back."

Jill bit her upper lip. "Um, we won't be able to pay you…until we get the money he owes us."

"I'll be fine with just a token amount from the settlement," Mallory said. "Look, I know what you've been through. You deserve to have someone on your side, to help make things easier for you for a change."

"Thank you so much." Jill pulled Jake into a hug. "Isn't this great, honey?"

"Yeah, it's cool." Jake looked away.

"Is something the matter, Jake?" Mallory asked.

Jake scrunched up his face. "Well…um, there's somethin' else." He unfolded the President's wish and handed it across the desk. "They wanted me to say this for the final wish. But I didn't."

Mallory scanned the single sheet and chuckled as she set it on the desk. "I'm guessing the President only wrote the last part about guaranteeing his legacy as the greatest president in the history of the U.S. And it looks like his advisors don't know much about what constitutes a single wish."

"Yeah. But there's more. See, the FBI agents who delivered it to me said if I made the wish exactly," he pointed to the sheet, "they'd secretly slip a whole lot of money to our family."

Mallory raised an eyebrow. "You know bribes are illegal, right?"

"Yes, ma'am. But they also told me that if I *didn't* do what they wanted, there would be dire consequences." Jake made air quotes around the final two words.

Jill turned pale. "They threatened you?"

Jake nodded. "Yeah. And since it's kinda obvious I didn't make the wish they wanted, I'm worried they'll send like assassins or black ops guys after us."

"Let me think about this a minute," Mallory said. She perused the document more carefully this time.

"I'm so sorry you have to deal with this, sweetie." Jill took Jake's hand in hers. "I just didn't know."

Jake blew out a sigh. "Nobody did, Mom."

Mallory removed her glasses, and held up the President's document. "With your permission, Jake, I'd like to release copies of this to all the major networks and independent news media." Mallory waved the paper in the air. "Once the public knows they tried to force you to make a Final Wish that insures political power in perpetuity, and that the President expected to cement his legacy the same way, they won't dare follow through on that threat. The whole world will be following their every move, just like it did for you, Jake."

"But won't they just deny everything and call me a liar or worse?"

"Probably. That's their normal strategy. They'll deny it all. But you're a lot more believable than they are, Jake. And once the public knows about the bribe and the threat, their credibility will take a major hit. Besides, you have nothing to gain by making this up."

Jill winced. "But won't that thrust Jake right back into the spotlight? He's already gone through so much."

"The media will want to interview him, of course, and there will be naysayers and bullies on the Internet. And lots of requests from the talk show circuit. But I'll do what I can to keep Jake's exposure to a minimum. And I'll be right there with you, Jake. Everything goes through me."

By the time they left Mallory Jameson's office, Jill was elated. Her heart floated, partly because their days of struggling to make it paycheck-to-paycheck were about to end, but mostly because Jake was smiling, really beaming. It had been a long time.

CHAPTER 50

On Sunday, ten days after the tumultuous town meeting, no crowd gathered in the street outside the Parker home; no unmarked van parked down the street; no news teams lurked nearby; no FBI agent stood outside Jake's bedroom door. The Command Center was, once again, a simple dining room.

In Jake's bedroom, a wad of paper flew through the air, struck the edge of the wastebasket, and settled among the others on the ground. Jake and Lester continued to crumple up letters from the stack on the bed. Most landed in the wastebasket. All were reactions to the Final Wish.

Lester grinned. "Man, your lawyer sure made the FBI and the President look like dicks."

"Yeah, everybody's pointing at somebody else and denying they knew anything about it."

"Looks like there's gonna be an investigation into it by Congress, though."

Jake puffed out a laugh. "It'll go on forever and probably nothin's gonna happen to the people who did it. At least everybody won't be watchin' every damn move I make any more."

"So, I guess you're not gonna be a big deal celebrity anymore, huh?"

"Nope."

"You're not gonna star in a video game or a movie...not even one of those totally lame reality shows?"

"Guess not."

"Bummer."

Both boys burst into a fit of laughing.

Lester glanced at the large screen HD TV and the stereo system set up in the corner of the room. "Damn, do you guys hafta give back all the cool home entertainment and computer stuff your dad got?"

"Naw, we're keepin' it. Bonus, my mom's gettin' a new Subaru SUV too. Dude, the thing totally parks itself. I guess you gotta look all successful and shit in the real estate business. Her old Fiesta isn't going to cut it."

"What about the Beemer?"

"My dad took that when he left."

"He's *gone?*"

"Yeah."

"But I thought you guys were back together."

Jake shrugged. "It wouldn't have worked. Anyway, both my mom and dad said it's gonna be much better for us all. He's gettin' a cool new apartment over by the Wood. Me and Kevin might be spending some weekends with him."

"But what about that hottie with the massive boobage who was in *Playboy?*" Lester wiggled his eyebrows.

"Dad says it's just gonna be him and us." Jake snickered. "I guess it'll be okay...if it really happens. We all gotta make adjustments."

The boys continued to toss crumpled letters at the wastebasket, content to let the quiet wash over them.

Finally, Lester broke the silence. "Jake?"

"Yeah?"

"Can I ask you somethin'?"

"Course."

"Well, I know what the rules are and shit. Like you can't ever reveal your wish or nothin'." Lester studied the laces of his black high-tops. "But, well, in the middle of that scary firefight? Didn't I get shot?"

Jake grinned. "Dude, if you got took a bullet, you must be one hell of a fast healer."

Lester scrutinized Jake for several seconds. "Yeah." He nodded, "I musta dreamed it. Anyway, so what's the deal with all this weird stuff happening 'cause of that Final Wish thing you did at the gym?"

"Weird?"

"You know what I mean. The Internet is full of stories about how people all over the world are acting *different* to each other—treating other people with…with—"

"Respect?"

"Yeah, just like it seemed you wished for at the gym. I mean no one knows for sure *what* you really wished for…that's totally your secret. But if…c'mon, dude, you know what I mean."

Jake stared straight ahead. "I been thinkin' about this a lot lately. One thing I learned from all the shit I've been through is that the only thing that really matters is what people wanna believe. Stuff like facts, or truth, or evidence…dude, they don't usually even count."

They sat in silence, reliving the last few days.

"Wow, Jake, I just figured out somethin'."

"Well, the pizza was an accident, but your other two wishes were totally for other people—not *you*. You never even used one of the wishes to get tons of money or turn yourself a six-foot-four total super athlete chick magnet."

Jake felt a shock run through his body. *So what if I'm a foot shorter than that, girls are definitely starting to flock around me. But I still don't have a clue how to deal with them. It'd be cool to have a girlfriend. Kevin has Angie. But look what happened to him. He's mostly forgotten his friends, and now he's sleepwalking around here like a grinning zombie. Don't want that to happen to me. Might not be a problem anyway, all those fangirls will probably lose interest now that I'm not a big celebrity any more.*

Lester chuckled. "Earth to Jake."

"Sorry, what?"

"I was just sayin' I'm not all that sure I woulda been able to resist the temptation to, you know, make me and my life a hell of a lot *better*."

"Come on, Les, why would you need to do that?" Jake grinned. "You're totally awesome just the way you are."

Lester's face flushed and he looked away. "Yeah, right." He sucked in a breath and looked back at Jake. "Hey, wanna do some cruisin' on the bike trails? Like old times? I mean, you're probably gonna be getting a stupid cool ride as soon as you get your license. So let's get in some serious trail ridin' while we can."

"Sure. I'll meet you over by the new ballpark. But give me like fifteen minutes or so, 'kay?"

"Cool." Lester rose from the bed and headed out. At the door he swung back around. "Jake, I'm never gonna mention any of this again. Ever. I promise. But, well, you're…you're totally the best friend a guy could ever have." He spun around and fled the room.

Jake slid off the bed and strode over to his desk. He gathered the wads of paper near the wastebasket and dropped them in. Just visible among the crumpled papers in the basket was his well-worn red watch cap.

———◦◦◦———

Jake pedaled along the street, relaxed enough now to sit tall on his bike. A huge weight had been lifted from his shoulders, and he could feel the difference. The pressure to make the right wish, to do the right thing, had taken a toll on him, but all that was history now. God, it felt good to be free.

When he arrived at the alley behind the restored Addison mansion, he slowed. Jake wasn't surprised that Ben's ancient truck and trailer weren't there. He just wanted to take a moment to kind of pay his respects.

As he continued down the alley, Jake could see Ben standing there protecting him from Buster and the Tweedles. Taking him to the only Giants game he'd ever been to. Teaching him how to hit the ball right. Revealing to Jake who he really was. But most of all he could see Ben's almost-a-smile. He'd always remember that.

When he reached the spot where the old man's trailer had been, he spotted it. Jake laid his bike down and ambled over to a wrinkled paper sack jammed into the corner of the new wooden fence. He pulled the sack free and peered inside. Jake broke into a grin as he liberated the old Brooklyn Dodgers cap, shook it into shape, and settled it on his head.

It fit like magic.

www.ingramcontent.com/pod-product-compliance
Lightning Source LLC
Chambersburg PA
CBHW030355020726
47493CB00003B/824